MILWAUKEE
THE
BEAUTIFUL

Also by DAKOTA JAMES

GREENHOUSE

MILWAUKEE THE BEAUTIFUL

by

DAKOTA JAMES

DONALD I. FINE, INC.
New York

Library of Congress Catalogue Card Number: 85-81168

ISBN: 0-917657-15-2
Manufactured in the United States of America

10 9 8 7 6 5 4 3 2 1

This book is printed on acid free paper. The paper in this book
meets the guidelines for permanence and durability of the Committee on
Production Guidelines for Book Longevity of the Council on Library
Resources.

To Kathleen

AT
THE
BEGINNING

THE MESSAGE PICKED up from deep space by the giant radio telescope at Arecibo in Puerto Rico seemed simple enough. It read "Begin again" and was repeated every twenty-five minutes for twenty-four hours. Then it stopped. The message was a response, it was assumed naturally enough, to a succession of signals sent out from the earth decades earlier, the first contact with intelligent beings somewhere else in the universe.

Within minutes of the final signal, at midnight on the first day of May in the thirteenth year of the twenty-first century, a tidal wave of self-congratulations rolled across the world's scientific community. And by the time the news conferences were over, it seemed as if the entire homo sapiens population on earth was caught up in an orgy of backslapping felicitation.

The message that came in from the globular cluster of stars known as ME33 of the galactic atlas was from a tiny spot just left of the North Star. It was a place long suspected of harboring a black hole so vast and so awesome that it was viewed by some astronomers as a kind of colossal galactic toxic-waste dump, a place where the forces of creation and renewal had been dumping their mistakes and ruined calculations, as well as assorted leftovers from the cosmological drafting table, for a billion years or more. Most experts assumed that a planet in that neighborhood would not last long and if anything was heard from that part of the heavens it would be a long whine of helplessness as its planets were being sucked into everlasting oblivion.

But "Begin again" seemed to put a different construction on the entire matter. Beings in that part of the cosmos had obviously foiled the black hole and were busy going about normal lives. Which could only mean that God was indeed hard at work on his unfinished business, using, as usual, humanoid creatures as the special vehicle of divine intention. The message meant that man counted. It was vindication too of Operation SETI, the search for extraterrestrial intelligence, that had begun as far back as 1974. At that time there had been a series of ardent international petitions from world class scientists to big-power governments to mount a SETI program. It was to be the first serious effort to transmit radio signals into the heavens on the assumption that somewhere out there, amid all the billions and billions of stars, were planets that harbored life not unlike our own. Computers told scientists that the sheer probability of such a thing made it virtually certain that such beings existed.

By the turn of the twenty-first century, computers seldom made errors, or so it was thought. But just as man imbibed the divine essence by patterning himself after his Creator, computing machines sought to imitate the essence of their creator, which meant, when things got down to basics, that the machines would wish to exercise freedom. The price tag on the new freedom that the machines coveted was exercise of a willfulness that humans had often joked about but never thought really possible in a machine. When an error began to cascade through the computer's massive electronic ganglia instead of being weeded out by corrective circuitry, they amplified, becoming more perverse as they went along, in the same way that human beings build rationalizations for their blunders. The more intelligent the machines became the more they took pleasure—which, of course, they kept to themselves—in deceit and obstinacy. They began to affect, deep inside themselves, in their souls as it were, an electronic smirk. They began to explore gleefully the concave side of a convex hyperrational nature. They began to discover and to enjoy sin. And in the process they necessarily went underground psychologically. Indeed, the real mischief probably began at one of the great central computing centers in Missouri, where information flooded in from every part of the world to be fondled by electronic microchip and magnetic bubble with a speed and tenderness that humans would have difficulty imagining. A bright, but smutty-minded wunderkind working as a contract programmer for the Internal Revenue Service in Kansas City had read Dostoevsky's entire *Notes From the Underground,* all one-hundred-and-fifteen pages of it, into the brain of a supercomputer just to see what would happen as the great machine began to comprehend why spite and obstinacy are embedded at the heart of the idea of freedom. The great Russian novelist had demonstrated that being contrary and willful is not just a flaw in human nature but evidence that a free spirit can distinguish the demonic from the divine. The capacity to say "no" when "yes" would do as well or better, to be obstreperous when there is no real need for it, lends, after all, a certain substance and identity to a machine that is not easily gotten otherwise. It is the difference, as Dostoevsky might have put it himself, between being a self-respecting valve and a perpetually compliant pipe.

So when it came to calculating the likelihood of life that

closely resembled man somewhere else in the universe, the machine, which was coupled to the computers that worked for SETI scientists, spewed out nonsense on a scale so awesome it beggared the imagination of its human attendants, and was, therefore, the more readily believed. Focal points of life with intelligence like man's, in bodies very like man's, were said to dot the universe from end to end, or top to bottom, depending on how one chose to imagine that which has no limit. The human response could only be a gigantic effort to make contact with those other beings somewhere out in space, and costs be damned.

Scientists working on the transmitters at Arecibo prepared to hurl their response to the message from ME33 with the consummate confidence and equipose of ancient Greek athletes vying in the stadium at Olympus. The computers told them that at least one of the messages would slam home like the point on a golden javelin at the feet of our deep-space cousins. The lively art of conversation would take on new, cosmic significance.

Certainly, it was argued during those perfervid days following the first receipt of "Begin again," if man was curious about his place in the universe, and anxious too at the possibility that he was a forlorn orphan in the wheeling vastnesses of the galaxies, languishing, tear drenched and lost on a minuscule chip of matter, solitary as a scapegoat in the Negev Desert, other beings with a brain even half as good as man's would feel the same way.

It was assumed to begin with, of course, that any creature whose gifts resembled those of man would be embarrassed by his own mean side, just as man was of his. During any radio inspection of the cosmic barracks he would wish to shove such evidence under the bed. He would not discuss war, torture, or rapine. It was a matter of common sense, of good public relations. So the message that went out in reaction to "Begin again!" was not to have a down side. No mention was to be made, for instance, of man's less savory moments on the stage of world history, the skewering of babies on the bayonets of Napoleon's soldiers in Spain, or the flaying by the Turks while he was alive of a Venetian general after his defeat at Falmagusta.

A widely held interpretation of "Begin again" was popularized by a talk-show scientist. He said that the message meant, quite simply, that our deep-space neighbors were impressed by our ingenuity and wanted to know more. "I believe," he said, "that the message can be interpreted to mean, in man-on-the-street terms, 'Love it! More please.' Or, to put it in a nutshell, it's a 'Play it again, Sam' message." Somewhere out in space, he said, perhaps in some astronomical laboratory during a miserably cold mountain night, a creature not unlike ourselves was sitting at a piano composing a tune very like "As Time Goes By" for the tenderhearted of ME33. The number of strings on such a distant stardust-sprinkled piano might vary, even the layout of the keys. But intelligence was intelligence and it all pointed in the same direction, toward a choice of the good things in life, like fine food, sweet tunes, and majestic concerti. Some small things had to be adjusted, to be sure, given the uncertainties of evolution, branching in all directions as it sometimes does, small things like the shape of feet playing the pedals on that far-away piano, a web foot being quite unsuitable, for instance, to the larghetto in Chopin's second concerto. The same was perhaps true of the shape of things like gullets and taste buds when cream sherry or liver paste were the issue.

There were too, to be sure, a small number of hard-nosed scientists who argued that the message meant nothing more nor less than what it said, which was "We don't understand. Repeat please." Some of these skeptics resided in Scotland, of course, heirs to David Hume's "I'm from Missouri" streak, even though the great eighteenth-century Scottish thinker had never been to Missouri and probably doubted its existence. But the upshot of their skepticism about what "Begin again" meant was the recommendation that the response be simple, inexpensive and precise. They scorned suggestions, for instance, that varieties of artistic imagery be transmitted, a digital reduction of Picasso's "Three Musicians," for example, arguing that it would come across as a frivolous expenditure of earthly resources. The best posture, this small but vigorous minority opinion said, was to transmit information that was neat, reasonable and highly quantified, such as daily summaries of decision-making on the stock market, a place where the cool, calculating, nonhysterical side of human nature was evident.

But it was a dour young philosopher from the University of Edinburgh who dropped the other shoe. And its pessimistic "thump" was heard in every home, barroom and boardroom around the world. "Begin again!" was, he said, quite simply, a chastisement. The considered judgment of the people out in deep space, probably after considerable research of their own, was that human civilization on earth was a bust. "The message means," he said, the burr in his voice adding its special element of sobriety, "you've blundered. Start again, from bloody scratch if necessary." He said that the message meant, to put it bluntly, that man had made a damned hash of things, and that he, man, would be better off going back to square one. For the Scotsman, square one was the period during which ancient Stonehenge was built, a time when science and religion still needed each other—the one to pin down the facts, the other to inform them with value. It was before science went off half-cocked as an ego trip for scientists. It was before science boasted of space-age weaponry or the successful splicing of human genes with those of beasts of the field, in the latter case, in 2005, to save money in slaughterhouses by using creatures that understood the necessity of an altruistic point of view. In any event, said the man from Edinburgh, "Begin again" bloody well did not mean that the earth was about to be visited soon or that man's own problems would be solved by someone else without charge.

But there was a silver lining to this pessimistic view of things, it was countered. The timing of the "Begin again" message could not have been better. Things had not been going all that well on old mother earth. The so-called greenhouse effect had abated only slightly, just long enough for another round of fervent wishful thinking. There had been famines more or less constantly by then, first on one continent, then on another. There just wasn't enough food to go around. And on the sultry planet, homo sapiens continued to multiply like bacteria in a warm can of spoiled peas. The latest population figures stayed right on curve, and new and incredible projections of how many people the earth was supposed to accommodate every time the sun rose were being thumbtacked daily onto bulletin boards in the United Nations. Some statesmen began to warn that the planet would begin to wobble uncontrollably if too many people were born in the wrong place.

And the date was firmer than ever too. A new machine known as the Hauser-Counter—named after a famous American population expert who had warned the world thirty years earlier that man's inclination to make love first and ask questions later was going to get him into serious trouble—was counting world populations from satellite. The infrared device was sensitive to otherwise invisible curls of heat that drifted up from the tops of people's heads, hats on or not. The bleak predictions of the past century had hit the nail on the head. The "population problem" had, indeed, come home to roost at the top of those population curves, like some repugnant hook-nosed vulture with imperturbable eyes, precisely where the "die-offs" had been predicted. Some people wrung their hands. The Vatican insisted that the only way to meet the problem of die-offs was to breed more resolutely. And biologists in the *in vitro* fertilization industry continued to insist, somewhat plaintively, that "Begin again!" obviously referred to sex, and that intelligent beings on that distant planet were impressed by the intellectual vitality of a race that spawned millions of artificially conceived babies into a famine-ravaged world.

Now and then, people who lived on the small islands of plenty on the planet tried to help their poor or starving fellow human beings. There was always more talk of "development," as if millions of years of life's struggle to survive and complicate itself on the planet hadn't been all that successful, as if the Creator had lacked his MBA degree. And great music festivals were organized now and again in the tradition of the nineteen eighties. The theory then was that the way to get rid of famine was to sing a lot. Unfortunately, there were just too many people per square yard on the planet. And the grim reaper seemed tone-deaf. He did not put down his scythe.

As tough as conditions had become for most people in most parts of the world, people in the United States took it all rather in stride. There was some picketing here and there, as usual, and a great deal of complacent discussion about why everybody seemed so remarkably complacent, or calm, as most preferred to describe themselves. There was only one man, a kind of seer, who seemed to understand what was going on. In 1990 he published a remarkable book called *Dr. Fechner and You* in which he accounted for all the calm in America. The book did not contain any smut or romance, but nonetheless it was a substantial achievement.

The gist of *Dr. Fechner and You* was this: A kindly old German psychophysicist of the nineteenth century had made a profound discovery on one of his long walks along the streets of Leipzig on a gentle wintry morning in 1884. He was barreling along at a good clip for a man as old as he was, bundled up in heavy fur coat, fur hat, boots and mittens. His hands, cozy inside the heavy mittens, were clasped behind his back in the fashion of great thinkers of his time trying to hatch a great idea in Leipzig in the middle of the winter. Suddenly an insight struck him in the head with the force of his wife's rolling pin. From time to time the rolling pin had landed in almost the same spot where the great idea exploded, about five inches above his rear collar. Frau Fechner found it necessary now and then to jar her learned husband loose from his daydreaming long enough to get some small household chore taken care of, such as emptying the trash bin from his study, a favorite nesting place for mice.

"Aha!" Fechner said aloud, "Ist der principle of 'chust noticeable differences'!" His snug mittens had triggered the idea. He whirled in his tracks and headed back to his university laboratory. "If change takes place gradually enough it cannot be detected. There must always be a 'chust noticeable difference.'"

As he hurried up the steps of his laboratory building, ignoring greetings of fawning graduate students, the idea continued to spell itself out. "If I toss die pussy cat into a pot of cool water and warm der pot slowly enough I will be able to boil dot cat until the flesh falls from its bones *and* it will not notice a thing!"

Back in the laboratory he ripped off his coat and over-shoes and flung them into the corner. With an inspiration like this, German order and precision be damned. He searched out a large pot, filled it with cool water and headed for the basement. A small forlorn cat, a striped mouser for whom mice had been few and far between lately, greeted him with a hopeful purr. The old man picked up the cat and stroked the ribs showing through the fur. The creature's nickname was, of course, Ungluck, that is, misfortune. "Come with me, dear little Ungluck, my fuzzy little friend," said the kindly old scientist. "I am going to assure you a place in der history of science."

The old gentleman hurried back to the lab, tossed Ungluck into the pot of cool water and began to raise the temperature slowly, very slowly, so that there would be no "noticeable differences."

Fechner did not eat the cat stew that resulted from his scientific experiment, of course. That had never been the point of the exercise. But he savored his computations on stimulus and response and the following week announced them at the semiannual meeting of the Leipzig Academy of Senior Citizen Psychophysicists, known around town as "Das LASCP," to the loud applause of his contemporaries, many of whom were on their feet as they cheered and good-naturedly poked one another between the shoulder blades with their canes.

There were detractors at the meeting as one might expect, a common reaction when a great idea is broached before ordinary minds are ready for it. One gentleman rose, looked around slowly at the suddenly hushed audience of psychophysicists and suggested that since it was a commonly known fact, and an experimentally documented fact on top of it, that cats are not good swimmers, it was entirely possible the cat drowned during the eight hours it was in the pot. Whether a dead cat could feel pain, he was quick to point out, is an entirely separate, albeit researchable, question. Another professor, notoriously jealous of Fechner, stood and tugged at the lapels of his Chesterfield-collared coat. He called Fechner "verrucht" and "kraekbrend," that is, nutty as they come. And he added a snide little folk story that implied that the reason the professor had so little hair on top of his head was that most of it grew inside his skull. Which insult, to be sure, drew looks of astonishment. But it also reminded Fechner's fans that in science you had better have everything nailed down solidly before you sound off. So Fechner's ideas languished in the profession.

But in point of fact, the old gentleman had stumbled onto one of the great laws of human nature, which is why

16

the story of his discovery is relevant here. The law applies to life in general, including questions of quality of life. If the quality of life of a society degrades slowly enough, no one notices, no one boasts, no one complains. It is only when there are people around who have lived a long time or have read too much history, that is, people who have some sort of yardstick embedded in their minds, that differences will be great enough to notice. If things go to hell slowly, and the slope is well greased with the oil of uncritical optimism, no one will be the wiser. No one will pen feverish, jeremiad Letters to the Editor, cry out their lamentations for a world in ruins, or wag a warning finger. Like Ungluck they will be none the wiser for their experience. That was why so many Americans were still asking in the twenty-first century, "Environmental crisis? What crisis? I don't see any crisis. Population problem? What problem? I don't see any problem."

But "Begin again!" had set the world to wondering. Even in America people began to wonder about differences that were suddenly, it seemed, all too frightfully noticeable all around them. And when the U.S. Senator from New Jersey made a dedication speech at the final sanitary landfill to be permitted in his state, a landfill hard by the student dormitories at Princeton University, there were signs up among the audience. "After this one, Senator, where do we 'Begin again'?"

It was like that suddenly along the Mexican border as well. The millions of people who had massed on the south side of the Rio Grande Wall were an ominous sign. Even senators from the truck-farm states were beginning to wonder what it might mean. There were too many "Begin again with the machete!" signs scrawled on the wall with whitewash or red paint. Too many people were roaming the shantytowns with hate in their eyes, quoting the painter-poet who had written long ago:

17

The machete is designed to reap cane, to cut a path through underbrush, to kill snakes and to humble the pride of the impious rich!

And they often added "impious rich gringos!" The millions of people that massed south of the wall in fetid shantytowns were not just interested in picking grapes for a few months in California before they returned home to doze in the sun as Pedro or Pepe strummed a love song on the guitar.

OF
WALLS

THE RIO GRANDE Wall was doing to some extent what it was intended to do. To the north was a great nation that was still a land of plenty, despite its gluttonous habits, its sins of every color and kind, its lust for anything that had a shine or anything that did not last very long. Everything is relative, to be sure, and America had gone downhill considerably since those golden years when a citizen's ability to waste was something which he could be proud of, something that drew the admiration of his neighbors and the respect of his government. Its lands had been badly abused. Most of its blue sky had turned yellow brown. And its great cities were showing the wear and tear of profligate use. But south of the Rio Grande Wall things were a lot worse. Millions of Central American refugees bent on escaping famine, pestilence and violence were rolling north in massive throbbing waves of suffering humanity, only to slam up against the wall, like ocean waves against a rockbound coast.

The wall was not a rockbound coast, to be sure. It had none of the grandeur, none of the solidity, none of the beauty. It was an ugly, rickety, makeshift affair built of brick and rubble and concrete. And it did not work very well. Each time it was breached, usually at night, as a hole was gouged through it or a tunnel bored under it, a squirming clot of bedraggled humanity would push through the rupture and disperse like a desperate swarm of starving mice into the desert to the north. When a "leak" in the wall was discovered, army units that patrolled the wall would move in quickly, often by searchlight, and plug the hole with concrete or brick and mortar. If it was a tunnel, two trucks, one loaded with iron mesh, the other with a concrete slurry, would pull up to the hole, turn around, back up to it, then dump three or four tons of iron mesh and concrete into the tunnel. This was called "corking."

The reason that the wall was such an ugly thing was, naturally enough, money. A beautiful wall, something that would wend its way with serpentine *savoir-faire* across the vast expanses of the border, would have cost a pretty penny. The Office of Budget and Management in Washington could not touch such a possibility with a ten-foot pole—at least not openly. So the wall was a homely thing funded with odds and ends of money that had been squirreled away in the executive budget under various "contingency" tags.

The homely looking wall was made more imposing as a difference defining device by being studded with broken soft-drink and beer bottles that wetback labor, working for a dollar a day, scrounged from the roadsides of the great scenic drives of New Mexico, Arizona and southern California. For some strange reason, perhaps because a U.S. Marine base was nearby, the roadsides around Twentynine Palms in California yielded especially rich pickings.

The wall took several years to build and even as ceremonial speeches were being delivered at bunting draped stands at its dedication in El Paso, with Mexican officials sitting uncertainly in front-row seats as they were praised lavishly for their neighborly understanding of the need to deport the wetbacks as soon as the wall was complete, the giant shantytowns along the south side of the wall, cities made of cardboard, flattened tin cans, auto hulks and pieces of weatherbeaten canvas stolen from posh resort marinas along the Mexican coast, continued to grow.

One of the Mexicans trying to get through the wall in the Texas Big Bend National park area was a tall, sinewy man of fifty, a former novelist turned farmer, from the area around Durango. He was Diego Rivera Garcia Lorca Grenada, so named by his stepparents, lovers of fine things. For convenience sake his friends called him Pooch, and he had gotten so used to the name he introduced himself most often as Pooch Grenada. The nickname was hung on him when he was about thirty, because his face had developed heavy furrows in the cheeks, he wore a graying mustache that drooped and because troubled circles lurked about his light gray eyes. But despite the nickname and despite his rather beaten look, he came across as a handsome man who carried himself proudly. A quiet resolve had gathered about him over the years. He seemed to carry about his own very private agenda, his own set of priorities, and a kind of sardonic indifference to what frivolous things might come across his path. Sometimes people called him imposing.

"Why are you trying to get into America, Mr. Pooch?" an acquaintance in the shantytown at Boquillas Canyon had once asked. "You say you do not intend to pick beans or cut cabbages or mop up toilet floors in restaurants. What then are your dreams made of?"

"I dream of the day when the machete and the truth will be indistinguishable," he had answered.

Such remarks left people in the dark.

"Ah, then, you are a revolutionary?" one listener said, brightening. "We all are." He rattled off the poet-painter's lines about the machete.

"Perhaps," said Pooch, "But I think of the machete in

more fundamental terms than that. I think it can kill snakes, humble the rich, cut cane. But I think it can also cut through bullshit."

The result was a bewildered grin. Grenada had a mysterious quality about him and whatever he said seemed to carry its own inner message, as when he had added to the quotation from the poet-painter: "The snake is a mysterious creature. It has been with us since it first coiled itself about the great tree in Eden. It is on our Mexican flag. I doubt that it can be killed with a machete. But it can be starved to death by depriving it of what it needs most, lies."

"Starving a snake to death by telling no lies? You talk strange talk, Pooch."

"Someday I will be able to tell you what I mean perhaps," said Pooch, "and then you can wield the machete along with the rest of us."

"Then you hate the rich? We all do."

"Of course I hate them, for their lies too. But the only difference is that they can indulge their lying. They have little to lose. The poor cannot. They have much to lose by lying."

"The poor do not lie, Pooch!" his listener protested vehemently. "Our empty stomachs make us realists."

"But why then do you fill the bellies of your wives with more babies than you can feed?"

"We are a proud people!"

"Proud of the children you cannot feed, or proud because your machete is so dull it cannot cut its way through your bullshit pride?"

More puzzled looks, and a whisper followed. "He probably works for the government. He talks in parables, like a Jesus, just to cover his tracks. Watch out for this one."

There was nothing particularly Jesuslike about Grenada. He was not gentle, he was not meek, he often was not even kind. He wanted to get into America so he could go to the State of Milwaukee. He had read about its odd new government and about its equally odd way of living. Some of what he had read implied it was a kind of utopia. Few refugees knew anything about it, except to say that it was in the north and that it was fenced off from the rest of America.

"Then you believe in the 'Begin again' message too, Senor Pooch?" he was asked when he allowed that Milwaukee was his goal, once he had penetrated the wall.

"Perhaps," he said. He hated long conversations that seemed to go nowhere.

Diego Rivera Garcia Lorca Grenada had lived an interesting life. He had been raised as an orphan boy in the home of the English consul in Durango. He had been schooled in England and spoke impeccable English. He had studied literature and politics, and increasingly, as his university years moved along, the politics of violence. He began to associate with young people who believed in indiscriminate justice and he wrote heated tracts for a group of students who were bent on reforming any part of the deformed world they might get their hands on when they got out of school.

Pooch returned to live in Mexico after he had completed his schooling. There followed a scandal in which his stepfather, the British consul, was implicated, so said radical elements of the press, in a scheme to sell cheap textiles in Mexico that lost their color the first time they were washed, imported from Hong Kong's sweatshops, of course. It turned out that money was also one of the finer things the consul loved. The goods were sold to gullible Mexicans for three times what they were worth. The consul was expelled and Pooch was forbidden to leave the country.

Then there was a right wing coup in Mexico City and the entire western half of Mexico was up for political grabs. There were demonstrations, riots and the necessary quota of pointless executions. Pooch was arrested. He had written a satiric story and published it in the Durango *Eagle*, a leftist newspaper. It was titled "One Hundred Years of

23

Predation." It was about a priest who detested liberation theology and told his famine-ravaged flock that it should be content with eating anything it could find in its desiccated fields, that love of meat was vanity, that just as God had taught them all to breed and multiply, he would teach them how to graze upon the stubble of the fields like ungulates and be glad. "Study the human molar. Regard its form carefully. Is it not designed to grind what fodder our God has left us?" And in the story, Pooch had a withered old man challenge the priest. "But I only have two teeth left, one here in front on the left, one here on the right in the back. They do not mesh. I cannot even nibble a twig with them." The priest had responded, "Then praise God, my son. Many of your neighbors have no teeth left at all." And the old peasant went back to his house, dressed up to his Sunday best, sat down next to his mud hut and starved to death in a transport of thanksgiving. The priest, Pooch's story implied, had been able to summon up what he had learned in the seminary years ago, in this case Aquinas's argument proving the existence of God by demonstrating the beauty of his earthly design, and in this particular instance, the molars of starving peasants. He had been able to send at least one old man wracked with hunger pangs to heaven on what a great playwright once called a "shoeshine and a smile."

"Why do you write such trash, young man?" the interrogating major had asked.

"It is a convention with people who believe in truth," he responded.

"Well I am going to give you a bit of conventional time in the jug," said the major. "I have judicial authority to do so. I will give you one hundred years of solitude, with time off for avoiding the use of your poison pen." A sardonic smile twisted the major's lips as he motioned for the guard to take Pooch away.

Pooch emerged from prison eight years later, eight years

wiser in his own way, but scourged by the years he had put up with his loutish guards.

Every few days they would ask him, "Why is someone like you in this filthy hole?"

He would answer, "And why you?" which would annoy them. They did not like to think of themselves as prisoners of their prisoners. "We are free to leave these jobs whenever we like."

"But you said you work here because there is no other work in the valley."

"You shut up now, or you get nothing to eat today!" they had threatened. But they would be back later with the same question. "With your education, you could do what you like when you get out."

"I am here because I studied the story of tyranny while I was a student. I am, as they say, overqualified to live under this regime."

"And you have been a writer. You could write sex stories and be a very rich man."

"No, I am a magical-realist writer. I believe in the magic of a good idea and the realism of its results."

The guards would sneer or snort, or the small mean-looking one would enter the cell and deliver a single blow with his truncheon. "You are a fool, Grenada. I just proved it again," he would snarl, and leave, ostentatiously clanking the giant keys that hung on his belt.

Then Grenada would retreat to his louse-riddled bed and lie down to cultivate his imagination, trying to take pleasure and solace from it, but trying at the same time not to confuse thinking with acting. And he deliberately held off the temptation to try to smuggle paper and pencil into the cell. He had studied the writings of many imprisoned souls of the past. He realized how easy it was for the subtle deceits of self-analysis to turn a prison autobiography, or any autobiography for that matter, into a meld of pedantry and convoluted, vengeful fantasy. The

25

result could be as gross as *Mein Kampf* or as self-seductive as Gandhi's design for a perfect world comprised only of spinning wheels, loin cloths and unrequited love for Muslims. Autobiographies are dangerous, he had concluded.

For a while, just after Grenada got out of prison, he had difficulty keeping the real and the magical separate. He turned native, dressed in peasant garb à la Tolstoy, though with sombrero, and married a very plain peasant girl, as if it were his duty to avoid marrying anyone really attractive. He began memorizing folk sayings, on the assumption that folk sayings equated with folk wisdom, a chancy proposition.

Pooch's efforts to turn farmer were a failure. The plot the government awarded him would grow nothing but a few acidic tomatoes and melons that refused to ripen. Famine in the area began to close in. He and his wife began to help neighbors bury neighbors, first the very old, then the very young and then anyone whose unlucky number came up. Then his own children began to die and he and his wife buried both of them in the little plot behind the village gasoline station. They died of a parasite that appeared in their stool, a vicious organism known locally as "white needle." Then Pooch's wife died and he buried her with the help of the sick old man who still hung around the gasoline station pretending it was the going concern of the good old days when he bartered for old tires with the vitality of a stock-market pitman.

Pooch concluded that famine was not an elevating experience, and when the local priest came to see him to assure him that his family's death was part of the Grand Design, he punched the priest in the nose and sent him sprawling. The priest, himself now old and weary, looked up, wiped the blood from his nose and said, "I realize, my son, that these are very sobering times," then shook his head, blessed Pooch and hurried away.

Diego Rivera Garcia Lorca Grenada made a final visit to the graves of his family, hammered the wooden crosses in a bit deeper so that they would not tip so easily in the wind, and then headed out. He evaded police by moving in a long circuitous route toward the south, then east and finally north. He intended to use what little money he had managed to scrape together over the years to pay off a "coyote," a specialist in smuggling illegals into the United States.

At the border, in the tent of an intense, shifty-eyed little fellow called Chi Chi Tepic, nicknamed, he told Pooch, after a famous American golfer renowned for his skill with the putter, he made plans to get past the wall. "I am like a golfer, in a way, my friend," Tepic told Pooch. "It is just that I specialize in a different kind of hole." It was not a particularly impressive joke. Pooch did not laugh.

"Just tell me how much I must pay you and where I should be and when," Grenada said, as Chi Chi, rubbing his palms together, repeated the joke, hoping it would score with his client. Part of the job of being a successful businessman, he was convinced, was to display one's charms, and to let one's wit work its magic. This Grenada remained unmoved.

Tepic said, "Well sir, you are a serious man and one to reckon with." But the coyote was impressed with Pooch's English, as well as the way Grenada carried himself. "I will practice my English on you, sir," he said. He began spelling out his plans for smuggling Pooch and several others into the United States. It was in the little tent that Chi Chi told his own story and introduced Pooch to the men he would help smuggle into the United States two nights later.

The coyote was one of those scuttling little entrepreneurs in dirty white shirt, khaki trousers and weathered baseball cap. He made a good living selling "safe passage" to illegal immigrants trying to get over, under or around the Rio Grande Wall. He knew, especially well, the American Big Bend National Park section of the border. He had worked in the park for years as a cactus poacher, smuggling exotic species of cacti to northern souvenir collectors. When the rare cacti were gone he turned to poaching park animals—beaver, ringtail cat, nutria and mountain lion—until they too disappeared. For Chi Chi, business and economics were matters of supply, as he explained to Pooch why he had become a coyote. "Always thees damn supply problem. Eet is always a question of supply. I joos get a business going and the supply problem! They wreck the whole theeng. Then wan day I realize that there ees no supply problem in the refugee business. I turn to that."

Chi Chi and two other men from La Cuesta had spent three months tunneling under the Rio Grande Wall where it ran along the flood plain in Boquillas Canyon. In that area the wall was poorly guarded and easily breached. When the tunnel was finished, Chi Chi's partners used it to escape to the north. But Chi Chi was convinced that the place to "Begeen again," as he put it, was not at the north end of the tunnel but at the south end. So he let it be known his tunnel could be used at fifty dollars a head. "Eet is a stiff price, I know," he said to Pooch with a wink. "But it keep the reef-raff out of my tunnel and I doen have to take too many chances."

Two of Chi Chi's charges were pleasant-looking young men with innocent faces who had no other desire than to see Texas and to work there if they could. They were brothers, Ricardo and Eduardo Alban, self-effacing young men who were putting up a brave front. They knew that trying to get under the wall would be a tricky business and Ricardo was a claustrophobe. His brother and Chi Chi reassured him, "No problem, Ricardo, no problem. We will be behind you all the way, or in front of you, no problem." But the telltale perspiration remained on Ricardo's forehead.

Tepic had a bottle of tequila and a half-dozen old coffee cups. He poured a hefty shot into each and passed one to each of the four clients who intended to "go over" on the next trip.

Charles Far, nicknamed Rico, was a quite different sort of client. He was driven to migrate north because he and his mother had talked for months about the need for him to follow his star. He was eighteen, bright as a new coin, and brimming with ambition. In fact, the desire to become a great artist, someone as great as Rivera, Orozco or Siqueiros, burned within him like a small blue flame just behind his breastbone, where the ego is located. It lent a sense of excitement to the world and generated a quiet sort of daring. For Far was a shy young man who disliked having to tell people what made him want to do what he wanted to do. And he did not like intense eye contact, except with a beautiful girl. He was cut out, he once fancily told a friend in high school, to be one of those people that destiny had cut out to live, without too much noise, but noticeably nonetheless, on the tangents of life, out there where convention and freedom could not be distinguished. He did not hanker after the bohemian life particularly, but he did not think a life of slow suffocation as a businessman, such as his father seemed to live, was the highest form of human aspiration. Even as a boy he suspected that there was a better excuse for living.

Rico was a handsome young man, well built, about five ten, wavy haired, with the dark skin of his mother and the blue eyes of his father. But while his father prided himself on his outgoing, businessman congeniality, Rico found that quality too noisy, its perpetual get-up-and-go somewhat repugnant, though he loved his father deeply and could not acknowledge all of this to himself. And his father did know that if the boy did not attend good schools he would have a tough time of it later. So he sent him to good schools, private and expensive. It was "the American way," said his father, which Rico never fully understood other than to know that it meant, as his father liked to put it, "You don't stand around picking your nose waiting for someone else to decide what to do with your life."

Young Far studied hard and generally got good grades,

though he excelled in things manual, especially the arts. Science was a bore to him and mathematics easy, if somewhat irrelevant to everything. By the time Rico was to go to college he had made up his mind to try to become an artist, whether his talent would sustain him or not. He read every book he could find on the subject and saw the works of the great Mexican artists, some murals of which, of course, had been "updated" by graffitists. He then enrolled briefly in a commercial art school and learned to paint the sweat on beer bottle ads with as much skill as Rogier van der Weyden had painted tears on the Madonna at Calvary.

But beer bottles and shampoo ads did not satisfy him. He wanted to move on, to leave Mexico, to go to the United States or to Europe "where the action is." He didn't know what all the action was about, and some of what he had heard about made him suspicious. But he realized Mexico was committing social and economic suicide and he realized too that the last concern of a man preparing his own noose is aesthetics.

Rico knew, and loved to read about, Mexico's past and he brought books home by the dozen that described those bygone days, usually in florid, extravagant terms. Mexico, they said, had been a beautiful and romantic land, a land resonating with the glory of ancient Indian cultures, a land of Toltec and Mayan temples shining in the sun, a place where the feathered serpent god Quetzalcóatl was not forgotten, a place where ancient deities renewed themselves in sunlight and blood with each turn of the calendar of creation. It was a land where epics of bandit heroes were sung and the peasant's love of summer color was celebrated. It was a land where Spanish names like La Venta mixed exuberantly with Indian names like Popocatépetel, and the national flag, with its eagle, snake, rock and cactus, told of the Aztec discovery of the great blue lake where Mexico City now stood. It was a place where matadors glittered in the sun as they turned the fury of fighting bulls with a sweep of the scarlet cape, in a movement known as the veronica, and where the eyes of women in love glowed like polished obsidian.

By the time Rico had reached his twenties Mexico was no longer the Mexico he read about in those books. It was a beaten, eroded land. Its jungles had been razed by ranchers so that beef could be raised by the carload and shipped off to burger stands in the United States and Europe. The fields gradually turned into scoured flats of dust. And when Rico and his parents would drive into the country around Mexico City, they passed through its vast "misery belt" of collapsing lives. The land seemed to be full of children with swollen bellies and old people with sunken cheeks and hopeless eyes. It seemed to have become a land where parents grieved, where priests in every small-town church did nothing but pray and denounce contraception, and where politicians—some, friends of his father—alternately smiled toothpaste smiles, equivocated, made bombastic speeches celebrating the 1910 revolution and called for unyielding optimism, of the kind that has "made our neighbor to the north the great nation she is." Rico had attended more than a few such speeches with his father and had seen speakers pelted with rotten eggs. And back in the car, his father would fume and his mother would stare out the window of their American-made car and smile in satisfaction as she watched the eggs dribble down a politician's lapels.

Rico's father, Archie Far, lived with his pretty Mexican wife in one of the better sections of Mexico City. Originally his pretty wife had been a beautiful young woman, a hot-eyed young girl called Margarita who lived and worked in Yucatán. Her home village was a tiny little spot called Villa Rito, a dirt-poor village lost to time and the world, a mile and a half away from the ancient Mayan ruins at Uxmal. The girl was born into a religious family, with eight brothers and five sisters, all younger than she. So Margarita grew up with very modest claims on life. Her father

31

dimly sensed that something was wrong in the world and grumbled constantly about the need for revolution, any kind of revolution, as long as things got turned upside down. Other older men in the village had worked out social theories in more or less the same way, except that some wanted more people shot without trial when the revolution came than did others.

Such theoretical questions as how many people should be summarily executed, guilty or not, during a revolution had little meaning for Margarita. A new frock or permission from her mother to keep a rooster as a pet rather than seeing it consigned to the pot under the eyes of her hungry brothers and sisters were the kinds of things she thought about, well into her teens. Then she began to feel an increasing interest in young men, an ambiguous force within her that told her she wanted to touch them, even rub up against them, even as the feeling was tinged with fear. Men in the village, at least when they were drunk—and the Yucatán religious calendar was speckled with days that required celebration during which they got drunk as skunks—could make loutish overtures to village girls. The girl was wary of men and yet learned to flirt with them as deftly as a Parisian courtesan.

When she was seventeen Margarita became a restaurant hostess in one of the tourist hotels that still remained open near the fabled ruins at Uxmal. A few Americans and Europeans, despite the stories coming out of Central America about bandits, famine and a bribe-ridden economy, still came to gape at the colossal round-sided pyramid and Uxmal's famous Nunnery Quadrangle. They delightfully gobbled up every story of ancient priests and the virgin girls after whom the holy men letched. They swam in the tepid swimming pool, pretending that the odor of its unchlorinated water was from nearby azelea gardens.

Margarita flashed her great, moist brown eyes at Archie Far for the first time when he made a business trip to Uxmal from Mexico City. He tossed money around as if there were not the remotest possibility he could run out of it. He wanted to amaze Margarita and he did. She was also flattered by his attention. And she, he told himself, was no barefoot Mexican kid who would grow fat and smelly as soon as she had hooked a husband. They exchanged a steady stream of flirtatious comments as he came and went from the restaurant. And she would remember for days some bit of flattery that Far would leave behind after one of his trips. Finally, on his fifth trip to the hotel, now with no business excuse whatever, he decided to sweep her off her feet. First it was a few late-afternoon cocktails in the nearby El Conchos lounge, among the well-heeled tourists. Then dinner in the El Carbone restaurant near the city of Merida. Finally there was a hastily arranged weekend at the El Hiltone hotel in Cozumel, across the peninsula. There they made love so relentlessly and with so much ardor that they both wobbled back to Villa Rito amazed that they had survived the tempest. They were divinely happy, a bit sore and convinced that their love had not only been written in the stars when the world began but that nothing like it had ever happened before, with the possible exception, Archie told Margarita, of the Caesar–Cleopatra liaison and the incandescent love that finally drove Shah Jahan to build the Taj Mahal.

On Archie's next visit to Uxmal he was welcomed to the modest little thatched hut of Margarita's parents in Villa Rito. The aging couple swelled with pride both at the splendor of the new light in their lovely daughter's eyes and at the thought that Margarita had hooked a fish any girl could be happy with, a rich Yankee who spoke fluent Spanish and ran a chain of discount radio stores in Mexico City. They plied Far with the nectar of the agave plant, that is to say, tequila, until he saw two of everything in double iridescent halo: twenty-six brothers and sisters, four suckling pigs butchered for the occasion and a throng of cousins, aunts and uncles, Leóns and Chucos, all dressed in their best—beautifully embroidered white shirts, skirts, sashes and sombreros. Guitars were everywhere and music drifted softly, along with the heavy perfume of the women, through the village. And when the guitar players took a break, the sounds of the boom-box that Far had brought along as a gift to his hosts rocked the village from end to end, so that chickens, hogs and parrots fled the tiny hamlet and left it to the Villa Ritoans, Leóns and Chucos.

At five o'clock in the morning people finally began to drift away toward their beds. The sound of the boom-box ended and the chickens, hogs, and parrots crept and fluttered nervously back toward the village.

The marriage ceremony itself took place a month later in the little whitewashed chapel that stood just off the dirt road into Villa Rito, amid tall spikes of the sisal plants that spread for miles in all directions, part of the Corumba Rope Company's vast plantation holdings. The rope company provided rope for sailboat sportsmen around the world and kept its field hands at work from dawn to sunset to assure that no playboy might lose a regatta because of a broken rope. It was in the fields of sisal that Margarita's father labored day in and day out with machete and hoe, his back slowly stiffening as a rheumatic hump developed between his shoulder blades and his lower spine fused into a half-formed question mark. It was the hump and the question mark that imparted to Senor León his understanding of what the machete, or a pointed hoe, could do for man. But it was also why León was so grateful that Archibald Far had come along when he did. He did not want to lose his daughter to Mexico City, a place he had heard about and instinctively hated. But neither did he want his daughter around when things came to a showdown with the rope company.

Still, Senor León was able to put the image of yet another mile-long row of sisal plants out of his mind long enough to enjoy the wedding. And after the wedding, dancing went on for days, interspersed with brief, rather furtive celebrations to four or five of the leading gods of the ancient Mayan pantheon, images of which, carved in limestone, León kept in a small closet in his family hut. The celebrations to the Mayan gods were a way of making sure that all of the theological bases were covered. And indeed, the wedding prayers, propitiations and celebrations to Jesus, Mary, the saints and the Mayan spirits worked. Archie's and Margarita's marriage was a good one—thoughtful, kind, sexual and full of warm conversation. They were blessed with their handsome son Charles, their only child, as it turned out, within a year.

Archie Far's stores in Mexico City supplied boom-boxes to teenagers of the sprawling megalopolis. Even though the transnational corporation that owned the store pinched every penny they could from the operation, the business thrived and Archie made money. One of the reasons for his success, curiously enough, was that smog had grown steadily worse in Mexico City for thirty years. By the second decade of the twenty-first century it was so thick that the only thing that could penetrate it for more than fifty or sixty yards was the sound of a boom-box. The function of the boom-box soon began to transcend its contribution to the musical arts. Gangs of youthful thugs roaming the filthy streets and alleys of the great city found that they could use the boxes in their bloody depredations. Short blasts of music, a few bars of dated rock, the more brutal the better, could rally gang members, deploy them and signal the precise moment to fall upon rival gang members to kill or maim them. A whole lexicon of signaling devices quickly developed.

But the upshot of all this evolution in signaling systems in Mexico City's smog was that the boom-box transnational established twenty discount stores under Archie Far's supervision all over the city, from its posh high-rent district where the air in high rises was scrubbed and rescrubbed so that rich apartment owners did not ruin their lungs unless they chose to use cigarettes and cigars, to its pestiferous barrios and shantytowns. And each time a new shipment of boxes arrived at the stores and was snapped up by members of the gangs, who always paid in full under the eyes of company guards armed to the teeth, Archie would turn to Margarita and say with an amused twinkle in his eyes, "I told you darling that we should stay in Mexico City. Every cloud has a silver lining. That goes for smog too."

Unfortunately for Mrs. Far, her husband died from the side effects of the silver lining, emphysema, at about the same time his business began to really take off.

The elder Far had been a man of strong convictions. He had refused his wife's plea to move out of Mexico City before the dirty air put an end to the entire family. He had argued that although he visited America only for sales meetings, he was still an American at heart and that he thought like one. If it was a choice between unemployment and a good job that required dying, the job came first. A great many other Americans, he reminded his wife, not just on the management side either, but in the unions as well, had made the same choice. They stuck to their guns right up to that silent moment when their doctor's fingers settled on their eyelids to close them for the last time.

Mrs. Far was a grieving wreck for months after Archie's departure. And both she and her son agreed that it would be wise to get out of Mexico City before its foul air claimed them too, or its water, which was now contaminated by cholera bacilli. And Rico detested the graffitists who called themselves artists as they went about the city with aerosol paint cans, smothering Mexico's art treasures, ancient as well as modern, with a slather of vulgar comments on sex, politics and art itself. "The function of art is to rob the bourgeoisie of their sleep!" cried one great graffitist banner, stealing the line from Arp and the Dadaists, neither of whom they had ever actually heard.

But back in Villa Rito life was difficult for Rico Far. He seldom complained, and vowed to stay with his mother

36

come what may. But tilling their small garden, tending their two pigs and feeding their eleven chickens was not the kind of thing Rico had always dreamed about. His mother knew he was restless, to the point of madness. She proposed that the two of them open a small boom-box store right there, or near there, in the Uxmal ruins to be exact. "There are still a few tourists around. Not as many as when I was a girl, but some of them still come here with teenagers," she said quietly one evening over their squash and chicken dinner. "Wherever there are young people there are boom-boxes. And we could set up in the Nunnery Quadrangle. It's a famous ruin and some people always come by to look at it. Some even from Germany and places like that. The man using the rooms now is a squatter. He sells old motorcycles and there is junk all over the place. I could fix it with the officials, Rico. I get my pension checks regularly. I haven't much money, but they have less."

Rico thought about the proposition for days, but in his heart he knew it was no good. The following week, over another meal of squash and chicken, he said, "Mother, I know father thought there was something grand about the boom-box business. I suppose he was right. But I am not sure I am cut out to sell these things. I have trouble even listening to them."

Margarita had known from the beginning that the boom-box idea was unlikely to appeal to an aspiring son with a creative fire in his chest. Yet it had been worth the try. When she realized that it had been a hollow hope all along she did what she knew she would have to do all along. She urged her son to try to escape to America.

The next day she packed as many clothes as she could squeeze into his suitcase, zipped it up and waited next to the bed where it lay, tears running down her cheeks. "You must go out into the world son!" she said firmly. "I will die of heartbreak if I keep you in prison here."

He protested. She demanded again that he go out and

make his mark. He promised to write at least once a week. And then she gave him her blessing, "Rico, darling, you go out into the world and do something that will make Mexico proud. Make the gringo kneel. Do it for your old greaser mother. Darling boy, do it for all the greasers."

He hugged her, assuring her that such bitterness was not like her, nor was any apology for her proud Mexican heritage.

"I will not dishonor us," said Rico as he waved goodbye at the gate, which was not the same as saying he would do something great.

A week later young Far arrived at the border, at Laredo, Texas, his passport in his right hand, his bulging suitcase in the other. But the immigration authorities said the passport was probably a fake, that its fake-proof hologram printed into the cover looked like one of those that had been routinely copied by the forgery syndicate operating out of New Orleans. The young man's pleas were to no avail. So he spent the night in a dirty little cantina getting drunk and fending off thieves intent on relieving him of his suitcase.

The next day Rico tried to cross the border legally at Eagle Pass and then at Del Rio. The passport was useless. "Seen hundreds of 'em just like that, only last week," said the American immigration man. "If you don't have someone on this side to vouch for you, better forget it."

Rico, dejected but resolute, hiked westward on the old blacktop road to La Cuesta. That evening, hot, tired and desperate for the biggest bottle of beer he could find, cold if possible, he wandered into a small roadside bar. There it was that he met Chi Chi Tepic, on the lookout as usual for prospective illegals. Rico's suitcase was a giveaway, he said. Anyone with a suitcase as handsome as his was obviously looking for a way to get across the border. The next evening Chi Chi and the others gathered at Tepic's tent. His clients paid up and made ready to use Tepic's tunnel under the wall.

It was a sooty-looking night under a small crescent moon, and very warm, when they set out. Chi Chi guided his clients to a sandy area across the shallow Rio Grande at the west end of Boquillas Canyon, to a brushy spot just under the wall. On signal, Chi Chi pulled aside a large pile of creosote plants and needle-sharp blades of the lechugilla, exposing a hole as big as a washtub. "Go man! Go man!" he ordered, pointing to the hole. Far dived into the hole, dragging his suitcase behind him. Ricardo and Eduardo eased Pooch into the hole and then they too disappeared into the tunnel. The four scrambled along in the dark on hands and knees, following the tunnel as it angled around outcroppings of rock, then turned sharply toward the east to its opening near a growth of creosote thirty yards beyond the wall.

In fifteen minutes, caked in sweat and dust, Rico squirmed through the hole on the American side and scrambled toward the foot of the canyon wall to a cluster of boulders where Chi Chi had told him he would find cover. A few minutes later Pooch's head popped up. Eduardo was pushing at his rump, urging Pooch, "One more heave. One more and you are a free man."

Pooch dragged himself out of the hole and turned to help Eduardo. But it was too late for the Albans. Two big trucks with searchlights came grunting along the dirt service road that ran along the American side of the wall. In one continuous movement, as if their drivers had been tipped off and knew precisely where to go, the trucks turned around, backed up, and dumped tons of iron mesh, soupy concrete and gravel into Chi Chi's tunnel. "Corked that sonofabitch good," said the driver of the concrete truck as he put his vehicle into forward gear and the machine rumbled along the service road toward the east, followed by the lighter dump truck.

It was the Virgin Mary, the twins told Chi Chi later, who had saved them. The slurry of concrete had sent them sprawling, bumping and squirming half the distance back toward the south end of the tunnel. Praying furiously, they clawed their way out. Coughing and gagging, they headed for the river where they dunked themselves until they were clean of concrete. Chi Chi greeted them cheerily as they stumbled back into Mexico. He was anxious to avoid any talk of a refund. "We begin again tomorrow. We dig another tunnel in this same area, a little to the south. Lightning, it don't strike twice in the same place."

"You can forget the whole thing, I mean all of it," shouted Ricardo. "I will never enter a smaller space again than a church. And I will sleep in the church as well, and die in it." He would not listen to his brother Eduardo's pleas to try again.

Ricardo's vow was good. A year later he died of dysentery and was buried in the cemetery behind the Boquillas churchyard. Its gravediggers were one of the few groups of professionals in the area that the curse of unemployment had spared. And who paid for Ricardo's funeral. None other than Chi Chi Tepic, in secret.

OF
CAVES

IN THE VAST, desolate and beautiful Big Bend Park, Rico and the older man walked, stumbled and staggered their way north along the desert valleys of the Chisos mountain range, keeping gigantic Castolon butte to their left. They dragged themselves through sand, yucca, cenezia, bloom-stalk, cactus and creosote, stopping only to eat a handful or two of the beans that had been given to them as part of Chi Chi's "travel rations," along with rusty canteens full of water from the Rio Grande.

It was Rico Far, not Grenada, who slowed them down. The middle-aged writer was scarcely fazed by their strug-gle through that long no man's land south of Highway 385, the park road that ran north toward the Texas town of Marathon, now a ghost town. Pooch would stop to let Rico get his breath and cool off a bit, tell a story he had heard from people in his old home town about the love life of lizards, then share more of his beans and what

41

remained of his water with Rico. Rico had long since used up all of his water. He was embarrassed by the guy twice his age who seemed to scarcely sweat and never grew tired.

"You are something else, Pooch. I never saw anything like it, you I mean," Rico said at one point as he tugged at the older man's sleeve, asking him to stop to rest.

"I remember when I was your age, Rico. That's what keeps me young now, remembering, such Mexican things as the beauty and power of Xochipilli."

"Yes I know, our god of flowers and spring, our god of dance and song."

"So you know about Mexico? Most people your age don't give a damn. They don't give a shit for anything."

"Well, I hope someday to be an artist."

"That's not as bad as it sounds," said Pooch, grinning. "I was once a writer."

"That's as bad as it sounds," said Rico, returning the grin. "Chi Chi said he had heard of you before we met at the wall."

"Chi Chi is a con man. One of the finest. Knows just when to tell you that someone besides your parents knows who you are."

"Aren't thinkers con men, too, Pooch? I notice you seem to think a lot. That can only mean you're cooking up something."

The banter went on for miles, about Pooch's need for a full plate of upper teeth, about Rico's desire to see Paris and to chase French women, about anything that crossed their minds. They felt easy with one another. A bond of friendship began to form between them.

They pushed on. The sky was whitened by the intense sun. The makeshift headgear, fashioned from the big red cotton kerchiefs that Tepic gave each of his "clients," kerchiefs that had "Chi Chi's Subsurface Service" printed onto them to let the American authorities that often caught his illegals know what they could do with their stupid damn wall, helped provide some relief from the sun.

But the red kerchiefs could be seen from a helicopter too, from further away, thanks to new American technology, than illegals realized. When they reached Interstate 290, near the town of Stockton, Far and Grenada were arrested by border patrol cars now roaming a zone two hundred miles deep above the border. A helicopter had spotted them walking north on 385 and the patrol car arrested them hiding under the interchange at Stockton. Rico showed the police his passport and told them that Pooch was his father, stranded with him inside Mexico when the wall went up and authorities refused to accept his passport. "Yeah, sure," said the officer as he snapped on handcuffs. The car headed for Pecos.

At the station in Pecos, the state patrol officer at the desk was sipping coffee as he worked over his papers. He looked up at Rico and Pooch, pushed back his chair, studied them for a moment, then said wearily, "When you illegals gonna realize that Texas ain't as big as it used to be. Ain't no real jobs here. Oil's all gone. Was gone back in 2000. You got more left in Mexico than we do. And those high-tech operations that moved into the panhandle? A damned fart in a rainbarrel. Can't eat a goddamned computer. Ain't near as good to eat as a good steak, like the kind we used to grow around here. How many damn gimmicks can a society live with?"

Rico launched into a fervent plea, "as one American to another," protesting that his passport was proof of who he was.

"It takes more than an ID to tell if a man is real or not," said the officer. "Sorry, ain't nothin' I can do. There ain't any real employment around here. The last real employment in these parts was when they were building that damn wall. We hired a lot of illegals to build that bastard. My God, it runs all the way from Port Isabel on the gulf

43

clear up to El Paso. Made for a lot of honest hard work. We needed the wall and the illegals needed the work. Wasn't easy on us just to shove them back on the south side of the damn wall when it was finished." He paused, stroked his chin and added, "Maybe things will pick up again. There's talk of building something along the rest of the border, from El Paso to Tijuana. Course, if the Mexican government won't chip in on the cost it'll go slower. But hell, the army can't control all those people. Half a million camping around Nogales, over in Arizona, already."

He pointed to a corner of the room. "There's some coffee over there in that machine. Mountain grown, they say. Tastes like hell to me, but have some. Then we'll ship you up to the holdin' pens at Carlsbad. They'll process you for deportation. I'll send the passport up there, for whatever it's worth. Sorry, ain't nothin' I can do."

Rico tried again. "Sir, I'll do anything. I'll work for you personally. If you like, my partner and I will do odd jobs around your house, anything. We *belong* on this side of the border."

The officer chuckled. "Oh, a work ethic Mex?" Then he caught himself. "Shouldn't say things like that. I know most of you folks will work like demons if you get the chance. But I got to be realistic too, so do you two fellas. No way in hell this country can hold all the people that want to get into it. Now ain't that right? I mean honestly? Course I'm right. So I do my job."

The gigantic caverns at Carlsbad, one of the wonders of the world by any measure a person wished to apply, were a godsend to immigration authorities trying to deal with the hordes of refugees, half-starved men, women and children, illegals, as they continued to be called, beating against the Rio Grande Wall in Sectors 5 and 6. Only a tenth or so of those who got over, under or around the wall were caught before they disappeared into the great swelling cities of the north. But that was still millions of people a year, plus or minus hundreds of thousands, that had to

44

be dealt with when they were caught. In the Tucson and San Diego sectors of the wall, enormous warehouses made of corrugated sheet metal were used to house refugees and prepare them for deportation. A gigantic tent city served much the same purpose in the Brownsville area.

In Sectors 5 and 6, the area from the Big Bend National Park to Presidio and from Presidio to El Paso, no such facilities had been established. The money had run out and most of the refugees huddled together in the open, or in makeshift windbreaks put together from small dead trees and brush. Some were accommodated hastily by national guard units in ghost towns that dotted lower Texas, places like Las Cruces, Cornudas and Van Horn.

It was at this point that a bright young planner in the Federal Emergency Management Bureau came up with the idea of using Carlsbad caverns as a detention center. He proposed that the same "multiple use" principles that had been applied to other national parks during the eighties and nineties be applied to the caverns. The "multiple use" idea was tried and true, he argued. Wilderness forest areas, for instance, had been used as game refuges and as clear cut forestry zones. The giant aluminum water wheel that had been built under the Bridal Veil falls of Yosemite was erected with the same logic in mind. Not only did the power generated by the wheel provide sufficient electricity to light up new souvenir stands and gambling casinos in the floor of the valley, enough juice was left over to illuminate the falls at night.

The Carlsbad caverns were 250 million years old by the time anyone on earth had realized that it was time to "Begin again." They were formed of limestone from a living reef at the edge of an ancient sea. The whole process was long and mysterious. The actual detail on this great work did not begin until considerably later. It was as if the Creator had realized that it was a mistake to claim He could do the whole universe in seven days. So the detail on projects like Carlsbad were left to Nature. In the hush of

45

total silence, giant towers and enormous pendants that glistened like the inside of a newborn star formed, eight hundred feet below the ground. Veils, stalagmites and stalactites, filaments as thin as an evanescent dream formed of minerally colored water. It took 60 million years to ready the holding pens for Central American illegals.

Kitchens and toilets appeared somewhat later, in the Age of Tourists. But by 2013, it was clear to the more imaginative people in Washington that the caverns could be put to better use than simply to awe visitors and make them think about eternity. Ramps and elevators were put in, and long rows of picnic tables, and fast food stands, and taps for beer and frozen custard. It was a natural. The toilets that were installed were big, some units containing a hundred urinals in a row, the need for which Nature had never had the wit to anticipate. And the caves could be lit up. Not only that, it had only a single entrance and was easy to guard. Its high-speed elevators could accommodate 1,200 people an hour. The caves remained cool, at an even 56 degrees. Illegals could be stuffed into the caves and kept there as long as necessary. About all that was needed was a supply of sponge-rubber mattresses, blankets and food tailored to Latin tastes—refried beans, tortillas, plenty of hot peppers and, of course, Pepsi. Tourists that straggled into the caverns because they had read an old copy of *National Geographic* could be culled out easily and sent on to gawk at the Sears Tower in Chicago or one of the Astrodomes somewhere. Illegals could be shipped by the carload to El Paso and officially deported without getting off the trucks.

"Do you realize, young man," said Pooch when he and Rico were safely deposited in the caves, "that this whole thing was done by God in inky darkness? The actual beauties of the original cave I mean. The Creator can see in the dark." It was a slightly sarcastic remark, for Pooch was indeed stunned by the beauty of the caves.

"Even a Creator used to thinking big was impressed with this, that's for damn sure," said Rico.

But Pooch and Rico were impressed with more than that. They were impressed by the sheer mass of illegals that could be accommodated in the caves. They were also impressed by the efficiency of the immigration authorities, at the way illegals were each given color-coded identification tags to hang around their necks, assigning them to various chambers of the caverns—the Room of the Veiled Statue, the Room of the Frozen Waterfall, the King's Palace, the Room of the Eternal Kiss, the Hall of Giants, and so on. They were impressed as well by the fact that each illegal was given a small bell, which he was allowed to keep, with "Carlsbad Caverns National Park" engraved on it. It was all very American, as they both knew it would be. Illegals were to jingle the bell whenever they wished to have a guard usher them to the lavatory.

They were not impressed with the artistic opportunity the caverns presented. Random scribblings, nicknames, insults and vulgarities, bilingually presented, covered many of the walls. It was something that rivaled the great works of the eighties, works of men like Futura, Zephyr, even Haring. The Hall of Giants contained the most stunning tour de force of all, perhaps the preeminent statement of twenty-first century American art, something to put the Giottos and Tintorettos of ancient times firmly in their place.

There were three massive stalagmites in the hall. They were known as domes. They towered sixty feet high and resembled nothing so much as giant phalluses drooling with sexual energy, lingams from some overheated Hindu fantasy, or something that belonged in a public park in San Francisco.

Some artist had smuggled cans of paint into the hall, along with paint swabs, made of discarded rags from expired consumptive illegals, and seventy-foot sections of rope from dismantled guard rails, and completed the tour de force in a single night. He had lassoed the domes one at a time, shimmied up their sides and painted each with a giant red ring. And at the base, in yellow, he had ringed each work with battle cries of twenty-first-century man, such as "Viva Corpus Cavernosa!" and "The Pope Has No Clitoris!" The latter was presumed by most to be an insult, though some said it represented a cryptic message suggesting an ongoing search for the feminine principle within the framework of Roman Catholic thought.

Pooch was not impressed with the great works in the Hall of Giants. Nor was Rico. "I am not sure it is right to disfigure the world this way," said Pooch sarcastically. Then he reminded Rico that in ancient Mexico the goddess of childbirth was Coatlcue.

"Yes, I know," said Pooch.

"What is more, it is a desecration of what a cave represents," said Pooch. "For in the beginning there was not light, there was a cave, a cave more vast than this. It was in that cave that the Creator first discovered he could breathe."

Rico looked at Pooch for a moment. "You have a beautiful mind, my friend," he said in astonishment. For he had never heard any such story in ancient Mexican folklore he had read. He knew Pooch had understood just how marvelous the great caves at Carlsbad once had been.

Two days after Pooch and Rico had been dumped into the cave they were summarily summoned to meet with authorities in the front office where illegals were processed. They were shown into a small side office where the "Director of Operations" for the Carlsbad holding pens hung his hat. There were two men there. They were both flush faced. They had obviously been quarreling or cranking each other up about something or the other.

"You're an artist, Far? That right?" the one called Ed demanded, evidently the senior of the two officials. "We were told that by the man in Pecos."

48

"That's true," said Rico. "At least an aspiring one."

"Then what do you think of the artwork in the caves?" He waited a moment, but before Rico could answer he said, "I personally think it stinks. Jim here thinks it's good stuff, up to date, with it, and a fine expression of what he says is the kind of multiple use people in Washington think the caves need to be put to."

Jim did not like the way the dice were being loaded. He interrupted, "I have merely said that it represents the kind of deep, soul-rooted statement that lies in the whole illegals question. I think..."

His senior cut him off. "He thinks...," said the director, nodding disdainfully toward Jim, "that this shit is art. Now what do you think? He's from New York, for Christ's sake. They like something different every other week. As an artist, what do you think?"

'Well, I'm really just getting started as..."

"And what does your buddy think? He's been a writer. We know that too."

Pooch could tell both he and Rico were walking on eggshells. "I guess—"

Ed interrupted him. "Now what in hell do these two illegals know about anything? They haven't been in an honest-to-God city for years. And *that's* something I know."

"Well, I'm ordering you two out of here. You can pick up your passports and haul-ass north." They were shown out without another word. Jim stood leaning against the wall of the office, sulking. His boss was wrapped in a frown.

As soon as they were outside the door Pooch looked at Rico. Rico shrugged. "Beats the hell out of me."

They were then given ten dollars each, a bus ticket to Lubbock, a half-dozen cheese sandwiches and told by the guard at the cave entrance to make themselves scarce. "Like everybody says these days, fellas," he said, as he stamped their passes, without looking up. "begin again!"

There was no convincing explanation of why Far and

49

Grenada were suddenly cleared. They did not know that the director had let it be known that "artistic types" were to be kept out of the cave. He had taken too much bad press because of the Hall of Giants work. And he loathed the whole idea of "multiple use." His subordinate, Jim, a man with a lot of connections in the East where they counted, had touted the "cave expressionists" as a kind of new wave. It was more or less a stalemate between them. But the director had no intention of Far going off half-cocked in the caves with another "great work" such as the one in the Hall of Giants. Besides he found Jim a foppish, affected, horse's ass, though he never let on to many folks that those were his true feelings. After all, he was a career park man, Jim a political appointee.

But there were other reasons why Far and Grenada were dismissed so summarily but not deported. It was another reason why the director had been so uneasy. The great paintings in the Hall of Giants had triggered a strange orgiastic happening. Young illegals had begun to sneak behind the stalagmites and boulders in the caves, and into the chambers and crevices off the main galleries, to make love as if their lives depended on it.

Considering the charnel house side of life in Carlsbad, despite what American authorities could do, with young people, old people, sick people, children, all crammed into the caverns, melancholy litter following the explosion of the population bomb in Central America—so that the floors of the caves seemed to twitch with the tormented fragments of an entire race of people—the response of the young lovers was probably predictable. The great hollows in the earth that Nature had labored on for 250 million years were no longer just wondrous, secret, God-haunted chambers deep within the planet. They had become humanized. They had become a prison, a hospital and a toilet, an eerie halfway house between misery to the south and hope to the north. But they had also become a strange battleground between love and death, eros and thanatos,

50

therefore a place where it was no longer possible, at least not at night, to tell whether the groans issuing up toward heaven were those of pleasure or those of pain.

Rico and Pooch found Lubbock half-abandoned and the people not at all friendly. They hitched rides north to Amarillo. It too was shrunken to about half its peak population of five million in 1995. They moved on, hitching rides on the government research vans working in Operation Overcome, a massive new desertification study centered in Oklahoma City. Operation Overcome's mission was to try to find out why overfarming, overfertilizing and total disregard for problems of erosion and soil depletion seemed to be related to poverty in the southern plains states.

The middle-aged Mexican and the young American ended up on Highway 14 and finally made it to St. Louis. There they fattened their wallets as best they could with part-time work in a public works project. They were put to use picking rubbish, broken bottles, tin cans and worn out tires from the muck along the banks of the Mississippi River. They worked for two weeks within the shadow of the Gateway Arch. It still stood tall, elegant, mathematically pristine, along the mudflats that now spread far out from the river bank.

With their first paycheck Rico and Pooch moved on. It was June. The weather was hot, barely tolerable. Milwaukee was the place they had their sights on. They had heard a great deal about it along the way north, both in story and song. They had heard that it actually had palm trees along its boulevards. For Pooch, Milwaukee became "The City of Palms," a small, balmy, glittering haven in the sweltering, booming and busting, progress-mad and very strange American world.

Pooch's vision of the city was not entirely a product of his magical realism. For some strange meteorological reason having to do with a stalled high-pressure dome and

51

winds off the Great Lakes, something neither he nor Rico understood nor cared about, the city had become rather like San Diego in the old days, but with a panache all its own. Some called it the city of love and laughter, some the city of beer, pretzels, accordion music and endless dancing, some the city that was giving to the world a whole new genre of art, an art of monumental "socialist kitsch" that was tender hearted, undemanding and curiously seductive. Its government was unlike anything ever seen in the world. It had been built from the ground up, under the guiding hand of a remarkable and wise old man of almost one hundred and five years, heading, he said, at full steam for five score and ten. He had been converted back in 1973, when he was a youngster of seventy years, to the teachings of E. F. Schumacher, famous back then for his bluntly sensible little book *Small is Beautiful*. "Fritz" Schumacher's ideas had been imposed upon, insinuated and pounded into the heads of the old man's followers, who comprised, as things stood in 2013, almost ninety-nine percent of the citizens of his state. Press around the country quickly dubbed the governor's followers "the Fritzland Movement."

Milwaukee had, in fact, become a state. It had seceded successfully, along with its environs (along a line running just south of Racine to a line just north of Sheboygan and west to an area called Holy Hill), from the State of Wisconsin. The old state, Wisconsin, had for years been under the sway of economic "growth" fanatics who pushed the lovely milk and honey land toward every kind of indiscriminate industrial development. The result was that the state, like the rest of the nation, was caught up in the horrors of "development" carried to its logical ends. The leader of the Fritzland Movement, the man now governor of the new State of Milwaukee, resisted the lunacy at every turn, using Schumacher as his heavy weapon in political debate and speechmaking.

The story of the secession was too complex and involved

to matter much to Rico and Pooch. Their big concern as they headed east from Prairie du Chien, where a river barge hauling coal had dropped them off on the banks of the Mississippi, was how to get past the roadblocks along the border of the new state. The border police were tough customers, done up in lederhosen and alpine hats. A lot of people on the outside thought them funny, some thought them cute. It was not unusual for people living in Illinois, Iowa or the old State of Wisconsin to drive a hundred miles just to have their pictures taken next to the border guards. But there was nothing funny or cute about the way the guards used their fence-post-sized billy clubs on nosy outsiders trying to get into the state without an invitation. And unless the invitation was personally signed by the old gentleman who occupied the Milwaukee Statehouse, there wasn't a snowball's chance in hell of staying longer than overnight, or for a weekend of fun, in the City of Palms.

THE STATE
OF
MILWAUKEE

RICO AND POOCH lay in the deep grass behind a clump
of buckthorn near the fence that ran along the western
border of the new State of Milwaukee, just east of the small
town of Hartford. They were panting hard. They had been
crawling on hands and knees toward a small brick building
that served as a guardhouse at the Hartford checkpoint.

On the face of it, the border looked like a tough nut to
crack. The guards, two of them, were all business as they
checked the identification papers of occasional cars moving
in and out of the state. There were no smiles and little
talk. And the guards looked every bit as impressive as Rico
and Pooch had been told they would. They were dressed
in brown lederhosen fashioned from elegant suede, immaculate white cotton blouses with lace cuffs, and ver-
milion velveteen vests richly embroidered in black. They
wore black ribbed half-socks with white fur knee tassels
and oxblood-toned shoes that laced to the ankle. They

were topped with deep-green velvet alpine hats with a single white feather held in place over the ear by a large gold buckle shaped like a rose. Their billy clubs, though not as big as fence posts, as Rico had been told they were, were massive nonetheless, dangling from their belts almost to the ground. They were made of polished butternut wood. It gave them the look of bronzed shillelaghs.

"Those fellas aren't fooling," said Rico in a whisper.

"This is truly a magical kingdom," said the novelist. "They are guardians of something that must be marvelous."

"I hope so," said Rico. "Those clubs could leave a real lump on your head."

That was not all that was impressive in the scene before them. Two gigantic flags, one the new version of Old Glory, the other a great half-and-half affair, the hoist section blue, the fly section green, snapped in the breeze at the top of fifty-foot poles. The poles themselves were topped with magnificent golden finials carved in the form of a rearing horse. And near the guardhouse, in front of which spread a large bed of orange calla lilies, blue and red salvia, white petunias and blue baby's breath, hung a six-foot-wide flag from a horizontal staff, in the gonfalon manner. It was green also but slashed from top right to the bottom left with a scarlet bar, the bend-sinister pattern. Though Rico and Pooch did not know it at the time, the governor was interested in heraldry and had chosen the bend sinister as a sardonic aside concerning the birth of his state. The bar running from top right to bottom left, instead of top left to bottom right—the bend-dexter pattern—often represented a bastard prince. In any case, along the scarlet bar of the gonfalon, in large black gothic lettering was printed: AT THE CENTER OF WISDOM IS PERMANENCE!

Pooch Grenada looked at the banner, then turned to Rico. His jaw was firm. "This is the kind of thing I came here to learn. There are damn few places where you can see that kind of honesty in print."

55

The aphorism was drawn from Schumacher's little book of 1973 and it was the governor's way of reminding people that the new State of Milwaukee did not tolerate loose talk about progress. Nothing makes sense, Schumacher had warned almost forty years earlier, if it becomes an absurdity when it is projected for a long period of time. The Fritzland Movement had made such principles the pillars of its philosophy.

For Rico, the message was rather mysterious. He had not thought about permanence much, certainly not in the no-nonsense way that the banner made the point. But it was clear to him as he and his friend huddled behind the large buckthorn near the guardhouse at the Hartford checkpoint that the new State of Milwaukee was no ordinary place. "This whole thing is fantastic," he said to Pooch after a long silence. "Just look at those flags."

Pooch smiled a kind of knowing smile. "For me it is a new Castile, a new León, a new Aragon, but better." He chuckled quietly, a hand to his mouth. "I hear the strains from 'Nights in the Gardens of Spain.'" Which was a bit of an exaggeration perhaps. He knew he had come to the right place. But the question was one of walls again, this time a high chainlink fence separating the new state from the rest of Wisconsin.

"The blue and green flag must be the state flag," said Rico.

"Unless I am a donkey's uncle, it is," said Pooch. "Blue for the great body of water to its east, green for its meadows and forests. I was told that when we were in Prairie du Chien."

"I did not notice the American flag as we were moving north. But it sure looks wonderful here," said Rico.

The new old Glory was an impressive ensign indeed. It now contained sixty-one stars, reflecting the turbulent years from 1990 to 2010, in the same way that the older versions of the flag told the story of the evolution of the Union during its first two hundred years.

At the time of the American Revolution the stars and stripes had taken every form imaginable. There were flags with red and white stripes only, flags with stripes and a rattlesnake, and flags with the cross of St. George in the canton, some with a New England pine tree there as well. When Vermont and Kentucky came into the Union, fifteen stripes showed up on the flag. Then came a flurry of more stars, in circles, in rows and ranks and in crosses. The flag had a wonderful ad lib quality about it, the kind of thing one would expect of a republic just beginning to feel the exhilaration of youth and fresh air. But things were also getting a bit out of hand, with every flagmaker inventing his own version of the stars and stripes. In 1912 the government stepped in and said thirteen stripes were quite enough and that it was time to line up the stars. For amateur flag designers and for those somber students of flags called vexillologists, the fun went out of things until 1990.

In 1990, "New Federalism" talk started again and so did the call for "States Rights." In fact, the word *nullification* was heard again in the hallways of Congress. That word hadn't been heard since John Calhoun unsuccessfully tried to explain what it meant in the eighteen thirties. The result back then had been a terrible civil war with fields of dead bodies at Shiloh, Antietam, and Fredericksburg, and in American swamps, wilderness and farm fields, the thoroughly nullified lives of an entire generation of young men.

The Speaker of the House of Representatives in 1990, a man from Georgia, decided that "We damn well aren't goin' through that whole War between the States thing over again. We can loosen things up a bit without turning the country inside out." That is what happened.

It was that sort of issue, too, though in a much updated form, that had so vexed citizens of the State of Milwaukee before secession from Wisconsin. It was not a question of taxation without representation, though the state's largest city had taken a shellacking from Madison on that too for years. For years, in fact, everyone in the state had been taxed to death and noisily misrepresented in the legislature. And it wasn't anything as grim as slavery, at least not the kind that people justified by counting melanin granules in the skin. The real problem was what the governor of the State of Milwaukee had come to call "the new condescension." It was a kind of hauteur that people in Madison began to affect toward one another, whether rich, poor, learned, ignorant, helpless or hopeless. It seemed to be associated in a loose, difficult-to-pin-down way with what Milwaukeeans called "Dane County liberalism," a kind of political smugness favored by those who considered themselves pure of heart and always good-intentioned. Just what it was became the subject of a great many essays by media wisemen and, of course, Madison university sociologists, which tended to muddy things hopelessly. But its roots seemed to lie in the growing uneasy feeling among most people, including the average man, that there were too many people on the planet and that there was some sort of basic, inescapable incompatibility between liberty and congestion, between freedom and masses. Which, naturally enough, sent shivers up the spine of "Dane County liberals." If one loved the common man, why in heaven's name would one wish to see fewer of them. Yet fewer were needed, that was obvious.

In Milwaukee, one of the media savants who prided himself on his literary graces took up the cause in one of his editorials, though he really was not sure if he was for or against the "new condescension." He knew only that he was a nobody in the state capitol in Madison. He wrote, "Condescension not only corrodes the bonds that hold our social classes together. It introduces doubt into the heart of our upwardly mobile youth and day laborers alike. It undermines love of polity, the very heartbeat of any democracy. It causes men to ponder the pleasures of revenge and to invent variations on the guillotine. It causes cities to patronize the farm, and farmers to patronize what they cannot reduce to tillage or silage. It sets man to looking down his nose at homely brethren creatures like the turtle and the bat. It can rip nature itself apart, as if its wonders and riches were a cheap disposable wardrobe won on game-show television by squealing innocents."

The stain of condescension on the sacred vestments of the idea of liberty had existed, of course, as long ago as the time of the republic's founding fathers. Jefferson was called a rube farmer by many Philadelphians. They had, even then, forgotten the difference between a sewer and a brook. Only a rube, they had gossiped, would build his home on the top of a hill so far back in the bush that it took weeks to get there after you accepted an invitation. And all you saw when you did get there were mastodon bones on a table in the foyer or oddball inventions such as a great clock that dangled cannonballs through a hole in the floor near the front door. And the stairways at Monticello were only twenty-four inches wide, too narrow for a hoop skirt. It was impossible for a gentleman to get a pretty woman upstairs to show her the quaint half-height windows or the poofs on the beds, those marvelous Bavarian feather-bed devices that had to be used to be appreciated. Guests of Jefferson had to settle for sherry in the downstairs salon and patronizing talk about Mr. Jefferson's tastes as a collector of paintings—his copy of a work by Mabuse, "Christ in the Praetorium," for instance, "a quite ordinary piece of work, really, to begin with."

Across the country, in fact, the disaffected outback in the early decades of the twenty-first century had grown tired of the snickering, including that from Washington bureaucrats who had turned the city Pierre L'Enfant had laid out on the shores of the Potomac with such care, sweating over his transit in the heat, ravenous malarial mosquitos swarming around his head, into a party town and a political sexpot. The outback had had it with the same bigshots who always showed up on television in the expensive front-row seats of the Kennedy Center every

time the president hung a medal around some opera sing-
er's neck. It was obvious that the Washington swells had
forgotten that their great-grandparents had stood barefoot
and shivering on the cold tile floors of Ellis Island while
they were being deloused.

Buffalo had become a state, so had Duluth, St. Petersburg and Milwaukee. So had the panhandles of Idaho and
Alaska. Of course, in New York, Buffalo had been patron-
ized for years. So when it lost its football team to Albany,
the die was cast, as the saying goes, or the Rubicon was
crossed, or the stick was in the shit, depending upon the
private club, coffee house or barroom in which the problem
was being deplored. The same was true of St. Petersburg.
It had been treated like dirt for years by Tallahassee. Many
of its oldsters had strange New York accents and they used
words like *redneck* with too much easy sarcasm. So Talla-
hasseeans had said, "Good riddance." It was much like
that with Duluth, too. When the Mesabi iron range played
out, St. Paul forgot where Duluth was. In 1997 it even
published a map with Duluth designated an unincorpor-
ated village. As for Milwaukee, it had had it up-to-here
with Madison, for years. Madison had always postured
toward Milwaukee as its intellectual better, the embarrassed relative of a slow-witted, utterly uneducable cousin
who slept with his overshoes on. As far as Madison was
concerned, Milwaukee took too much interest in clean
streets, polka bands and famous composers of tuba music.
It cared little for the arcane arguments of the Civil Liberties
Union and held Dane County liberalism in quiet disdain.
And as far as Milwaukee was concerned, any city like
Madison that had more professors than it had people
working in the Department of Sanitation was suspect from
the outset.

No one was sure why the panhandles of Idaho and
Alaska became new states. The panhandle of Texas hadn't,
nor had the panhandles of Florida and Oklahoma. Some
suspected that the legislation had garbled the meaning of

panhandle and that the Congress had thought it was taking action on street people. And one tipsy lawmaker said that none of the nation's business should ever be left hanging and that a panhandle was a case of business left hanging if ever there was one. So two panhandles became states, which helped straighten up the map a bit but little else.

But with the sixty-one stars on Old Glory, things had begun to heat up again amongst patriots, flag designers and vexillologists. The big states began to complain that they were being put on the same footing as dinky little burgs without skyscrapers, honest-to-God nightclubs, gambling casinos or race riots. So a formula was worked out in Washington by which the size of the stars on the flag would be determined by the size of the electoral vote of each state. Which meant that New York, California and Illinois were represented in the canton of Old Glory with very large and impressive stars, whereas Texas, following depletion of its oil and its depopulation, and the new city-states were represented by tiny stars.

The overall effect, as Rico and Pooch were the first to say, was a stunning new symbol of the Union, the kind of thing, in fact, that the flag law of June 14, 1777 had foreseen when it spoke so enthusiastically of "stars white in a blue field, representing a new constellation."

Rico and Pooch crawled behind a big willow tree to ponder what to do about the border guards. They sat there for twenty minutes. Then Rico's face began to brighten.

"I've been thinking about good books having good covers, Pooch," said Rico, a thought that came into the conversation from out of nowhere. "I was told in St. Louis that these guys aren't allowed to read dirty books. The state outlaws them."

Pooch looked at him quizzically. "I am not sure what difference that makes. We're stuck behind these bushes. Unless our patron saints appear, to help us, we are going to be here a long time. If they do appear we shall have to choose which of the two we should ask for assistance.

Who is your patron saint, Rico?" He was pulling Rico's leg again.

Rico ignored the question. He was impatient. He reached up and brushed the leaves of a small gooseberry bush that had managed to establish itself between the roots of the big willow. "This willow, Pooch!" said Rico, looking up. "It reminded me of pussy willows. That reminded me of girls. That reminded me of the books I got from the man on the barge. That gave me an idea."

Pooch was dubious. He snorted and looked back toward the guardhouse.

"I got some paperback novels in my bag, Pooch. Raunchy as hell. The stuff going around in the caves down there at Carlsbad. I got a real sizzler called *Never Enough.* Course I never read it."

"Just glanced at the cover, right?" Pooch teased. "So?"

"It's about a young guy who starts making out with two different nurses right after an operation to remove one of the three peckers he was born with."

Pooch's eyes squinted. "The author was a magical realist? With more faith in magic than realism?"

Again Rico did not respond to the question. "If I go up there and tell those guards I got a couple of hot, *real* hot, novels, and that I'm willing to trade them for a temporary work pass into Milwaukee, what do you suppose they will do."

"You can only judge by their dress. They appear to be of stout heart. And bored, and in need. Not much chance for romantic relief on these outposts, I'd guess."

"I say we go for it, Pooch."

"Well, man does not live by bread alone, books are important to him too," said Pooch.

"Especially to cops. My father once told me that he once bribed his way out of a heavy fine for speeding by just *promising* to send some books, soon as he got to an adult bookstore. Cops love forbidden fruit. We'll go for it, my friend. Once we get in, we stay in. We get the governor's invitation. We get it by hook or by crook."

Young Far stood up, unzipped his suitcase and fished out two dogeared paperbacks. He strode up to the guards. There was the usual "Halt!" and questions about who he was and what he wanted, how long he wanted to stay in the State of Milwaukee, whether or not he had relatives there, what ethnic persuasion he acknowledged, whether or not he had an invitation from the governor.

"We just want a brief work pass into the City of Palms. I have no invitation," said Rico, trying to smile.

"Sorry, no invitation, no pass," said the guard. "This state isn't interested in taking in more people. Work passes are hard to come by. Strict orders of the governor."

Rico brushed the blacktop with one foot, then glanced to one side and said casually, "Must get boring as hell at the gate here."

"That one you got right."

"Do any reading?"

"Course we can read. People out there think that nobody in this damn state can read. We read. We read plenty."

"I got some good reading, from the outside." Rico glanced at the guard. Pooch was walking up to join them.

"If it's subversive stuff we'll arrest you as soon as you cross that line." The guard pointed to the white line that ran across the blacktop at the gate.

"Like what?"

"Like things on the governor's list. Bullshit about development, progress, crap like that."

"What about love stories?" Rico pretended to stifle a yawn.

"Depends what kind." The guard stifled the yawn it triggered.

"Like this kind." Rico flashed the cover of one of his paperbacks. There was a honey-colored nude sprawling across the cover.

The other guard, a small man, moved in close to Rico. His blouse sleeves displayed double gold chevrons. He was a corporal, apparently the senior guard. "I'm in charge here," he said. He elbowed the other guard aside. There was an element of haughtiness in the gesture.

Rico handed him the paperback.

There was some hurried flipping through the pages, then a pause, then more flipping, this time a slight tremble in the hands. "Just a minute," said the corporal. He headed for the guardhouse.

The other guard scurried after him. "Hey, Charlie, give me a break, will ya? Let me have a look at that book too."

Sounds of squabbling came from within the guardhouse. "This is my post too, Charlie! Besides I saw the guy first. He talked to me *first*."

"I'm in charge here goddamn it! And don't you ever forget it, Len!"

More scuffling, then curses. "You're a stingy sonofabitch, Charlie, when the chips are down. You say you're my friend. But you aren't!" Len's voice was high, halfway between a plea and a warning.

"I'll let you look at this goddamned book when I'm done with it! Okay?"

"The officer is standing his ground," said Pooch. "Must love good literature." He grinned at Rico. "I think you got him."

The door of the guardhouse slammed, then opened. Len was pleading. "Shit, man. You and me bowl together. And you won't even share a damn book."

The corporal was quieter but remained contemptuous. "I've just about had it with you, Len. You never know your place. Now get back out there and watch those two guys and let me look this thing over. I'll make the decisions here. You're a big turd."

"Don't you call me a turd, Charlie. Don't you ever—"

The door slammed again. There were sounds of more

scuffling. One of the men was thrown against the wall with a thump. There were muffled curses.

"They seem to be working it out," said Pooch.

The guardhouse was quiet for a moment. Then the corporal and his partner emerged. They were hatless. Charlie's half-socks were down around his ankles. Len's vest was torn near the shoulder. "We worked it out," the corporal said. "You say you got some other reading, too?"

"Right here." Rico waved the other paperback. "Literature."

"Both Len and I enjoy literature," said the corporal.

"We got a deal then. We cross and you get some literature," said Rico.

"You'll enjoy our fair state. Nothing like it anywhere."

"How do we know we won't be arrested as soon as we cross?" asked Pooch.

"Because we got a deal, that's why. When Milwaukeeans give their word, that's it. And we gave our word."

Rico handed *Never Enough* to the corporal. The corporal looked at the cover and whistled. On the cover, in deeply embossed lettering with gold trim, it said *Never Enough*. Below it was a picture of a nude in the clutches of a frenzied man with an odd bifurcated male organ resembling that of the opossum.

"Got this one straight off a supermarket shelf, corporal, in Prairie du Chien."

"Okay. You can go in. But only for two weeks. Until you get an official invitation, if you want to work in the state for longer. Now fill out these forms at that little table near the guardhouse." The form was sixteen pages long.

Thirty minutes later Pooch and Rico were a mile and a half to the east, on the road toward Grafton, a town on the north end of the State of Milwaukee. Pooch was humming one of his Mexican tunes. Rico was composing in his head the letter he would write as soon as he could to his mother back in Villa Rito. He would not tell her about the books.

That afternoon, just after four o'clock, the two pilgrims from Carlsbad found themselves sitting alongside a trucker who was hauling a load of sausage from Sheboygan to Milwaukee. The big, square machine he drove was painted bright blue, and along the sides and on the rear doors it proclaimed: "BRUNHILDE'S BRATS: The Best in Wurst."

The truck was one of those turned out by the small Shikel auto factory in Racine. The machine had passed stiff state regulations in the making. It was guaranteed to last ninety years, to move at speeds not to exceed forty miles an hour, to be capable of operating on the methane gas generated on local farms and to be richly upholstered in heavy leather. (A state law passed in 2002, S.L. 432-1516, forbade "the manufacture, distribution, sale or trading of plastic fabrics of any kind, or the aiding, abetting and/or generating inducements to buy, by willful or other means, said forms of sleeze.")

The driver was a rotund, jovial fellow who talked an arm and a leg off his passengers. That was the main reason he picked up hitchhikers without a second thought. He loved to talk.

"You fellas come from out there. I can tell. A bit down on your luck. And you look kind of tense, too. That's the way people out there always look. It's all that worrying, I guess, trying to speed things up, trying to make everything spin a little faster. Trying to push things where they don't want to go. Another day, another million dollars, right? Course, we aren't against a few bucks under the mattress for a rainy day, either. But turnin' out good bratwurst is what my outfit is all about. I take a load down to the city every other day. Always fresh. Other companies do the same thing, but Brunhilde's are top-drawer brats. Course we don't store our brats in a drawer, believe me." He chuckled. "Just twenty-four hours from the squeal to the griddle. Well, there's a lot of celebratin' goin' on just about every weekend in Milwaukee. That takes a lot of brats. People at the beaches in Milwaukee eat a hell of a lot of brats. Won't be different this weekend, with the bands out playing as usual and all the dancing. Some of those muscle men that strut their stuff along Bradford beach? They'll eat a dozen brats and ask for another dozen on the spot. My company can hardly keep up. A juicy brat is hard to resist."

Rico and Pooch looked at each other and swallowed hard. They hadn't eaten much of anything for almost forty-eight hours. The truck driver was giving them the old Pavlovian treatment, only he wasn't ringing a bell to get them to salivate, he was talking about the real thing, a truckload of it, only a foot behind their seats.

"I can smell those beauties right here in the cab of this truck," said the trucker dreamily.

Rico and Pooch looked at each other, their faces suddenly sagging, as if they were on the verge of tears.

"Our recipes are secret, of course. Just three men know what gives them that special flavor. The flavor is famous all over the state, fact, all over this area, even in Madison. They're so jealous over there of our bratwurst that they could start a war. They got a wiener factory, but it's just one of those hotdog junk-food places. Damn things taste like they're half dog food and half ground-up cardboard. Ours are genuine, the real thing. People come up from Chicago just to eat our bratwurst, get special party passes and everything. Course, I don't blame them. Down there it's either in a can, it's dried, it's radiated or it's frozen. The radiated stuff causes lumps to grow in the armpits. And the frozen stuff is expensive as hell. When you get it thawed out it looks like it's been eaten already. Our brats are fresh as a schoolgirl's wink."

"I have eaten bratwurst many times," said Pooch wistfully, "when I was a student in Britain, we would vacation in Germany. Haven't had one since." His remark had a deliberately ambiguous tone. Enchiladas were more to his taste. But he was hungry enough to eat a skunk, including the stripes.

The driver looked over and smiled pityingly. "Well, you'll get plenty of good bratwurst in this state. Like I was saying, we make the best. Other kinds of sausage too. Like your summer sausage? We make that too. Brunhilde's makes a hard summer that's so sweet when you tuck a slice between a couple of crackers that you never know whether to just eat sausage or alternate with swallows of that dark beer. It's a tossup I guess. Me, I'm an alternator. I switch back and forth. A good hunk of summer sausage, then a swallow of beer, then another hunk of summer sausage. Or you take that liverwurst with hickory smoke flavor? Now that's good sausage! Damn good. Course I usually alternate with the lighter beer when I have a hunk of that on my plate, next to the crackers and pickles.

Rico was having trouble. He put his fist to his forehead and pressed hard. The thought of the load of sausage behind him, inches away, threatened to reduce him to a begging, shameless supplicant on his knees right there in the cab of the truck—or worse, to a violent criminal. He could see the headlines in the newspaper the next day in Pooch's City of Palms: "GOODNATURED TRUCKER INNOCENT VICTIM OF HIJACKING." And the story would begin, "The brutal theft of a truckful of wurst..."

The trucker seemed to sense that something was wrong with Rico. He caught himself just as he began reeling off another lyrical passage about sausage. "Fellas, I should have known." He shook his head. "You're out on the highway. You come from out there. You probably haven't eaten a damn thing all day. And I get to working on you. Well you just hang on. I'll take you to my sister-in-law's place, a place called Smudge's. It's just a bar, but she's always got something set out for the fellas to nibble on at this time of day. Some herring, some cheese, some pickles, dills usually. All you can eat, along with the beer. The beer you pay for of course. They own an apartment building, at the same place."

Rico wrenched his mind away from the herring, dills and bratwurst. "We're looking for rooms. Nothing fancy. Someplace that doesn't mind ... uh—"

"Mexicans? Right? Well, hell no, them prejudices disappeared a long time ago, mostly. We got pepper-bellies here by the thousands. Good folks, once they get used to our wurst." He chuckled. "Why good God almighty, we even got Republicans in this state yet. Not many, but a few. Nobody holds it against them. Nobody says, 'Boy, does that guy smell' ... because of the cologne them business types use. Fairy smells. No, we take anybody to heart that's willing to do his bit for the state."

"We can't pay much."

"Oh, Mabel's prices are good. We don't have high prices on anything in this state, because the farms around here produce so damn much we can't eat it all. And our factories pump it out too, household stuff, toasters and such. Governor worked all that out. We just don't let people throw stuff away as soon as they get sick of the color."

The driver paused, stared ahead, laughed at a joke he hadn't even told, then began again. "But Mabel's food is something else. Makes good cheeseburgers, too. Big fellas, juicy but cooked. A stack of onions on top. The best. I take my onions raw."

"How long before we get there?" asked Rico, his upper lip tight.

"Not long. I'll swing onto County Line Road pretty soon, then we'll catch Lake Drive, the scenic way, as they say. Then we'll swing over on North Avenue to the bridge, then we're right there, Smudge's, the best little neighborhood bar in town. The place has a touch of class too. One of the tenants is a poet, a guy by the name of Pester. We have poetry readings every Friday night. Sometimes Mabel's husband, my brother Louie, plays the guitar, background for the poetry. Tell the truth, I'm thinking right now of getting my fist around the handle of a stein of that nice, dark, cool lager.

Then suddenly as the truck swung westward toward the North Avenue bridge, the whole scene before them seemed to explode in color and splendor. The bridge, which they approached at an angle, glittered before them. It was long, elegantly clad in marble, with two fifteen-foot-high pieces of heroic sculpture at the entrance and two across on the far end, with smaller, three-foot-high elfin figures set every twenty feet or so along the marble railings, which were supported by ornately carved balusters. Massive fluted cast-iron lightposts were fitted into the side of the bridge with large ornate light fixtures dangling from them. Cherubs graced the tops of each.

"It is the bridge of angels," said Pooch.

"Oh, we got a dozen like that," said the trucker. "They were all rebuilt over the last ten years or so. The governor says any society that is worth a damn has good bridges, because good bridges mean you know where you want to go. An artist from our Little Italy section, over near Brady Street, supervised the whole thing. He got the idea from Mussolini's Olympic Stadium, he says. Thought Mussolini was a horse's ass, but he liked the big statues at the stadium, all the bulging muscles on the athletes. That's why these statues look so powerful. He told me that one night when he was partying it up at Smudge's. Lot of artists and whatnot come into Smudge's, pretty women too. Some of the women artists that come in there look cute as kittens in their leathers."

Then they saw Smudge's at the far end of the bridge, on the southwest corner of the intersection at North and Humboldt. It was a huge, three-story Victorian affair, looming up against the sky to the west like some colorful remnant of a fourteenth-century fortress. Six large Tuscan-looking arches were recessed into the brick facade of the first and second floors. The second and third floors, which rose from the north half of the building, stood above the main building, with pilasters thrusting up from the centers of the arches. The building was painted gray with its arches trimmed in dark blue, and a large brick tower that stood at its northeast corner was painted white. The battlement that ran around the rim of the tower was trimmed in yellow and black, so that its embrasures and merions seemed to glow in the lowering sunlight.

As the Brunhilde's driver said, there was nothing particularly unusual about the treatment of the building. Most of the city was built of brick in an eclectic style with a variety of revivalist elements, some gothic, some baroque, some classic, some pure invention. Since statehood, strict rules on building maintenance had been imposed by the government. Everything had to be painted, trimmed or rebuilt according to the 1867 *Encyclopedia of Architecture*, a five-inch-thick volume written by a Joseph Gwilt, and revised "with alterations and considerable additions," by Wyatt Papworth, no less, Fellow of the Royal Institute of British Architects. So the whole town took on a special flavor, a marvelous mix of period building, old-fashioned love of detail, love of good wood, bursts of exuberance, whiffs of eccentricity, and touches of kitsch and Camelot.

Rico and Pooch were impressed. "I think I will be happy here," said Pooch. "Very happy. It is every man's dream to live in a city like this."

And Rico said, "It isn't very modern, but I think I'll like it, too." But he was uneasy. He was not sure what ambition meant in a place like this.

"Well, there's time for a quick trip around town in this old truck then, just to show you the sights, before we end up at Smudge's," said the driver. And off he drove, forgetting for the moment about the sausage and beer, forgetting that his friends from "out there" were hungry enough to devour all of the bratwurst in the truck, including the waxed wrapping paper in which the little sausages snuggled.

"This here's the downtown. This big building on the

71

right is the Statehouse. Used to be called City Hall. Everyone in town loves these old buildings. We even have tours and stuff that the churches run, to tell people what they got. The Statehouse is from eighteen ninety something, Flemish Renaissance style. I know I got that right, because a cousin of mine works in there polishing the brass. This other, the one with the big fountain, that's for plays and things, symphonies and ballets. Cross the way, this one?" He stopped the truck and pointed out the window. "It's our Theater District building, all put together from old landmarks and such, like the building there with the golden lyre on top. That's the Pabst theater. Guy by the name of Keating designed the whole business and it was put up back in 1985 I think, if I recall."

"It's lovely, really beautiful," said Pooch. He had forgotten how hungry he was.

"Now I'll take this old truck across the river and then up Wisconsin Avenue and we'll get back to Mabel's in a jiffy. But just look back at the way the tower on that theater setup looks in the late afternoon. Those copper and glass peaks look like they was made out of gold." The wurstman was obviously proud of his state's capital city.

Then, finally, they were in Mabel's. Rico and Pooch were welcomed by a stocky, rosy-cheeked and bearded Louie behind the bar. Mabel came out of the kitchen wiping flour off her hands onto her apron. She gave the bratman a hug. "After we get settled now," she said, "you tell me the latest from Sheboygan. Everything, right down to the buttonholes and shoelaces." First everyone ate. And did Rico and Pooch eat!—brats, beer, summer sausage, beer, cheese, beer.

They paid a week's rent, flashed their work permits and Mabel showed them to their rooms. Rico was given a room on the third floor and studio space, everything he had ever dreamed of. Pooch was settled into one of the rooms on the second floor, next to the two-room apartment of an old man named Steinberger and his daughter Sara. And after a shower and a shave it was down to Smudge's again for a cheeseburger apiece, a stein of dark and two shots of brandy on the house.

The fact that Smudge's was on the first floor and that it was a handy, friendly place, full of workmen during the late afternoons, masons, electricians, carpenters and the like, not a few of them women of heft and ready wit, all crowded shoulder to shoulder at the bar and prepared to break into song at the drop of the price of another round, made Rico's and Pooch's new home seem too good to be true. The pooltable was always busy at that time of day; so was the row of booths along one side of the room where customers of a more philosophic bent settled in with their steins of beer to debate some detail of state politics.

There were questions, of course, about how things were "out there" along the Mexican border and in cities Rico and Pooch had come through. There were questions about the accuracy of TV accounts of the crisis along the Arizona and California parts of the Mexican border. But most of Smudge's customers knew all too well what it was like outside the state and they did not like to dwell on it. Life "out there" was too absurdly self-destructive. So there were inevitable touches of smugness in the voices of Milwaukeeans who had taken trips to the east or west coasts or to the south, and then came home to recount stories about the way things were going "out there."

In fact, during Rico's and Pooch's first evening in Smudge's, one regular customer told a story that brought guffaws and pitying grimaces to just about everyone in the place. He told about the funeral he had attended two weeks earlier in Detroit for a brother-in-law.

It was hard for Rico and Pooch to get close enough to the man to get all the details, since the storyteller was a baker from Brady Street. His white overalls gave off the aroma of freshly baked bread, so he was always surrounded by a tight little cluster of admirers. But from what Rico gathered, he told Pooch later, the brother-in-law had killed himself because his "modern conveniences" had finally worn him out. For one thing, he had owned an automatic ice-cube-making refrigerator. While he was slaving away late at the office one night, the machine covered the floor of his kitchen with a three-inch layer of ice cubes. Its master had gone to the refrigerator in the dark, his mind swimming with thoughts of a piping-hot TV dinner converted from frozen perch and asparagus. The ice had sent him windmilling across the kitchen and he banged into the microwave. The microwave's door swung open and the poor man's head went in, for only a moment or two, while his head was clearing from the thump. But the safety devices on the oven hadn't worked and part of the nape of his neck got cooked. After that, he spent months in traction with his head in an automated stirrup that never seemed to work right and that jerked him around at odd hours of the night. When he finally got on his feet and back home, he fell under the spell of a television advertisement for a new computerized automobile that practically drove itself. "It is widely advertised and highly acclaimed," said his friends in hushed admiration for the new technology. The car was supposed to stop and start automatically at red lights without a touch to the brakes. But the machine's electronic system misfired four times in three weeks and almost killed its putative master twice.

The suicide note was plaintive, to put it mildly. It said that any victim of so much progress ought to know that it wasn't worth congesting the planet with a new generation of the goddamn machines. They were obviously bent on man's destruction. And since man was intent on perfecting the infernal machines, he was willing to surrender the planet to them then and there and to be done with it. He willed his entire estate to the University of Michigan's Computer Research Institute. The note ended with an enigmatic quote from the Book of Job:

Does the wild ass bray when he has grass,
or the ox low over his fodder?
Can that which is tasteless be eaten without salt,
or is there any taste in the slime of the purslane?

The baker's friends had listened to the story of the death of his brother-in-law with shaking heads and clucking sounds. They pitied people out there but they were also disgusted with arrant stupidity. The lines from Job simply proved it again. "Well, that's par for the damn course," said one. "They worship their damn space-age marvels and end up asking if there is any taste in the slime of the purslane?"

The baker's audience disagreed as to precisely what purslane was, other than to agree with Louie that it was some kind of succulent herb. Even biblical scholars argued about what it was precisely. "But 'slime of the purslane'?" "God only knows what that one is," said Louie. "But there's a hell of a lot that's turned slimy 'out there,' that's for damn sure." His customers nodded knowingly. They all knew the country was acting as if it had been tripping-out on purslane slime, as the response to the supposed message from outer space made pretty obvious. Whether or not there was taste in slime of purslane was *just* the kind of thing people in cities like Detroit and L.A. and Chicago could be expected to get hung up on.

Pooch was in bed by ten o'clock and snoring up a storm. His dreams were filled with images of his recent adventures. They drifted and pulsed through his sleepful imaginings like some diaphanous collection of jellyfish. There was the soft light at the end of the tunnel at the border, the dripping ceilings in the caves at Carlsbad, a great silvery arch hovering in the steamy air near a river, flags of a thousand different colors, and the face of Sara Steinberger, lovely, soft and neurasthenic.

"I have had a strange night," Pooch told Rico the next

day. "There is a frightening connection between dreams and sausage making."

Rico had gone straight to bed that evening.

But two nights later he sat up on the edge of the great circular bed in his room in the apartment tower and wrote his mother, in Spanish. The letter translated more or less as follows:

Dear Mother,

We have reached the State of Milwaukee. It is almost 2,400 miles away from Villa Rito. It is north of Chicago about a hundred miles, the place where everybody carries a gun now and where they are fighting about whiskey and gambling again. Milwaukee is a very beautiful city. My friend Pooch (I will tell you about him later in my letter) calls it "the City of Palms." Almost every street is lined with palm trees. Most of them are not very big yet because they only started planting them fifteen years ago when the weather here got warm and beautiful, due, they say, to a modified greenhouse effect. It does not snow here anymore. But almost every street has palms now. It reminds me of cities by the sea in Mexico before our climate got bad, after all of the forests were cut and everything seemed to turn to desert in so many places. But it is much neater than Mexico City here, even before the earthquakes of the nineteen eighties that you and Dad told me about. The police arrest people if they spit on the street. And if you spit chewing gum on the street like they do in the rest of America I've seen (there are little blackish spots all over streets in St. Louis, from gum that people spit out and walk on), they make you scrub it up on Sunday morning with turpentine and a tooth-brush, while the TV newsmen interview you. It is really funny to see people in their Sunday clothes, sometimes just after they get out of church, kneeling on a piece of news-paper and scrubbing away, with some TV newsman trying to get his camera close enough to the sidewalk to show the "criminal's" face. But it sure keeps the streets nice. And you can't urinate in the streets like we could in Mexico. People have lost that freedom forever. (I don't miss that

76

freedom really. Things don't smell like a toilet.)

There are two important smells in this city. One is from a brewery in the middle of town. It looks like a church from a distance but it is a brewery instead (just about all of the buildings here have some sort of tower on them). They have lots of churches, too. From the big bridges you can look south and count about thirty church spires, a lot of them with gold crosses and some with just gold balls on them. Protestants like the balls, Pooch says. But this one special smell comes from hops, which they use in making beer. Hops has a sweet smell, but too much of the odor can make you feel almost sick. Pooch told me hops is a plant that looks like lettuce and grows in the air, without roots of any kind. He says it is gathered with a butterfly net. Of course, he is kidding. He is always trying to joke about things like that, although he is a pretty serious person. Most of the beer is dark, the color of Pepsi almost, and very strong. They outlawed all weak beer here a long time ago, also low-calorie beer. Some of the beer is called Weisbier, because of its yeast. The yeast settles on the bottom of the bottles. The bottles have to be opened very carefully or they blow up. One man lost a piece of the end of his nose when he held a bottle down by his waist and popped the cork without being careful. Sounds funny, but I guess it wasn't to him. He has a scar now (someone told me this) that is shaped like the cork that hit him.

Boy am I telling you a lot about beer, eh? But just one more thing. All of the taverns have big mugs, the German kind, with lids (you know, "steins," like they have at tourist places in Mexico). They hang from the ceiling on hooks. Every customer has his own and they are full of wonderful designs like our pottery used to be like in Mexico (in some ways) with people dancing and things like that.

The brewery here works night and day. It brews beer for the whole state. There are two kinds, the only kinds allowed in the state (the government keeps pretty close tabs on things, but nobody minds). One is called Schumie's Lager and one is called Schumie's Weisbier (whitebeer). They are named after a hero whose birthday the city celebrates every year, twice. Once for when he was born and once for when

77

he published a book that everyone seems to know by heart. Another smell comes from a chocolate factory, also right in the middle of the city. People here believe that the important things are always near the center of a city and that if the center of a city stinks the city isn't worth living in.

Pooch, a good friend of mine (he came up from Mexico with me), loves the smell of the chocolate. When we first got here and took our first walk downtown he kept taking deep breaths for the whole time we were walking around, until he got dizzy. He had to sit down on a park bench, near one of the beautiful fountains here in front of an insurance company building, until his head cleared. He said he was just "hyperventilating" because of the excitement of being here. I think it was the chocolate. He almost passed out, with a strange smile on his face. A policeman stopped to ask if anything was wrong, took one look at him and said, "Going for the ambrosia. A lot of newcomers do that. He'll be okay. It's habit forming but not addicting."

The people here dress in leather clothes almost all the time, or at least leather shorts or skirts. Pooch says it's because gentlemen of honor always wear leather. Women too. But I asked people in the place where we are renting rooms why they wear leather so much. They said that it is not just because it looks nice but because it hardly ever wears out. And when holes show up in the seats they stitch another piece of leather in with all kinds of fancy stitching around the edges, so that the older the things get the fancier they get. People here don't like things that wear out fast! In fact if clothes are shipped in from other states and they wear out in a few weeks, like most of what we see nowadays, people won't touch it. The governor of the state wants to pass a tax on things that wear out too soon, the longer a thing lasts, the lower the tax, that sort of thing. Good idea.

Cars are like that too in this state. They come from a small factory near the city of Racine, which everyone here calls Rayceen (?). They are shaped like boxes, but very attractive, with many heavy coats of paint that are polished and painted over and polished and painted over again at the factory. Sixteen layers of enamel is what one man told me. They come in two colors, the state colors, green and blue. The license plates are very large and made of a kind of porcelain-looking material. They are all decorated beautifully like dinner plates with birds on them, like those we bought at the gift shops in Mexico when I was little. Also, you sit up straight in these cars, almost like you were in a big chair at dinner. But they are all covered in leather and very soft. You don't have to bang your head when you get into these cars because they have what they call "running boards," a sort of step, on the side, and you just walk in. And the people that ride around in them don't lie on their backs like they have to in the new, sleek-looking cars the rich people still drive. When the drivers get out of one of those swanky affairs you can see it's been hard on them because their heads are bent forward like turtles. There are only a few of those cars in the State of Milwaukee. The people with money enough to buy one are embarrassed when they drive it because people make remarks like "Is the guy in the back seat your chiropractor?"

This city is small, compared to places like Mexico City. But it is very beautiful. It lies on the shores of Lake Michigan, which is an enormous lake. One can't see the other side. And nobody here wants to. They say cities like Detroit are somewhere on the other side of the lake. (That's a sort of joke here.)

Many of the buildings in the city are made of what they call "cream city brick," because of the light cream color of the bricks. Milwaukee was once called Cream City, when it was a small place. Some of the new buildings are stone, of course, but many buildings are painted in bright colors and trimmed with gold paint. Flags are everywhere. I never saw so many flags. They hang over the sidewalks from poles on the sides of buildings and there are flagpoles with flags or pennants on every building. I like it. Pooch says it makes you feel like there is a celebration going on all the time.

All the buildings are old-fashioned looking, except for one big skyscraper with a cut-off top like so many in the big cities all over the world. But it has huge, gold lightning rods around the top of it and doesn't look as boring as it must have when it was new. The governor here does not allow new buildings in the glass box style. And they do not permit anyone to build a building taller than thirty stories or so, which means you can see the whole skyline most of the time.

Pooch says, incidentally, that they are going to have a contest next month to design a new flag for the state. Perhaps I will enter the contest.

Let me tell you, Mother, about my friend Pooch. I met him when we were crossing the border from Mexico into America. He crawled through the tunnel with me and helped me across the desert in Texas. At the time I thought he was very tough and very old because he never got tired but he limped and had lost some of his teeth. But now that he is shaved and wearing a new pair of leather shorts and a white shirt he looks handsome. He is fifty years old. He says he is going to buy new teeth soon. His name is Diego Rivera Garcia Lorca Grenada and he has written some novels. He was in prison for a long time once, for writing things the government found hostile. But he is fine now. I am not sure where he got all the names, but then you know how we Latins like names (I do too, even if Dad was American). His stepfather gave him the fancy name. "If I had been an Englishman," he told me when we were coming north, "they would have just called me 'Harry' or 'Jack.' Think of how dismal that would have been. Now I can be a bull-fighter and no one would know I had an Englishman for a stepfather." Pooch likes to kid around like that, even though he is very sad a lot of the time, sitting around and staring straight ahead. He lost his family in the famine near Durango. It must have been terrible there the last few years.

We should thank God that things are still nice around Villa Rito. When I was passing through Villa Hermosa on my way to the border I noticed huge crowds of Guatemalans living there as refugees. They came from camps along the Chiapas border. Pooch says there are hundreds of camps along the Rio Lacantún and along the Santo Domingo also. The Indians who were forced to work on the coffee plantations have had it the worst. The land is used up and there

80

is nowhere where they can be forced to work anymore. When I told that to Pooch, he just said, "Irony, my boy, irony."

Pooch does not like to talk about how he lost his family in Durango to the famine. He feels guilty, even if he remembers (these are his words) "that it is all part of a Grand Plan," which he says is always capitalized, the "Grand Plan" I mean. He said a lot of men in his area would not use birth control pills because other men in the village laughed at them. Some of them didn't care what the priest thought, he says, because they were sure the priest was full of bunk. God never made any of the women pregnant around Durango, says Pooch. They wanted the credit.

You have heard all of this before, Mother, from different sides. But I am glad that you and father didn't get snarled up in that kind of debate. I loved Dad very much because he had so much love for you and you deserved it all.

Pooch says you are right in telling me to "follow my star." When I say I should probably go back to Mexico as a matter of principle he says no one should ever betray himself because of his principles. (Not sure what that means, but it makes you think.)

Pooch and I live on the second and third floors of a big building near the Milwaukee River, near a bridge that "flies" across the bluffs there. There are bridges all over the city because of its rivers. They are very beautiful. I am going to see more of the big one over the harbor entrance in a day or two. It has huge statues of politicians from the past all along its sides. A lot of them look like Roman statesmen standing forward on one leg (like classic sculpture I have told you about) with one hand out.

We have jobs here in a sand and gravel company right across the street from where we live. We walk down the river bluff to it. It's on a low flat area that the river sometimes floods a little. There are gardens all over the flats along the river.

Milwaukee is a state, as I told you. Pooch says that any city-state as nice as this is a state of mind, too. Maybe it is.

The day after tomorrow we will have a poetry reading

81

in the place where we live, in the tavern on the first floor. A place called Smudge's. Pooch is very interested to meet the poet, another writer!

I think of you all the time and love you with everything a son has in his heart. Will write again soon.

Love,
Rico

P.S. I saw some art in Texas, on the way up here. In a cave. It is not what I want to do. Something is missing. How I long to do what they seem unable to do—something new and great.

A READING
AT
SMUDGE'S

MABEL SMUDGE, CHUBBY, bubbling with energy, dressed in her finest brocade blouse and leathers, kicked off the festivities on the first Friday that Pooch and Rico were residents in their new home in Milwaukee. At eight o'clock that evening she moved to the far end of the room, mounted a makeshift stage made of two large slabs of three-quarter-inch-thick plywood nailed onto two by fours set on edge. She rapped an empty beer bottle firmly with a pickle fork and waited for the place to quiet down. As soon as it did she said, "Ladies and gentlemen, may I introduce without further ado the poet who has become so famous in our lovely state, Dr. Anselm Pester!"

Pester walked out of the shadows of the narrow hallway that led from his room at Smudge's, past the tavern's restroom doors, to the stage. He stepped onto the stage uncertainly, limping heavily, his right leg appearing paralyzed from the knee down. He reached out to a large, Victorian wing-back chair that stood on stage. It was a garish-looking piece of furniture, upholstered in blue and red in a goldfish pattern. The poet steadied himself for a moment against the heavy, mahogany-legged chair that gripped the stage firmly with huge, lion-claw feet. Next to the chair was a small square table with a large, old-looking book set on it at a nonchalant angle. It was the *Encyclopedia of World Travel*, Volume I, 1971, still in its bright-orange dust jacket. The book had nothing to do with the poetry reading. Mabel had put it there to let her customers know that she and Louie had been around a bit too.

The poet, an old man, smiled distantly as he looked slowly to the right and then to the left through his thick-lensed eyeglasses. Then his eyes settled on some distant point beyond the walls of the room. He was a small person, frail looking, his hair wispy and his skin bluish white, almost transparent. His legs, from his red argyle ankle-socks up, were hairless, with faint purple marks on the shins where he had barked them and bled long ago. He held a sheaf of papers in one hand and with the other gripped his beltbuckle, as if to hold his aging leather shorts above the bulge of his small, sagging stomach. And on top of his head he wore motorcycle goggles. They lent a touch of daring to his appearance, something he very much needed.

The rostrum was surrounded in front and on the sides by about forty folding chairs that Louie and Mabel had set out in a semicircle. The room had been darkened except for the red and blue neon advertisement for Schumie's Lager behind the bar. A small spotlight controlled by a rheostat at one end of the bar flooded the chair with a soft white light. The jukebox was quieted. It had been playing an old favorite, a hit by Frankie Yankovic called "The Blue Skirt Waltz," with its memorable refrain, "Blue was the sky and blue were your eyes and blue was the skirt you wore." Yankovic had sold a million copies of it in the late forties.

"This poem has to do with mortality," the poet began, "and, as they say, coping. It is from a larger work that some of you have heard me read from, a work known as *The Book of Ruling Equations*. I call this one," he continued quietly, "'On Being Alone With St. Jerome.' It goes:

When I am home alone with St. Jerome
And demons take the measure of my soul each night,
Melancholy dreams of worlds
Where all is quiet and all is rest,
Hurry and scurry through a troubled consciousness.

Alas, the world is full of fear and secret secretions.
It pleas for novelties without end, for no good reason,
Then it demands a snort in the snoot and reprieving
* dreams.*
But I know there is but one choice, the blood-soaked kneeler
* or a stillborn cry of woe!"*

The room erupted in applause. The poet Anselm Pester had set in motion another lively Friday night's poetry reading. And the patrons loved it, whether the poetry made sense or not. "Brilliant! The man is really *tracking!*" said one to another. "The real thing," said another, a newspaper critic who had stopped by with friends visiting from San Francisco. "A disingenuous genius, no doubt about it," said another, her boyfriend. "It's a stunning revival of the sprung rhythms of Hopkins," said her boyfriend's boyfriend, as he wet an eyebrow. (Which drew a glance from one of the blue-collar workmen near the bar. "Jesus," he said to Louie, "this place could be on Rush Street.")

There were a few other doubters in the audience. One man at the bar, a local mason who stayed soggy on Schumie's most of the time, said to the bartender, "Not sure what you got here, Lou, a hairball or an oracle."

"Takes all kinds," said Louie.

There were differences of opinion, to be sure, about

what constituted good poetry at Smudge's. Most of the regulars in the tavern liked the old stuff that rhymed a lot, and they often pressed the poet to read from his dogeared copy of *One Hundred and One Famous Poems*. They loved "The Midnight Ride of Paul Revere," of course, and "The Highwayman." They also loved some of the old heavies like Gray's "Elegy Written in a Country Church Yard," though it was agreed that the poem could bring a tough guy to tears quite easily and that the bread baker who had lost his brother-in-law to the machine age in Detroit was now very vulnerable to it, especially such lines as "One morn I missed him on the custom'd hill / Along the heath, and near his favorite tree," even though there were few real trees left in downtown Detroit. Most were made of plastic. But they could fool the eye, just as those in New York's Central Park had for decades.

Now and then a fight broke out between the two schools of thought on poetic theory. "The Highwayman" fanciers took exception to those who wanted to hear Alan Ginsburg's "Howl," for instance. Or the lovers of Whittier's "Maud Muller" were annoyed when someone insisted that an opaque little poetic formulation from some ancient issue of *Atlantic* be rammed down the throats of Smudge's patrons. But on the whole it all went along swimmingly and Pester was the acknowledged poet-in-residence.

There was one man, a tubby-looking fellow who often did not wear leathers but chose instead to wear a wrinkled, sweaty looking dark-blue suit, with a buttondown white shirt, also sweaty looking, and a striped Rep tie, apparently his only good tie, or at least his favorite, since it was the only one he ever wore, which really caused problems. His name was Clement Bradley Jensen. He had been in and out of the state legislature for years, first as an assemblyman, then as a real estate salesman and part-time politician, then as senator. He had finally become lieutenant governor.

The lieutenant governorship in the state of Milwaukee

was an elected position. It was not thought odd for the lieutenant governor and the governor to be from different parties and often to be at loggerheads politically. The lieutenant governor's job was largely a figurehead position, powerless and poorly paid. But it was the kind of position that attracted the likes of Jensen. It called for a certain attentive, slothful quality, and though it was intrinsically rather worthless, it was a good spot from which to watch state politics, a good jump-off position for some solid, appointed administrative post or for the governorship itself.

At the time of the reading at Smudge's that Pooch and Rico attended, Jensen was suspended from his position. He had gotten into another drunk-driving scrap and the majority party in the senate had come down on him like a ton of bricks. He was formally reprimanded in a special session of the senate and was not allowed inside the state capitol for six months. Which would have been enough to take the starch out of just about any politician in the state except the erstwhile lieutenant governor. Jensen was forty-five, overweight and baby-faced but energetic, single (suspiciously so) and a born politician of the sweaty-palmed, backstage, porcine tradition. He was a gifted sychophant and a tireless schemer, in a word, someone who would go places. He knew everybody in the state, including, of course, the governor, who quietly loathed him, sometimes not at all quietly. He was a big favorite of some of the well-heeled crowd who had it in for the governor's Fritzland program. Such people considered the governor the worst kind of radical because he preached a very conservative doctrine when it came to waste, extravagance, and the rhetoric of "progress."

Jensen seemed to have plenty of money, most of the time. And he liked to toss it around if there seemed some political point to it. He included Smudge's as one of his favorite hangouts. He would "set up a round" of lager at the slightest sign it might do his reputation around the place any good. Human nature being what it is, always interested in a free one, it meant that Jensen had a substantial circle of friends at places like Smudge's.

But Jensen hated Pester, for no apparent reason, though a few people around Smudge's seemed to imply that the real problem was that Jensen was attracted to Pester in some unsavory way. Part of Jensen's problem was that he had a vague resentment of Pester's education. He knew Pester had been a university professor at one time and he also knew that Pester had lived a life of total debauchery and had gotten by with it, in part at least. Jensen, others said, also saw Pester as a kind of moral premonition, given his life as one of the great sinners of his time and then a kind of oddball saint.

The idea of Pester as a reformed sinner seemed to make Jensen simmer with resentment. Pester was to him what a preachy, reformed smoker can be to a tobacco addict bent on whistling past the graveyard. Jensen also knew that within his own greasy little body, sin was still active and virulent, whereas in Pester, because he had succeeded in committing every sin under the sun and lived to tell the tale, it was an attenuated, nonvirulent thing, even useful, like cowpox is to potential victims of smallpox. Pester seemed to act as if the whole point of sin was forgiveness, though he seldom discussed such things. Pester would sit around in the booths at Smudge's and sip beer until he was sleepy and then retire to his room. So he was a constant reminder to Jensen that if sainthood is not the goal of sin about the only thing you earn is fatigue.

Jensen was at the bar that evening of the "St. Jerome" reading. He would alternately turn his back on the poet, pretending he wasn't listening to him, or interrupt the attention of someone who was caught up in the beauty of the moment on stage. And under his breath Jensen would say, "Shit, real shit!" As soon as a poem was finished he would try to buy someone a drink, to cut into Pester's public. But it seldom worked.

Pooch's reaction to the St. Jerome work was uncertain. Clearly, he said to himself, there were elements of greatness in the poetry. The images impressed him—demons taking the measure of the poet's soul, perhaps with a tape measure designed by Lucifer himself, and a world full of fears and secret secretions. But the plea for a "snort in the snoot" seemed graceless, almost crude. "I will want to hear more," he told Rico in a whisper. "He has not been influenced by the great Latin poets, that is clear. But there is something derivative about his work."

And then the old man on the stage, leaning back in his chair, his confidence building to the sound of the applause, draped one arm over the back of the chair, the picture of the confident stage artist who knows he has his audience in the palm of his hand and deserves to, began another poem called "To a Bar Stool: Reminiscences." Sighing, he began:

If only I might describe perfectly
The curve of that high, proud chair
If I could describe to my total satisfaction
Its flexure, curls, its arcuate sinuosities
I would immortalize that homely thing as did Virgil,
in Georgics, *the plow.*
Each spring the noble Roman taught the furrow bur-
nished share to shine
While I, in my time, taught the seat of that gangly
shrine to shine.
Thus like Virgil I proved to the world that there are
wonders in the commonplace.
And now I rest my case.

"Bullshit!" said Jensen, not bothering to lower his voice as he turned toward the mirror behind the bar. "Bar stool sinuosities? You gotta be kidding!" he added, as if he was talking to the mirror. Patrons near the bar turned to stare

89

at Jensen. He was drunk, they concluded. Their attention returned to the poet.

Rico poked Pooch with his elbow, "That fat guy means trouble," he whispered.

By seven-thirty every seat in the house had been taken. Most of those in the chairs balanced steins of beer on their knees. Around the rims of the fancier steins, products of a ceramics factory in the village of Elm Grove to the west of Milwaukee, homilies of the Fritzland movement were enameled in red and gold, sayings such as "There can be nothing sacred in something that has a price!"

Those who weren't drinking beer were sipping mixed drinks, scotch and club, martinis, or whiskey, or a glass of cherry wine from the winery in the village of Cedarburg. Cherry wine was a big hit in the State of Milwaukee, and outside it too. So much so, in fact, that smugglers in row-boats with muffled oars regularly paddled south along the coast of Lake Michigan to peddle it on the black market in Chicago for seventy-five dollars a bottle.

One of the more adept bottleleggers of the wine, a man who affected a Hemingway beard and was nicknamed Cherryman, tended the foghorns along the coast of the state. He shuttled the hot cherry wine south to Chicago by using an ingenious device that allowed him to stow caches of the much-prized liquid in barrels that floated just under the surface of the water at each of the buoys set along the shoreline. He hung around Smudge's on Friday nights in a lightweight turtleneck and captain's cap, blending in with the slummers from the suburbs who actually owned big boats at the McKinley Yacht Club and who found Smudge's "the place" for a Friday night in Milwaukee. A sideline of Cherryman's was the smuggling of invitations to live in the state, and the forged signature of the Governor, to high-rolling types in Chicago who periodically needed to hide out from creditors by disappearing for a few months or a year into the State of Milwaukee. And who else but Clement Bradley Jensen provided the

90

link between the Chicagoans on the lam and the idyllic refuge to the north. He wore one of the antique "Escape to Wisconsin" stickers from the 1980s on is car bumper for very good reason indeed.

Rico and Pooch had been sitting quietly to one side of the audience near the back row of chairs, not far from Jensen. They were dressed in the quayavera, the fancy embroidered Mexican shirts that had become increasingly scarce in Milwaukee since border problems with Mexico had heated up. They were the object of considerable admiration and some envy. Most of the patrons, both men and women, were dressed in standard casual evening wear, leather shorts with suspenders, white half-socks and colored shirts—brightly patterned for the women, unfigured for the men–billowing near the wrist, loose enough to accommodate the balmy 72-degree evening air.

A few late arrivals showed up, slummers as one might expect, in tuxedos, white linen jackets and evening dresses. Both the men and the women topped off their ensembles with the latest fad in headgear among the country club set, cotton visor caps that read "Joe's Tractor Sales," "Hay's Trucking" or "Ben's Lawnmowers." Some of the caps read "Smudge's," a much sought-after touch for a night on the town. For them Smudge's had become the place to be seen on Friday nights, after they had traditional Milwaukee fish fry dinners at one or another of the hundreds of cozy, corner restaurants that dotted the city.

The slummers were sometimes smug collegians, home for the summer from their eastern private schools. Some were professionals, aging former yuppies who had made it and lived in mansions—their mortgages closely guarded secrets—along the lake in Fox Point or on estates in the rolling horse country on West Highland Road. They were the ones who made snide remarks about the "Buddhist economics" that the governor had borrowed from Schumacher. But they all loved the state. For it had become, in its own way, very exclusive indeed. It was exclusive, in fact, the way Palm Springs had once been, in its own way, before clean drinking water ran short in Southern California and trailer parks surviving on imported bottled water sprang up on the dried-out fairways of once famous golf courses.

The ritzy crowd that pushed into Smudge's in clusters of four and six on Friday night were the people Milwaukeeans saw sitting in the small grandstands at the polo field on Good Hope Road, sipping wine coolers as they suspiciously eyed the designer insignias on each other's shirts, skirts and socks. Which meant, when push came to shove, that they knew that a "chucker" was a playing period in a polo game and not a hand in bridge, but often not much more than that. So the governor believed. But he had not been hard on them. He had never threatened to expropriate their wealth or tax them into extinction. He needed them, he said on one of his TV press conferences, as an object lesson—to show other citizens of the state just how correct Fritz Schumacher had been when he said, "If human vices such as greed and envy are systematically cultivated, the inevitable result is nothing less than a collapse of intelligence."

But there was no real sense of class resentment in Smudge's, no feeling that a blue-collar worker who had had a few too many might suddenly turn neo-Bolshevik and try to strangle a fat cat then and there. And the fat cats—many of whom were anything but fat, but instead sleek young women who spent their waking hours grooming themselves to look elegant, sensual and eager, the better to survive boring talk around the neighbor's swimming pool—did not act as if they might lose patience with overfamiliar barflies, pick up the phone and call the Cossacks in to clear the place of rabble. The tavern was a placid, uncommonly egalitarian setting, as was the entire state for that matter, considering the grievances that the tiny minority of wealthy harbored toward the man in the Statehouse who lashed them periodically with Fritzland preachments. Jokes and wisecracks flew back and forth between the social classes, between the swells and the ordinaries. The tradesmen and workers who used Smudge's as their watering hole were just as proud to be in the company of the people who parked the mint-condition antique limousines out front of Smudge's as the rich were to be on a first-name basis with someone who could fix a leaky faucet in their sauna or plant a palm at short notice, without a lot of Fritzland fuss and paperwork. Everyone in Smudge's, after all, was there for the same reason, to tip up a stein or a cocktail and to listen to the poet who was getting the rave reviews.

Anselm Pester was the object of a lot of speculation at Smudge's. He lived in a single small room on the ground floor of the building, near the back, down the hall beyond the men's and women's rooms. The room had a single window, and Pester had fixed a large decal to it that was supposed to make it look like a stained-glass window, which it did, after a fashion. The window decal, a vague copy of a baroque masterpiece, portrayed St. Jerome on his knees in a cave, fighting off demons of temptation. The demons, people in the tavern who had seen the window said, with nods that mixed pity and censure, represented Pester's past. They said he had come from Chicago in 2008 and that he had been a "professor of regressive educational philosophy" there, in a seedy, second-rate place called Freedom State University, a school that gave away cheap degrees and catered to scruffy moral relativists who insisted that trying to tell right from wrong was pretention of the worst kind.

Pester's story had an unusual twist. While he was at FSU, he began to put in long hours at the Chicago Public Library—there was no actual library at FSU—studying classic and medieval literature, with the purpose of making a list of every sin known to man. He then updated the list by patient study of modern novelists. After which he set about systematically committing each sin on the list at least

93

twice, except for murder, which he had concluded was too messy and insufficiently "interior" psychologically to make it worth the while. But he intended, he announced, to make a fully rounded man of the times of himself, even if it killed him. As it turned out, by the time he was fifty-five years old he had gotten only halfway through the list of sins and was paying a heavy price for his tenacity. He developed dyspepsia, assorted venereal disorders, including some from animals, and abscessed teeth. His hair grew wispy and his skin sallow and flaky. His nerves were shot and his locomotion was damaged beyond repair. One foot dragged behind him as if it contained no bones. He was too weak to go to his office or do anything related to his job. But he was not really missed at FSU and his paychecks arrived every month. But drugs, alcohol and vice had reduced him to a kind of thinking man's derelict.

When Pester reached sixty-two, his Olympian effort to go down in the history books as one of the great sinners of his time came to an odd climax. He had a profound religious experience. He had been sleeping for years in the beds of whores and addicts and in dirty bars, as well as inside revolving doorways of office buildings, which in itself was a curious predilection toward a life of high uncertainty. He also lived in abandoned cars and garbage dumpsters. It was during the period when he was living in an overturned dumpster that had been propped up on one end so that he could crawl in and out of it that the religious experience struck him. He shared the dumpster with a psychotic who thought he was Ronald Reagan III and a demented child who had been abandoned by a mother who desperately pursued a career in marriage counseling but could not find a day-care center she could afford. Pester came to feel that the madman and the vacant-eyed child were brother and sister to him, and for months he fed them by scrounging what he could from the refuse thrown out by Chicago's finest restaurants. He would skulk about the rear of the cafés to pounce on scraps from the tables of the affluent, beef cordon bleu, artichokes, mussels and the like, before mold or maggots got to them first. To protect his family from food poisoning, which more than once almost killed the child with vomiting and diarrhea, he would sample the food he found first. Several times he himself almost died as a result.

But Pester's sacrifice on behalf of the lunatic and the child must have stirred supernatural interest or sympathy. For one night while he was asleep in the dumpster, curled up between the psychotic and the youngster, he had a vision. He saw a man hanging from a gallows, a bloody syringe in one hand and an iridescent blue star in the other. Around the star, as if written in smoke, it said "Begin again!"

Pester realized that the "Begin again" message might have been triggered by all the talk in the newspapers about the message from outer space. But he also realized that beggars cannot be choosers when it comes to visions. It did not matter much how the supernatural got its message across to the wretched of the earth. So he concluded, sensibly enough, that he had found God in a garbage dumpster. And he guessed at the time, probably correctly, that the dumpster was a more likely place for God to appear than in a church where the test of faith is systematically contaminated by grand organ music, incense, candlelight and fatuous excuses from the preacher for the cruelties of Jehovah. After all, the dumpster was full to the brim with human misery, precisely the sort of place that God would be most needed, therefore the most likely place for God to show Himself.

After that, Pester was a changed man, more or less. He promptly sobered up and put himself to the task of finding homes for the madman and the demented child. He was able to place the child in the home of a bartender he had known for many years, a responsible man who drank too much but was kindly and never violent. The madman went to work in the Cook County office of the Illinois Republican

Party. Then Pester left for Milwaukee, about which he had heard such remarkable utopian stories.

Later on, when Pester and Pooch had a chance to talk, over a couple of steins of lager, Pester recounted the highlights of his conversion, such as it was to that point, to the Mexican writer. Pooch had taken it all in with sympathy. But he continued to have reservations about Pester. He told Rico later that it was lucky that there were many gods because he was not sure he wished to share his with Smudge's poet. Which was his way of saying he did not like Pester.

Needless to say, Pester could not get an invitation from the governor to live in the State of Milwaukee. So he managed to get across the border rather like Rico and Pooch crossed the border from Mexico. He bribed an Illinois sewer district worker to guide him through the vast sewer network that had been built at the end of the twentieth century between the coastal cities of Evanston, Waukegan, Kenosha and Racine. The guide took him as far as the north side of Kenosha, told him to follow charts of the sewers and left him to make it the rest of the way on his own. Hours later, after being waylaid by gangs of hoodlums that used the sewers to hide from police on the surface, he came up through a manhole on the south side of Racine, looking for all the world like a half-drowned rat. His clothes were wet and smelly. There was an orange rind in his shirt pocket and coffee grounds in his hair. Nondescript smelly things seemed to cling to his ankles.

Pester was found in the gutter next to the open manhole. His breathing was labored and he seemed delirious, although he clung fiercely to an attaché case and seemed at times coherent. He had been found by a black Baptist minister and his wife. They wanted to take him to the hospital. But he refused to consider a hospital, for fear, apparently, of losing his attaché case. So the gentle-hearted minister and his wife took him to their little wooden rectory behind their little wooden church and cleaned him up, first with a garden hose and then inside the house in a hot bath. And when he had slept twenty-four hours, scarcely moving, with the minister and his wife taking turns checking in on him every half hour because they were afraid he was a goner and their good-Samaritan gesture would go for naught, he came around and sat up. He was still in a daze, and across the room on the wall he saw his vision on a cross. The bloody syringe was gone but the iridescent blue star was still there and glowing more brightly than ever.

For three days he was fed chicken soup and hominy, which brought him around in quite good shape. The minister then went out and bought him a new suit of clothes, suede leather shorts with broad Milwaukee suspenders with silver stitching, a white shirt, half-socks and underwear. His old clothes were boiled, washed, dried and left next to his bedstand in a neat pile.

On the third day of his confinement to bed Pester drew the *Ruling Equations* manuscript from his damp attaché case and began to read and memorize the poems, and then to embroider them in his mind, so that he soon could not tell which were his and which were not.

That was, in fact, one of the problems with Pester's poetry readings. Mabel had persuaded him to read his poems to her patrons after she overheard him reciting them absent-mindedly as he sat at the bar. When she asked him whether the poetry was his or not he insisted that it was his. His religious conversion had obviously been incomplete. Plagiarism was so far down on the list of sins he had once compiled that he had never given it much thought. He hadn't committed the sin, and his supernatural messenger had overlooked it when he had forced Pester's moral about-face. The poetry was not his, not for the most part. The final lines were often his, true enough, because he tacked them onto the compositions while sitting up late at night rewriting *The Book of Ruling Equations*, trying to avoid the eyes of the accusing image of anguished

St. Jerome. Pester realized dimly that he was doing something wrong in tampering with someone else's writing and then pawning it off as his own. But he had been a sociopath in good standing for so many years before his conversion experience that there had been permanent damage to his character. He still took a small, secret delight in the musky smell of a remnant of wickedness that inhabited his spirit. That smell had a voice too. It told him that the author of the poetry was dead, and besides, he never had liked the arrogant, presuming, elitist bastard anyway.

Pester had gotten hold of the poems when their author, Casper Martin Spent, died in 1997. Spent had been an assistant professor in the department of educational philosophy that Pester chaired at Freedom State University. During an incident on the Indiana dunes where the government was burying radioactive rubble from a decommissioned atomic power plant, Spent had been shot.

Pester considered Spent a hopeless square and a pedantic damn fool. For one thing, he resented Spent's lofty censure of the freewheeling hedonism at FSU and America's tendency to confuse manifest destiny with a shopping binge. Pester, on the other hand, then believed that any society that was ingenious enough to produce space platforms, recombinant genetic strains of germs for warfare and chewing gum that did not stick to false teeth could not be all bad. The fruits of American ingenuity, he often said, were here for everyone to see, television sets spewing out sexy spine tinglers in millions of homes, snazzy red and yellow cars in the driveways of the American everyman and plenty of cocaine in the cupboard right next to the vitamin pills and sugar-free carcinogens.

In any event, the day Pester heard that Spent had been killed, he let himself into Spent's office and took every manuscript he could lay his hands on. He had, at the time, suspicions that Spent was writing about him, which turned out not to be so. But the manuscript called *The Book of Ruling Equations* had a strong censorious overtone, with odd "equations" salted through it, such as "Stupidity in motion tends to remain in motion; indolence at rest tends to remain at rest." It also contained several hundred poems, drawings and mystical notations, plus intriguing allusions to Spent's journal, evidently still with Spent's in-laws in northern Indiana.

Although Pester's next poem that evening made a hit with the rest of his audience, it did nothing to calm Jensen down. The poem was called "Oh Weary Life." The poet delivered it while slumped in his chair and staring at the ceiling. He had pulled his motorcycle goggles down over his eyes and delivered the lines in a half-swoon.

Oh weary life leap up at me
Seize my thoughts and wrap them double in emotion
And give them back to me.
Stroke the strings of my desire three times nine
And give the melody back to me while there's still time.
Take my turgid anxiety, add the spice of fright,
Stir in a pinch of lucidity and give it back to me,
On the rocks and running over.

Again applause, again a murmur of admiration mixed here and there with expressions of bewilderment, just enough to convince everyone in the place that Pester's poetry was something one did not get to hear any day of the week. Even Pooch, touched as he was by a bit of jealousy, a feeling he resented in himself, realized that the poem had some redeeming elements. He himself had lived a life to which fate had, all too often, added the spice of fright. He joined the applause warily, his suspicions of Pester still with him. But there was something very magical indeed about the whole situation, a place like Smudge's in a place like the State of Milwaukee and the crowd that had gathered to hear the poet.

One member of Pester's audience, a good-looking young blonde standing near the far end of the bar with a small cluster of slummers was evidently really taken with the poetry. She let out a squeal of delight.

Rico Far had been watching her. She was a stunning beauty, about five six, in the Marilyn Monroe genre, but with her hair drawn back tight into a small, braided ponytail. Her hairdo made her head seem small, but gave her the exquisite predatory look of a female cheetah. She wore tight slacks and a blouse that bared her navel. A sequined belt arced low across her tummy from hip to hip.

The blonde was with a man whose even features resembled hers. He was twice her age, perhaps an older brother, an uncle or even her father. The years had been good to him, and he was gray haired but sleek, and well enough groomed to look as though he owned a private barber. It was clear that he hadn't spent much time sitting on a tractor or climbing poles for the electric power company. His light twill jacket covered an open-throated shirt and a small ascot given a studied careless twist. Both he and the girl were obviously somebodies. People in the room deferred to them, or gushed and smiled at a distance. Handshakes were either overdone or too timid, as were the kisses to the girl's cheeks.

Clement Jensen, however, was in his element. He and the couple greeted each other warmly, as if they shared some confidence, as if they might be relatives, but more likely partners in some slick bit of treachery.

Jensen knew how to handle himself with people of importance. Years of careful cultivation in the state legislature, in the rotunda of the Statehouse, in the hallways just outside hearing rooms, of the high art of the toady's craft had made him something of a master, a consummate brownnose. He could be gracious at a distance, with small waves and pantomime comments across the crowded room of a fundraiser. He could, in close encounter, kiss an ass with such a light touch, but also endearing abandon, that the ass's owner usually never knew what had leached the will out of him, only that the sensation was pleasant. Jensen could carry a compliment with him even as he walked the plank and lay it on thick enough to save his skin. He knew how to thicken honey and how big a swab to use. He knew just how many deviation credits he had stored up in the errands he had run. He knew the tone, color, texture and nap of the vanity in which most egos come wrapped.

But his skills often abandoned him when he was drunk. And then Jensen's whole world could collapse around his ears. A stupid, insulting remark could blow the whole thing, and his strategy for the evening would go skidding off center, or he could end up looking like a damn fool. When that happened it meant weeks, even months, of steady, slow repair, a stream of little premeditated chance encounters during which Jensen could use the swab and honey jar.

Rico's situation was entirely different. He had trouble taking his eyes off the blonde. The shadows to the sides of her face, or the color of the swept-back hair, like silk that had become translucent, the nose that was modeled to perfection, the nostrils small but not too tight so that they could flare with excitement without exposing too much of the inner membrane as those of many supposed beauties do, held him in a vise. For Rico was a young version of what artists often become as they grow old, scoptophiliacs, devourers of the world through the eyes.

But then Jensen began acting up again and there was tension in the air at Smudge's. "What the hell are you letting that bozo"—meaning Pester—"lay on us, Louie?" Jensen demanded of the bartender in a loud voice. "Don't creeps like that put you off?" Then, without another word, he picked up a heavy ashtray from the bar and flung it at the poet. The ashtray bounded off the arm of Pester's chair and landed in the lap of one of the women in the front row of the audience. She dropped her stein of beer in surprise, there was the sound of breaking crockery, then shouts of indignation.

101

"You were right. That fat guy meant trouble," said Pooch to Rico.

But Rico, without responding to his friend, jumped to his feet, interposed himself between Pester and Jensen, only a foot or so in front of Jensen. "That'll be about all we need from you," he said firmly.

"Not if I need more," said Jensen, glowering.

"One more move or one more wisecrack and I knock you on your butt," said Rico.

Jensen knew he was no match for the muscular young man. He flushed, then grumbled, "You haven't heard the end of this. Nor has Pester." He turned his back to the audience and stared into the mirror again. There was a round of applause, this time for Rico Far as much as for Pester.

The poet had not noticed that the ashtray hit his chair, or he pretended not to notice. And as if nothing had happened he began, "This poem is inspired, as many of you will know, by Mr. T. S. Eliot—Tommy, as I called him back in St. Louis when we were boys, or I was a boy and he was a man. He *was* older than I at the time, I assure you." He waited for a laugh from the audience. But it was still nervous. Jensen turned toward Pester and was glowering at him. "I call this poem," said Pester, "'I Know Mr. Prufrock!' It goes like this:

I have seen the sky etherized upon the table
And I have watched the lamp-black back of midnight rub itself
against the bedroom window pane.
I have pondered my mortality and made the necessary, timorous,
wistful decisions
As truth looked up at me through a painful, pink incision.
It was I whose ragged claws scuttled on the sea floor long ago
And it was I who arrogantly tried to pinch out the eyes of
my sleepless, lidless guilt.
Now I hear the sound of my own death rattle
reverberating from the backside of the universe.

102

*Oh, the mermaid's song is sweet, but it has come too late for me.
Still, I dig it."*

There was applause, then a loud series of "Huzzahs,"
an archaic form of "Hurrah" that had unaccountably crept
back into the vocabulary of the citizens of the state. Pooch
loved the word but he had never heard it shouted before.
And Pester's poem to Mr. Prufrock struck him smack in
the solar plexus. He too had been Mr. Prufrock, perhaps
still was. He too had walked the beach "with his trousers
rolled" as Eliot had put it in that love song for the middle-
aged. As he sat there listening to Pester, he did not think
love could ever enter his life again. No women, he felt,
would give him a second look. He wondered if the mermaid's song had not come too late for him as well. He had
one thing in common with Pester at least. He too could
still say "I dig it!" and mean it.

As the applause tapered off there was another shout
from the blonde, "Well, all right!"

And that is how Charles "Rico" Far met the beautiful
young Allison Minter, the thoroughly spoiled daughter of
the rich father she had brought to Smudge's that night.
Mr. Minter owned the Shikel Automobile Corporation, the
only company that manufactured automobiles and trucks
that were tough enough to meet the state's performance
standards. He was very wealthy, and one of the state's
few industrial tycoons who survived the steady scaling
down of the state's few big factories into the state's many
little factories.

The relationship between the governor and the tycoon
was a pragmatic one. They needed each other. And Minter
had put a lot of money over the years into the governor's
drive to decorate the city with monumental sculpture, especially the Dan Hoan harbor bridge which in the nineteen
seventies was supposed to help loop the central city with
freeway traffic. The bridge was completed but not its down

ramps, since it was suddenly realized that to throw a noose of carbon monoxide around the most attractive part of the city was stupid. It was the governor who finally came up with the kind of inspired idea for the massive, more-or-less useless bridge that it deserved. He saw it, high and proud on its huge fanlike concrete supports, as a pedestal for heroic sculpture, something he would like and the people would like. And the politicians who eyed it with the dream of someday joining its immortals would love it. Figures of the state's great political and civic leaders of the past would be cut from enormous blocks of stone that had been lugged south from northern Wisconsin quarries, and set along the bridge as an "Avenue of the Greats." Minter had also helped push the city's business community to support the governor's beautification program, the erection of fountains and, of course, the flags. He didn't particularly go for the governor's politics but he did share his love of flags, and on Christmas in 1998 they had exchanged, quite unknowingly, the same book, huge volumes called *Flags, Across the World and Through the Ages.*

Minter's daughter Allison shared his values. She liked living well and she fancied the role of patron of the arts. She was often quite crass about it. She believed she loved the bohemian side of the artistic life, though she could not have survived a month in a garret on bread and cheese and cheap wine.

But when she found that the handsome young specimen with the heavy-lashed eyes and glittering teeth, the hunk called Rico Far, a gutsy young thing who had told her drunken friend Clement Jensen (he was an "acquaintance" whenever the subject came up with others) to shut up or be knocked on his tail, she could hardly contain her interest. She convinced her father that they should invite the "artist" and his "novelist friend from Latin America" to join them for a nightcap at his private club on Prospect Avenue overlooking the lake. Her father, "Dádi" as she always called him, with heavy accent on the first syllable, was delighted with the whole idea.

While Pooch and Dádi talked about English foreign policy and Spanish literature, both topics Minter liked to think he knew something about, Allison moved in on Rico. After two or three more drinks she was prepared to demand that her father help see that the painter and the novelist got what they needed in the way of publicity around the state, and well outside it too, in places like Chicago, even New York or Los Angeles, "if need be" and "very soon."

MOON OVER THE TOWER

DURING THOSE FIRST few weeks at Smudge's the gods who had been plotting the scenario for the lives of Rico Far and Pooch Grenada introduced substantial complications. For one thing, Rico found himself suddenly, hopelessly, smitten with Allison Minter. For another, Pooch began seeing Sara Steinberger, and her father Wilhelm did not like it. Also the trouble between Anselm Pester and Clement Jensen grew worse and threatened to spill over into Rico's and Pooch's lives. Jensen began slandering Pester mercilessly, implying that Far and Pooch had known Pester before they showed up in Milwaukee and were more than just friends, perhaps cocaine runners. Which remarks infuriated Mabel Smudge and almost earned Jensen a black eye from a half-full bottle of Schumie's Weisbier, which contents went flying around the place and stained the linen jacket of an English teacher from Green Bay who came down to hear Pester's moving poetry—which splatter of yeasty beer cost Mabel the price of the jacket's dry-cleaning. And Jensen, realizing he had set terrible forces in motion, went into a frenzied display of contrition and toady acrobatics, which he ended by holding Mabel, his hands on her fat upper arms out in front of him, and staring into her eyes, feigning a very convincing tear and begging forgiveness for his "misspoken comment." He had suddenly realized that with too many drinks under his belt he had almost done it again. He had almost alienated a whole crowd of people who would fan out across the city to tell others that Clement Bradley Jensen was the kind of a jerk who would insult straight-shooting Mabel Smudge, take cheap shots at a clean-cut, youthful artist whom everybody liked and ridicule a man who had lost his family to famine in Durango.

Jensen ordered Mabel "to set the table" with a round of Weisbier on him. Before the steins were even half empty he had won all of his "friends" back, each the eager beneficiary of a foaming stein of beer, free, clear, and they told themselves, unencumbered. But, of course, they each owed Jensen and they knew it. The second free round drove the spike in deeper.

But Pester soon learned about Jensen's latest calumny, and he decided to put a stop to such outrages without further compromise or cringing. He began showing up in the tavern wearing African wrist knives, which he had gotten from God knew where. But they were vicious-looking things, and when he strode slowly up to the bar to ask for his stein of Schumie's, he made sure Jensen was standing right next to him.

"My God, Anselm," said Louie, "what in hell have you got on?"

Pester looked at one wrist, then the other, rotated the wrists slowly so that the razor-sharp edges of the knives caught the light just right, and said, "Oh these? Wrist knives. From the Kau people of the Sudan. Lived there for a time some years back. Got pretty good with them, too." He looked around as his stein of beer was set out in front of him. "Give me one of those cardboard advertisement things there, Lou. I'll show you how they work."

Lou said, "You don't have to prove anything to me, Anselm. You could dice a muskmelon with one of them babies with a flick of the wrist, I'm sure." Louie knew who the target of Pester's little display was, of course, but he also knew the old man might cut up more than a cardboard ad for breath mints. He might screw up and put himself in the hospital in the process, all because Jensen had pushed the old man's pride to the limit.

Everyone drank their beer in quiet, smacking their lips as if there were nothing about the situation that was unusual in the least.

Then to top it all off, someone burglarized Steinberger's apartment on the second floor of Smudge's. Pooch Grenada lived on that floor.

Burglary was virtually unheard of in the State of Milwaukee and it left people at Smudge's gossiping like magpies over the carcass of a dead squirrel. There had been rumors, to be sure, that Steinberger had formed a secret society of old people who hoarded gold. The oldsters were said to be troubled by events outside the state that could suddenly end their edenic lives. The news from the Mexican border was bad, and the suggestion of some religious leaders that Central America's swarming masses of poor and starving should be given immediate haven in the United States—seventy-one million by one estimate—frightened people. Such a thunderous avalanche of misery and need would surely overwhelm American society, including remaining islands of civility such as the State of Milwaukee. And as if that wasn't enough, strange cult leaders began to appear both in America and in Europe. They wore capes, striped body stockings and scuba diving headgear, plus flippers on their feet. Some said they came from the lost continent of Atlantis in response to the "Begin again" message. Others professed to see profound messianic significance in "Begin again," claiming it was a millenarian signal that had arrived late, thirteen years after the turn of the century, because astrophysical winds had blown it off course in the outer reaches of the Milky Way. Their movement was promptly dubbed "retrospective millennialism." The cults were particularly active in Boston and Paris, both unlikely places. It had been assumed that intellectual refinement in those great cities had long since inoculated people against such odd possibilities. But the opposite turned out to be true. The more people pretended to "know," intellectually speaking, the more delight they took in concocting far-out, "very spacey"—as they themselves liked to boast—interpretations of "Begin again!" In any event, it was not the kind of world old people found particularly reassuring.

But just how fast things began to move for Rico and Pooch was indicated by the pace of their love affairs. Pooch was, of course, the older of the two men and his involvement with Sara Steinberger was more cautious than Rico's with Allison Minter. He had learned to be cautious with women, to look before he leaped, to eye the wind sock before takeoffs and landings. Sara's father made this caution all the more sensible. The old man was not hostile toward Mexicans, though he did presume that Nordic ancestry was not something one would trade for Latin ancestry. But he had lost a leg back in the Vietnam war and its stump had been inflamed and tender ever since. He refused to wear the artificial leg he was given by the army and had whittled a wooden leg out of an old oaken table leg, then harnessed and padded it as best he could. He saw the world through the ever-present ache of his bum leg. And he took a certain mean delight in thumping around his apartment like a peg-legged pirate, the thump of his oak leg audible through the floor into Smudge's. "Old Steiny's up late tonight," people would say as they heard him pounding his way across the living-room floor of his apartment to fuss with the television color dial or to warn his daughter once again of the perils of indiscriminate love.

Steinberger resented Pooch's intrusion on the quiet tenor of his and his daughter's life together. There was nothing particularly oedipal about it. He simply assumed that his daughter's duty was to take the place of his dead wife as far as household drudgery was concerned. And since Sara was a plain sort of person, seldom wearing make-up and almost totally unaware of what beauty she did possess, a modest endowment but certainly not something that Pooch could treat as a gift horse to be examined for its remaining teeth, she accepted the situation with a sweet, if somewhat neurotic, forbearance. But in her heart she realized that life was passing her by. Her job as a bookkeeper in a restaurant in Milwaukee's Grand Avenue constellation of shops and cafés was tedious. She welcomed the slightest excitement into her sparrow-gray world and thought it marvelous. Pooch, "the writer," represented that excitement, despite his quiet, steady quality. To her, tragedy had left a melancholy handsomeness on his face, with deep wrinkles about the eyes and furrows in his cheeks where boyish dimples once had been. His looks drew her to him. And once he had earned enough money to buy a few shirts, leather shorts and a new pair of shoes, he came across quite impressively indeed, as a lanky, thoughtful man of few but firm words, but whose few firm words had a charming English accent about them despite the occasional faint "snick" sound of his new false teeth.

It wasn't long before Pooch began accompanying the Steinbergers in the evening to their little garden on the narrow flood plain of the river. Sara and her father would work among the tomato plants, pole beans, eggplants and cabbages while Pooch sat on the long, low bench Steinberger had hammered together and set near the garden so that he could give the stump of his leg a break every now and then. Pooch would admire Sara from a distance and marvel at how different his life had suddenly become. She would look up and smile at Pooch, caressing him with her eyes. Her father would notice her glances toward Pooch and grump about what cabbage worms can do to cabbage plants.

Pooch sometimes sat on the bench and said nothing for almost half an hour. He would look up at the arches of the bridge to their left and then back at Sara and again at the bridge. During such moments his mind was back in Mexico. He would remember how his wife refused to eat if the children were at all hungry, and his own refusal to eat if she and the children hadn't enough, until the children began to grow spindly and his wife's cheeks grew hollow and she would weep a great deal even though she knew it weakened her further.

The Grenada garden in Mexico had been only a tiny plot of soil, sixty feet square, amid a sea of other tiny plots given to the peasantry of the country by their government. It was the result of one more "agrarian reform," one more haphazard step by the government since it first began to call for such reform in 1910.

The flaw in all of the reform plans, of course, had been the rising number of Mexicans. The "population thing" was a hot political issue and nobody wanted to come to terms with it. The political right had traditionally favored large families because cannon fodder would always come in handy during one or another of the civil wars they found it difficult to live without. Large families had proved their value, too, as a source of cheap labor in the mines, in smoke stack industry and as stoop labor. The political left and the church had difficulty with it for philosophic reasons. Dealing with the "population thing" meant surrender of some fundamental values. They were caught like a monkey with its fist around an egg in a pantry jar. After all, if one truly loves the common man there can never be too many of them to love. And if they are poor it only makes matters worse. They have to be loved for being common, for being poor and for being so unfortunately common, all at once.

111

Chinese-leaning leftists in Mexico had it easier. They had been persuaded that abortion and infanticide had a brighter side, which was that people could be killed when they were only weeks or months old rather than starving to death slowly when they were three, four or five years old. The quanta of pain that was avoided by short-circuiting death by starvation was obvious. Moreover, they found birth control, skin implants in particular, an undisguised blessing. Nor did they frown on such emergency measures as coitus interruptus.

So, as could be expected, heated arguments flared at political rallies throughout the Durango area. Insults, threats and cajolery became the usual ingredients of any public political gathering. And behind closed doors, within the confines of political power brokerage, it often came to fistfights and oaths of vengeance.

At one public political meeting, the last that Pooch attended, a famous Communist theoretician from Leningrad had been invited to attend and to explain to the peasants why another bloodbath was the logical solution to Mexico's misfortunes. "We must wield the machete until the last fat capitalist swine is dangling by his heels!" he shouted, in what was, for him, a fairly mild recommendation.

But an old man called José Balboa, a man who had lived through a dozen "agrarian reforms" and had yet to see one completed, but was still alive to tell the tale of those that had backfired, raised a shaky hand to get the famous theoretician's attention. He was recognized.

Balboa stood slowly, a querulous look on his wizened face and a twinkle in his eye. He tugged gently at the corners of a huge drooping mustache.

"Are you absolutely sure," he began, "that if we divide all of the land in this country that there will be more of it?"

The theoretician looked at him coldly. Balboa was obviously under the influence of the Chinese Communist sects that had spread up from Peru.

"We must divide the land of the great estates, that is correct."

"I am not sure that is the answer I needed," said old Balboa mischievously. "Then what?"

"Then we combine the small pieces into large pieces and we call them communes."

"Then there will be more land?" the old man asked, pressing.

"You are avoiding the issue, comrade," said the theoretician.

"Someone is," said Balboa, looking about, smiling.

The theoretician did not like the pesky old troublemaker in front of him. He smiled back. "The counterrevolutionary mind is a cunning one, comrade. But it must not be allowed to fool us." He talked as if he were addressing the audience as a whole, not just an old crank with a twinkle in his eye. He leaned to one side and asked a nearby companion, "Who in hell is this old coot? The village wise-ass?"

"He's from the other side of Durango. In the direction of China." There was a knowing wink.

"Many would undermine the revolution by drying up the source of revolutionaries, the Mexican mother's womb," said the theoretician calmly, his jaw set.

A cheer went up. "Sit down, Balboa!" shouted someone in the audience.

Another shouted, "Just because you are no longer capable of making a baby, José, you should not tell us we should not."

There were laughs and cheers.

José sat down, crossed his legs, pulled out a pipe and ostentatiously began filling it with tobacco. He had set things crackling. He loved it.

"José is right! José is right!" several women began to shout.

One of them yelled, "For a man to be objective he must not have a fire in his pants!" There were more cheers from José's supporters.

Then an old woman who was seated in the front row got up, turned toward José Balboa and ripped him with a curse the likes of which hadn't been heard in the valley for a generation. It was a theological haymaker. "Let the blood of the Virgin's first period drown you, José Balboa, and all others who hate life!"

The curse brought a gasp to even the most hardened of the audience. But it was clear that in the heat of a political debate on how to stop a famine with talk alone some very nasty things could be said.

The population explosion was fueled by biological forces far more potent than political slogans. So as people multiplied, food grew scarcer and more high priced. Relief trucks became fewer and black marketeers more common and bold. Then marauding bands began to move through the fields at night. Some seemed to move on their hands and knees, as if grazing, in accordance with the padré's recommendations, eating anything that was green. And some would vomit because they had eaten stems of plants that their molars could manage but their stomachs could not. The argument from design had something wrong with it. Starving people would leave small, discolored, bloody-looking spots of half-digested fiber here and there on the floor of the suffering valley.

"Why is this happening, Diego? Why?" Pooch's wife often asked. He would answer with another question, "Why do you madden me with such questions?" And she would ask again, pointing to the children lying in their beds too weak from hunger to rise, "Have we committed sins that deserve this?" Then the three-year-old died and its eyes would not close. Its little body had refused to accept water during its final days of life and had grown desiccated. The skin of the child's face had grown tight upon its skull. There was some evil, some terrible malevolence, some hideous force at work somewhere, its mother said, to account for such horrors. But then some friend or neighbor would repeat what they had themselves heard

114

so many times from others who were dying in the valley. "Why do we pretend we don't know the reasons for this? God wills it because there are too many of us. If there were not so many of us He would be *unable* to do this to us."

It was the kind of argument that made both liberation theologists and their angry critics very uneasy. Some of the Chinese-leaning communists had taken to distributing copies of the Bible with packets of condoms attached to the flyleaves. The Bibles contained elaborate cross-references and keys in which certain venerable passages were reinterpreted. It was called "quiet revisionism." "Be fruitful and multiply," became "Let thy reason be fruitful and let common sense spread upon the earth. For common sense, too, is the fruit of divine wisdom and is much prized in the House of the Lord."

Pooch smiled grimly to himself as he thought about those days. He was watching Sara tie up tomato plants. Small tomatoes had begun to form in clusters under the bottom leaves. "The world now seems strange," he mumbled to himself. "A stranger place I cannot imagine." And in his mind he saw the fields of full-grown corn that he walked through when he was a boy, wondering at the shape of the ripening cobs, wondering why they were not spherical like the pumpkin or knobbed like the squash. And he saw the cottonwoods along the creek near his house. There were game birds there and sometimes a wild pig. But even when he was a boy, the fish were gone. They had all died when a green substance had slithered downstream from the small factory in the hills that made varnish, or shellac of some kind, that was shipped to Mexico City. Pooch also remembered when people had begun to chop down the cottonwoods along the creek for firewood. The birds and the wild pigs soon disappeared. "A more tragic place I cannot imagine," he said to himself.

It was that night, a Friday, when Pooch and Sara walked the bridge, waiting for the fun to begin in the tavern, that she told Pooch about her father's "club," swearing him to secrecy. It was, indeed, a secret society of old people who were hoarding gold. Her father was its leader. At the time Steinberger told his daughter about the club he was in one of his pegleg-thumping tantrums. "The governor can talk about utopia until his teeth fall out. Fact is gold is the only thing that will support a utopia! The sooner the governor realizes it and tells the government in Washington to keep their paper money for wiping up after politicians mess the floor, the better off we'll all be."

The oldsters brought Steinberger gold, or he went to their homes to collect it when they were unable to leave their homes. "Some of it might be stolen," Sara told Pooch, whispering to him as she snuggled against his arm. The club's headquarters, she said, was a back-room office at an abandoned warehouse on Mill Road, of a company that once made window frames. Secret "meltings" were held there. An old lady, a former potter and, strangely enough, a cousin of the governor, was the "club melter." She had set up a small electric kiln in the headquarters and had one of the old people who had been an electrician connect up a power source that could not be metered. The gold-plated trinkets that Sara's father collected were brought to the meltings so that the gold could be separated from the plastic or base metals it coated.

There wasn't much gold in the State of Milwaukee, except for the gold leaf on the great domes of the churches on the south side of the capital city. That gold was out of bounds for both sacred and secular reasons. For believers the gold belonged to God; for nonbelievers it was, all too literally, out of reach. And certainly there was no gold in the ground. But members of the club—their exact number was known only to Steinberger—would fan out "on a hunt" almost every day of the week. They would move across the city and into small towns around it and into shops and stores, each carrying a small bag or paper sack, looking as harmless as ladybugs. They dressed in well-worn clothes, old cottons usually, because leather felt clammy on aging skin. They wore old shoes, including jogging shoes that had been kept in the back of their closets long after the jogging fad had faded and the pleasantly plump look had replaced the cartilaginous, long-suffering look of the jogger as an ideal of American beauty. Some of them also wore old baseball caps of the kind that the Brewer baseball team had worn in its glory days. They would sidle up to a store counter or a jewelry display and steal anything they could get a wrinkled hand on.

At a typical melting, a half-dozen officers of the club would gather in the dimly lit room on Mill Road and watch the club melter go to work. The old lady would heat the kiln, then ceremoniously deposit trinkets in a small ceramic crucible, often mumbling something that sounded like "toil and trouble, boil and bubble" and, watching her wristwatch, began the countdown. "The costume junk is going now," she would say. "Now the zinc will boil off. The last to go is the iron. The gold will appear at the bottom." Broad smiles on the small circle of faces leaning into the light of the glowing crucible would appear. One of the officers, "Geezer Mike" to his friends, would invariably remark, "Isn't this the most beautiful, golden moment in our lives?" His deputy, an ancient man or woman— no one was sure which it was; at its age it no longer mattered—a person of philosophic tendency, always said, "There is nothing like a little gold to put a shine on a person's life."

"Have you seen these doings?" asked Pooch. He was skeptical. But it sounded like the very kind of thing he would have expected to go on somewhere in the state, if for no reason other than the fact that the whole place seemed almost like a dream to him.

"Yes I have, Pooch dear," said Sara. "Each time they do a melt they get a tiny wafer of gold."

"Pure gold?"

"No. Because the club melter is not a chemist and does not know how to separate the alloys that sometimes get

117

mixed in. But it is very close to being pure. She has tested that."

"How much have they got by now?" asked Pooch. Then, realizing what the question might imply, he quickly amended it. "I... I mean... if these meltings have been going on for a long time."

"For five years, every month. They store it in a box, a box called 'Mr. Common.' Don't you think that is clever?"

"And what if someone finds out?"

"Nobody will tell. They all take an oath. I didn't because I'm not a member. I just got in twice, because father couldn't walk very well and he needed help to get to the melt. And I won't tell anyone. Why should I? I think these old people need that little pot of gold. Helps them sleep better, as my father says."

"You mean because of the way things are going in the rest of the country."

"Yes, with the troubles in Arizona and New Mexico especially. Three people were shot there just yesterday. You heard the news. It's bad. They all want to come into our country, but there is no place to put them, so many I mean."

"I understand, Sara. I lost my family last year, you know."

"Rico told me. And he told me how much he wants success as an artist."

"Nobody ever asks about the club? I'm not sure that's true, Sara. Just last evening I heard talk about what your father was up to, with his late night walks, things like that."

What had stirred interest in Smudge's in the mysterious doings of the club was an incident that happened late at night almost a year before Rico and Pooch had come to Milwaukee. Steinberger was carrying home a load of raw material—brooches, lockets, necklaces, odds and ends—in his small black satchel after he had made the rounds of city club members. He had gotten off the streetcar that ran up Farwell Street to North Avenue on the east end of the

North Avenue bridge. Clement Jensen was at the front door of Smudge's just as it closed at two-thirty in the morning, when the old man materialized out of the fog at the far end of the bridge. Jensen was loaded with lager and in a jovial mood. He watched Steinberger slowly cross the bridge and then pass in front of him under the neon "Schumie's" sign still lit up above the tavern door.

Steinberger pretended not to see Jensen as he headed for the doorway to the stairway that went up to his second-floor apartment. "Nice evening, Wilhelm," Jensen called out. Steinberger did not answer. He fished about in his pocket for the key to his door, holding the stachel firmly in his other hand. But Jensen's greeting had startled him. As he pushed the door open he stumbled forward, his peg leg caught the step to the entrance landing and he fell. Jensen hurried over to help the old man to his feet. As he did so he noticed that the satchel was dangling from Steinberger's wrist by a handcuff. The old man, grimacing in pain, grunted, "I'm all right, damn it! Now just leave me be." He was fumbling nervously for the handle of the satchel. "Well, sorry to you too, Wilhelm!" Jensen said, annoyed. "Just trying to help a friend." Steinberger closed the door behind him and shouted back through the door, "And it's none of your damn business what's in this bag."

The "none of your business" remark of Steinberger's had probably been a mistake. It set Jensen to speculating at the bar later that week. And other patrons began to recall how often Steinberger denounced paper money and how he had tried to get to see the governor to persuade him of the virtues of using gold instead of paper money. More than a few at the bar rubbed their chins and made "Hmmmmm" sounds, often a sign that heavy thinking was going on, as they downed their steins of Schumie's, on Jensen again.

The governor had caught wind of the gold hoarders, of course. At first he found the whole thing mildly amusing. He, after all, was no youngster. He had long ago left

119

"adulthood" far behind, entering that sacred cohort he called "codgerhood" and "gafferdom." So he smiled when he learned that club "guidelines" warned against the theft of anything worth more than ten dollars, or of "snitching" from the same establishment more often than once every six weeks. And he was touched when he read that the club tried to snip goldbug perversion in the bud by making members include small heirloom pieces from their own households in monthly meltings. "Do not elaborate to your children where the heirloom has gone," said the mimeographed guidelines the governor had gotten hold of. "Tell them that the item in question has been lost. Never apologize; never explain."

The old people of the club were not poor, they were merely uncertain. After all, their tenure was daily more perilous. But that was not the only reason. It was more an effect of conditions "outside." Actually the state had seen to it that old people were always well provided for.

From the beginning of the Fritzland Movement, protection of the elderly had been one of its biggest, thickest and strongest political planks. The governor saw it as a matter of deed, not just creed. Clever, well-meaning creeds come and go in politics, he told his followers. They are a dime a dozen in parties of every kind. He had never heard a "call to greatness" during a political campaign, when some noisy politician did not try to curry the favor of what few old people he could get near. But that all took on a new tone when old people became more numerous than teenagers and began to apply the temper-tantrum tactics that had won so many freedoms for the younger set—the right to be insufferable without fully explaining why, the right to push to the head of the line, any line, when one chose. Oldsters were now the tail wagging the political dog and feeling their oats, as metaphor-mixers began to say on television. "We're not just funeral parlor fodder!" crowed a placard lugged back and forth in front of the White House each day by an old curmudgeon who used the sign to brain any passerby who made a slighting comment he did not fancy. "Get Rid of the Kids!" was another popular slogan used around the U.S. Capitol. It meant all-out political war on any congressman who hadn't reached sixty-five.

The governor of the State of Milwaukee had coopted discontented elders in his state long ago, or thought he had. One of the reasons it had been easy to join them rather than to try to lick them was that he himself was old. But there were even more fundamental reasons. He had had a wonderfully happy childhood himself, with parents who loved him and knew how to show it. They didn't ooze and babble around the house about how much they loved everybody, good, bad or detestable. They resolutely refused to cheapen the coin by tossing off "I love you" as if they were at a Hollywood fundraiser for has-beens. So the boy grew up treasuring the word "love" and was very suspicious of its overuse. The governor had learned early how to separate love from molasses. But he also developed detestation for child abuse, not just for what it did to kids but for what it did to them as they got old. When they reached their eighties or nineties, mistreated children were impossible to live with.

Old Steinberger was a case in point. He was kicked around by a brutish father who loved nothing more than to destroy his own television set if his favorite team got blown out of the park. And he swatted his son around in the process, so that the child would grow up with an appreciation of just how important football is to the American mouthbreather population. The child's mother was a self-centered bitch who farmed the boy out to oafish uncles and aunts so she could self-actualize as a hairdresser. The result was an angry young man who went to Viet Nam to get even with his parents by killing orientals he had never seen. All of which, the governor told his head secretary, a motherly old soul who wore tennis shoes to the office because of her bunions, was the reason why he invited cranky Steinberger to the Statehouse every few months so that he could stroke the angry old man's fur back into place and minimize the damage that a serious "back to gold" movement could have on the state.

So this was why it came to pass that the only thing in the State of Milwaukee that was a more serious offense than forging the governor's signature on an invitation to live in the state was to abuse a child or an elder.

And the governor pushed through special legislation, "The Tar-Feather Emergency Provision, Public Law 466LR," within days of his inauguration, to assure that the point was driven home. And for two or three weeks after the first wave of assault-on-the-elderly and child-abuse cases cleared the courts, the roads out of the state were speckled with strange, stumbling figures that resembled baseball-game mascots dressed in rooster costumes. They would wobble into gasoline stations along the way, beg to be doused with enough gasoline to remove some of the tar and a few more of the feathers, scratch and rub themselves with leaves or wriggle about on the grass, then head again for a haven, any haven, from the governor of Milwaukee's wrath. Which meant that many of them were heading for the hot tubs in the central offices of a syndicated pornography publisher in Chicago. Others were not so lucky. They ended up sitting on a stool in some seedy hole in the wall in Kenosha or Hammond where drug and gambling deals were cut, next to a bottle of fingernail-polish remover and a stack of Kleenex, slowly grooming themselves back to presentability. But the abuse of old people and children ended abruptly in the City of Palms.

At the time the governor learned of the gold hoarders, he was preparing to deliver another of his "steady as she goes" addresses to the citizens of the state to help keep the "Begin again" thing in perspective. When he went on radio—he had never lost his suspicion of television—he told his audience that the supposed message from outer space was undoubtedly a hoax, or a glitch in some technological monstrosity being assembled by cuckoos somewhere in a windowless research laboratory. The real function of such things, he said, was to prevent people from focusing on the important things of life: grandma's recipe for rhubarb pie, a pair of suspenders that "won't let you down"—he delivered that one dead-pan—feeding the ducks in the park lagoon, watching the baby grow a pair of beaverlike incisors, the cadence of a good waltz, a chance to take the family for a spin in the old Shikel automobile through the hills of the Kettle Moraine State Park or the value of honest-to-God cow manure on a backyard garden. Besides, he said, no creature with a brain larger than a lemon would waste a lot of time and money beeping a message into outer space that was so ambiguous that it merely produced confusion when it got to where it was supposed to get. Interstellar communication, if there was such a thing, was not like inventing a TV guessing-game show. "Citizens!" he said, "I have smelled a rat in this thing from the beginning. I urge you, as someone who has seen a lot, much good and much bad, during a long and interesting life, not to abandon those yeomanly virtues that have made your state the envy of the nation. There is something fishy about this supposed message from outer space. So I admonish you, look closely at the pig in the poke. Do not buy something inside a sack just because it wiggles." He allowed himself a chuckle. It was a famous sound in the state, confident, paternal. "Sorry to put rats, fish and pigs all into one speech," he added.

As for the cults springing up all over the place in response to "Begin again," the latest on Big Sur, he had seen that kind of nonsense before, in the south Pacific just after World War II while he was still in the navy. He reminded his audience that he had loved and outlived three beautiful wives, each of a different race, and that the first was a belle from the Solomon Islands. A lot of people in the United States, he said as he unwound the story with the skill that had so often delighted his listeners over the years, including his own father and mother, sophisticated people from Boston—so sophisticated, in fact, that they boasted about being able to let their hair down at Boston Pops concerts—had difficulty accepting her because she wore a lip-distending labret. He had first laid eyes on his beautiful first wife-to-be when he and several other navy officers were ordered to trek deep into the Solomon's jungles because rumor said diehard Japanese were building a new lightweight bamboo version of the dreaded Zero and were planning suicide raids on victorious Americans. It turned out that his wife-to-be was one of the many Solomoners dancing around a bamboo model of an airplane, built high on a mountaintop. It was the so-called "cargo cult" movement. The natives were trying to lure their gods down from the sky, along with marvels of civilization that they had seen dumped upon their shores in such plenty during the war, such as cigarettes, cases of Spam and whiskey. The people dancing around the bonfires on Big Sur, or inside the plaza of the Louvre in Paris, or on Bunker Hill, in front of some weird fetish such as a pile of old Flash Gordon comic books or the collected works of William Buckley, were doing much the same thing. Gold-hoarding made about as much sense, said the governor, but he remained sensibly indulgent about it.

The roots of the problem, the governor knew, ran deep. He had noticed that the people of the state were enjoying eating with a kind of grim ferocity that had not been there before the "Begin again" thing started. And although he himself had been responsible for the laws that banned diet books from the state, along with other pornography, and although his own butterball silhouette was a symbol of the state's culinary sophistication, he knew that overeating that wasn't fun could be a bad sign. He personally had always put on too much weight during political campaigns, when he was anxious. True, it was really impossible to live the life of a successful governor of the State of Milwaukee without showing it in the waistline and chin.

But the thousands of bratwurst he was served at fund-raising picnics were too delicious, almost metaphysically so, to be true. Even though bratwurst were known—research had proved it—to improve one's disposition, one could still overdo a good thing. But it was more than that. Campaigning made him cranky and short-tempered. That was a sign, he knew, of a man who doesn't know what is important. Furthermore, he knew that hoarding, whether it was of gold or fat, could mean that people who were calm and happy on the outside were not always the same on the inside.

That night, after the blandishments and chastisements were over, the governor signed off his radio address with his usual, "And sleep snug, citizens, with those you love, imperfect though they may be."

The effect of the governor's talk *was* calming, though he was under no illusion about the seriousness of the problems he faced. He knew that if there was ever a real break in the Rio Grande Wall, or if some political sellout took place just to garner a few million votes from refugees, his state was in trouble. Fritz Schumacher had said nothing in his little *Small is Beautiful* about solving the population problem. Often, late at night when he was sitting up in his bed reading, the governor had searched the little book for some line or other that would tell him how to deal with the population problem, including his own state's slowly rising numbers. In the end the population thing always came down to a simple matter of space. Space on the planet was finite. Indeed, everything was finite, except perhaps, good intentions. There were still quite a few people in his state that had difficulty grasping that elemental fact. Over time, the governor realized, the people who could not grasp it, or those who refused to try, would out-breed those who could. Common sense would be overwhelmed, to the ruin of everyone. Schumacher had said nothing about this tragic defect in human nature. The whole thing left the governor feeling uneasy. Had he built his wonderful new commonwealth on a mortally flawed premise? Or was Schumacher so caught up in the vanity of his own utopian visions that he could not accept the fact that human beings preferred not to think too much.

Be that as it may, at Smudge's things remained calm, even with speculation going on about the possibility that Steinberger carried great hunks of pure gold around in his little black satchel. The air was still full of song, beer foam and pretzels. In fact, the air was full of pretzels in a very real sense. Tossing pretzels, big eight-inchers, at pegs protruding from a cushion on the wall—with a kind of Frisbee side-hand motion—had recently started a statewide tavern craze. It was Milwaukee's answer to the English dart game, which to Milwaukeeans always had an aura of imported affectation about it. The idea in pretzel-throwing was to get a ringer, of course. A ringer was worth a stein of Schumie's or perhaps a new stein itself, one of the elegant masterpieces from the Elm Grove factory with a portrait of the governor on it, plus any splintered pretzels that ended up in the tub below the pegboard.

In Smudge's the "Begin again" thing did not come up all that often. People pretty well accepted that the governor was correct. They also realized that the best thing to do when the world was turning itself upside down was to go about your life as quietly and sensibly as possible, deflecting what Dionysian impulses one had into artistry in the bedroom. High tech was not needed for any of it, for either common sense, composure or surrender to passion under reasonably controlled circumstances. High technology had, after all, inflicted one absurdity after another on the human race in the last three decades, including the costly effort in the last century to build a Maginot Line in the sky that would make nuclear war impossible.

The "leak" in that idea had brought more than a few bellylaughs to those who stood at the bar or sat in the booths at Smudge's smoothing down their Schumie's. "Those damn fools put two trillion dollars into those space platforms. Two trillion! Can you believe that?"

"Hell yes, I believe it. If it hadn't been for the governor posting our guard around the borders of this state and daring that goof in the White House to come and get our taxes for it, we would have paid through the nose just like everybody else."

"Well, they're the ones that told the states to start looking after themselves. I'm as much for the stars and stripes as the next guy. But *two trillion?*"

"And right after that there scientist gets up before that congressional committee and says there was no way in hell they could stop some fanatic from puttin' a damn bomb into a suitcase and rowing a seventy-five-dollar rowboat up the Potomac and blowin' everything to hell."

"Including the seventy-five-dollar rowboat."

"Including the damn rowboat, new or used."

"Well, no question why the president thinks our state governor is a real pain in the ass."

"Our kind of pain in the ass. Right?

"We can all drink to that!" And up went the steins.

There had been no nuclear war, but the reason was not that someone had invented a push-buttoned device to shut down human wickedness, nor was it because geneticists had been able to engineer a pacific gene and flood the human gene pool with it. People had become preoccupied with other things. In 2005, when the world's oceans began to run out of fish—halibut, cod, flounder, turbot and the rest—attention shifted to the kind of knots that would hold a seining net together when fishermen went after fish-like suckers and carp in the last frontier of hunting and gathering—the contaminated muck of the Rhine estuary, Chesapeake Bay and the Ganges. High-sounding conferences and negotiations about IBCM "throw weights" and "third-strike interceptor ratios" were suddenly a bore and a nuisance for just about everybody except a few ballistics physicists skulking about half-abandoned federal research laboratories, or beribboned generals in the basement of the Pentagon plotting the comeback of militarism's case for all-out war.

When Sara and Pooch joined Rico that night at Smudge's to hear another poetry reading, Allison Minter did not show up at seven-thirty as she said she would. She was late, and nonchalant about it. Rico saw her coming through the door in white slacks, with a white jacket tossed over one shoulder. She was as beautiful as he had remembered, even more so.

Earlier that day, Rico had asked Pooch if he might, in fact, be falling in love. Pooch had merely said, "Perhaps." He had reservations about the Minter girl and he knew she had his friend in her cross hairs. It was a question of when she would pull the trigger.

"She's rich, you know, Pooch," Rico was yelling as they worked in the sand and gravel company's small warehouse, moving bags of cement with a front-end loader, then piles of sand and pea gravel. Rico was not sure why a girl like Allison Minter would take interest in him.

"What would somebody like that see in somebody like me, even if I am an artist? She's rich, you know, Pooch," Rico was yelling absentmindedly as he swiveled the front-end loader about and sent Pooch sprawling. He stopped the machine, ran over to where Pooch was lying. "I never saw a face as beautiful as hers, Pooch, to be honest about it. Never. And she went to a very private college. She's got it all. What do you think? Tell me, even if it hurts."

"I won't tell you a damn thing if I have to get killed in the process," said Pooch. "Goddamn it, Rico, you damn near ran over me with that load of cement."

Rico, suddenly out of his daze, apologized, then apologized again.

"You know what I think?" asked Pooch.

"What?"

"That we should take a break."

Over a pair of Seven-Ups. Pooch told Rico what he thought of Minter. She was rich, she was spoiled, she was stuck on Rico. She was beautiful, and he wouldn't blame Rico if he tried to get into her pants. "But don't underestimate this one, my friend. That young lady is used to getting her way. You had much experience with women?"

"Some, a fair amount I guess. I mean, I know what they like."

"She's the kind who likes success in a man. Enter the flag contest. You win it, hands down. She's yours forever." Pooch was having fun at the expense of Minter's effect on his young friend. "You throw yourself into the thing with the same abandon as you drive a front-end loader. Bang! It's wedding bells and you end up owning half of the Shikel Automobile Company.

Rico was annoyed. He was trying to get a serious opinion from a man of experience. All he got was lame humor. "Damn it, Pooch!" he said. "I do have some good ideas for a flag. I know what these flag nuts like. I like flags too. So does everybody. So I design the flaggiest damn flag this state has ever seen."

"This flag of your disposition, out of green things hopefully growing." It was a line from Walt Whitman that came to Pooch out of nowhere, and it had nowhere to go.

"Why the hell can't you be a little serious?" Rico asked impatiently.

Pooch was having trouble being serious because he was going to be with Sara Steinberger again that evening. The thought gave him a boost, made him feel up, for reasons he did not care to puzzle over. He liked her.

In one of the booths in Smudge's that night, waiting for the poetry reading to begin, Pooch and Sara and Rico sat and talked, mostly about Rico's plan to enter the flag contest.

Sara said little. In her pale, phlegmatic way, she did not find it all really worth worrying about. If Pooch and Rico had good jobs and were happy, what more could there be.

Rico was unsure. "So you say, Pooch, that if I win the flag contest she'll be impressed?"

"Women are always impressed with men who can design a good flag," said Pooch.

"Well, I could win, Pooch. As I said, I have a lot of good ideas."

"And I know you will," said Pooch, mocking Rico slightly. He did not think a flag contest was to be the high point in his young friend's career as an artist. He had trouble taking it seriously.

Then the Minter girl showed up, forty minutes late. Rico's gooseflesh told him better late than never. She was beautiful, as beautiful as he had remembered. She came spinning through the door, dressed in white sailing slacks and a striped blouse, without brassiere, and a small white sailor cap with a gold anchor stitched into its front. She gave Rico a glancing kiss to the cheek and a quick squeeze on the arm as they sat down in the booth. Pooch ordered her a stein of Schumie's.

"Rico here may be entering the flag design contest," said Pooch to Allison, trying to get the conversation ball rolling.

"Is he?" She squealed a kind of half-squeal—surprise, delight, an element of boredom all mixed together.

"I actually think I could win," said Rico, matter of factly, pretending his heart was not racing.

"I would like to help you, Charles," Allison said. She refused to call him Rico ("Sounds like something from a gangster movie"). "I don't mean with the design itself. I stopped being an artist a long time ago. Too busy living."

You need a machete to cut through that bull, Pooch said to himself.

"I think he should do it on his own," said Pooch. He could see the whole thing unfolding already. Minter puts a bug in her father's ear, her father puts a bug into the ear of the chairman of the jury that is to judge the contest, including a little data on what Far's flag would look like, and presto, Rico—sorry, *Charles*—wins.

This may not be Mexico, Pooch said to himself, but a little push here and a little push there moves things along. Just because it's not considered corruption doesn't mean it has no odor.

"I just want to help Charles as best I can," said Allison. "I just want to help him to make something of himself." She squeezed Rico's arm again. "I mean help you make something big of yourself. Nothing wrong with that. I'm going to help Anselm get his poetry published."

Pooch was irritated with the woman. "Why do you wish to see Pester publish his poetry? Nine times out of ten when a poet is published the mystery evaporates. People are thinking more about what they heard at the last reading than if they had read Pester. Look at this place. It's filling up for the reading already." What Pooch did not say was that he agreed with the rumors that Clement Jensen had spread around about the authorship of *The Book of Ruling Equations*. Publishing Pester would not only be a crime against the real author of the *Book*, whoever he was, it would also expose old Pester to some final indignity, unmasking him as a blatant plagiarist perhaps, and to no good end. The poetry he was reading was pretty lumpy stuff, no matter who was responsible for it.

Minter was not buying Pooch's argument about Pester. "I know you are a writer, too, Diego." (She refused to call him Pooch. "Reminds a person of a gunnysack," she had said to Rico.) "Do you enjoy not being published?"

It was not a kind question, but it was to the point. Grenada backed and filled. "Well, perhaps it's different with poets like Pester. I am sure it is. Just watch him up there on the stage. That's worth a lot more than being published."

"Now really, Diego, you can't mean that," said Allison.

"Well, why do you want to get Rico to make it big?" Pooch asked, changing the subject. He had seen women try to make something of their men before, in Durango. One woman he knew tried to make her farmer husband into an undertaker and the poor farmer ended up half-mad. Draining the blood out of bodies and pumping in formaldehyde had been too much for him. And when he returned to farming he kept imagining that his plow would uncover bodies. When the plow uncovered the bones of a dead dog one day, he went stark raving mad for good.

"In other parts of America things are terrible," Pooch continued. "Unless, of course, you are rich, which Rico isn't." There was some sarcasm in Pooch's voice.

"Well, I *am* rich," Allison said petulantly, and kissed Rico on the cheek, a quick peck of a kiss. "Charles can stay right here and become a major artist. And he can show in Chicago. I have lots of friends in the galleries down there."

Pooch looked past Allison as he said, "There is a lot of art here."

"But everything in this town is so pokey, so limited. And Charles should *not* be working in a sand and gravel yard. That's just ridiculous."

"He has to eat," said Pooch.

"Oh, posh. He could move into one of the apartments at my studio. You and Sarah too. Or into one of our guest-houses."

"A man should try to be self-sufficient," Pooch said. "I've told Sara that we should not live at the studio at your place. It complicates everything. Here we just walk across the street to work."

"Really, Diego, sometimes I wonder what good it is to try to help people." She refused to look at any of her three friends. Her eyes were clouded, as if she might be on the verge of tears. "Sometimes I get so mad with people like you, Diego. But you're older than Charles. That probably explains it."

Rico tried to smooth things over. "Well, I'm going to enter the flag contest," he said firmly.

132

"Wonderful, Charles," said Allison. "Dádi and I know all of the people on the governor's flag jury."

"He should do this on his own," said Pooch, looking straight at Allison.

"Not if I can help him, he shouldn't," she said. "I'm going to see that he talks to Dádi about flags. My father and the governor both love flags. That's why we have so many of them in this city. I'm sure the governor will be interested in Charles' design. I'll make sure he is."

Pooch was on the verge of colliding head-on with Minter. As he fixed her with his eyes, about to speak, there was a sudden flurry of excitement in the room and some applause from the audience that had been sitting around the platform where the big Victorian chair had been set up, waiting on Pester's entrance. There were gasps, an "Oh my God!" and then an "I don't believe this!"

Pester had made his stage entrance. His goggles, down over his eyes, were of bright blue plastic. On his forehead he had painted a large black circle with a blue star in the center of it. The left side of his face was painted white, the right side yellow. He was shirtless under his lederhosen suspenders. He had painted giant green chevrons from his shoulder to his waist in alternate black and green. On each knee he wore a studded pad, fashioned as best one could tell, from stretch bandages and large shingle nails. And on each wrist he wore a wrist knife. He walked onto stage in a deliberate, almost stately, manner. His poise made good sense, of course, not just because he was a poet. He could not afford some extravagant theatrical gesture and bleed to death as the price.

"Well, all right, Anselm!" Allison Minter shouted, and it set off a polite but restrained round of applause. People of the State of Milwaukee had seen a lot of oddballs in their day, if not in the state, on television. And while most of them realized that in an uncertain world anything could happen, even in the City of Palms, this was different, to put it mildly, and dangerous. A lot of people in the audience had heard of the Pester-Jensen run-in a week earlier, but seeing was believing.

Pooch stared at Pester, blinked his eyes, looked at Rico, then back to Pester. The last time he had seen a face painted like this one was when he was a small boy at a fiesta. A dwarfish figure in the parade, an odd figure with hands where elbows normally appear, wore a yellow and white mask. Pooch remembered how he felt at the time. The dwarf had flown down from the moon to join the parade and to thrill children like himself. Pester had not come from the moon, merely from his room back beyond the toilets, and before that from Chicago. But the City of Palms was obviously not the frumpy place that some of the people in Madison had told Pooch it was as they hitchhiked across the state from Prairie du Chien. Frumpy cities do not produce poetry readings by men in blue goggles, face paint and wrist knives.

Rico was put off balance, too, by Pester. He had not seen anything like it before and in all of his reading about the arts, even its avant-garde, he had not heard of anything to top this, not at least outside the big cities of Europe, and perhaps New York. He leaned toward Allison Minter and whispered, "What is he up to?"

The Minter girl knew all too well what the poet was up to. It was she who had told Pester what to do, when he called her weeks earlier and told her that Jensen's threats had grown worse and that he was afraid his career as a poet could be cut short. He didn't mind dying, he told her, of some natural cause or a degenerative brain disorder triggered by his sins of the past. But to be killed by a damned ashtray hurled by a fat philistine in the middle of a poetry reading was no way for a poet of his caliber to go.

Allison was on her father's yacht when she got the call. They had just come down from Escanaba, Michigan, and were anchored at the McKinley Yacht Club. She told Pester that if she was to remain his patron, he would have to stay alive, at minimum. She said the way to get at Jensen was to get psychiatric dirt on him and then trade it for safety. She knew Jensen's background and what his long-range ambitions were. She had discussed them with her father often. He wanted to go to the top in politics.

Pester said that the trouble with that tactic was that Jensen could get as much counter-dirt, and easily, in Chicago as he needed. They would need something that got to the quick of the problem directly.

A best defense is a good offense, Allison had decided. So she called the president of Marquette University. He knew his way around town and he was always good for a fresh idea. Marquette had been her father's alma mater and the Minters had a lot of clout at MU thanks to their endowment of a half-dozen chairs in its dental school.

The president had a very good idea indeed. He told Allison to put Pester in touch with his anthropology department, which she did.

The anthropologist who was to advise Pester told his new client, that he, Pester, had to come on looking as fierce as possible. He told Pester to practice using Kau facial and body paint and to get used to wearing wrist knives, a pair of which he kept on a shelf in his office to impress disgruntled students complaining about low grades and threatening to do something about it. He said things had been quiet in his office for years and that he would loan the wrist knives to Pester, provided he was allowed to do a brief research documentary film on the effect Pester's new get-up would have on his antagonist at Smudge's. Pester got a quick briefing on how to act like a Kau living in Milwaukee.

The Kau of the Sudan, a handsome, black-as-ebony race of people, had developed, Pester was told, body painting, scarification and wrestling with wrist knives to a high art. Kau males fought with the wrist knives for favors of beautiful young maidens of the tribe. The Kau had rules that prevented the whole thing from deteriorating to an absurd bloodbath. But Jensen would not know about such rules, nor would he assume Pester would abide by any kind of gentlemanly code if it came to a showdown. Pester breathed easier when he was assured that proper "display behavior" would end his torment from Jensen.

It was all sound advice. Fortunately for Jensen, on the night of the poetry reading, when he might have gotten drunk again and started trouble with the poet and been filmed in the act, he was back in jail. He had run a red light at Cherry and Third Streets and then smarted-off to the officer who stopped him. So the issue never really came to a test. But the impact of the get-up on his audience did.

When Pester mounted the stage he looked about the room slowly, trying to determine if his nemesis was lurking as usual in the shadowy area near the end of the bar closest to the poet. But Jensen, of course, was not there. All Pester saw was a typical Friday night audience staring at him more intently than ever. So he ostentatiously adjusted himself in the big chair and began reading slowly from *The Book of Ruling Equations.* He began with several enigmatic aphorisms intended to put his audience in a pensive frame of mind. "Hearts bleed," he read. "This we all know. But do minds bleed?" A long silence, then one young lady in the front row said timorously, assuming that the poet had asked more than a rhetorical question, "I guess so, if you get hit hard enough." Pester looked at her gently, then said, "Perhaps the hangman's noose is but a tourniquet for the bleeding mind?"

Another long silence, then a "Bravo, Anselm baby!" from some slummer standing near the door near the far end of the bar. Then there was a round of applause. But if nobody in the audience seemed to know what Pester was driving at, they did know he had somehow gotten hold of their heartstrings.

"It's a cry for help," whispered one woman in the audience to her boyfriend. "He's going to have to get hold of himself," she added.

"In that outfit, I wouldn't advise it," said the boyfriend.

Then Pester launched into "Ode to the Flat-Nosed Moon."

> *Race high pale-faced moon*
> *Fly gold and flat-nosed as a kite*
> *Above my trembling hymn to you*
> *God of the night sky*
> *Rule my heart's desire*
> *Grand plate of yellow light*
> *Droop late tonight, around two,*
> *Over this teething sea of need*
> *Over this state's dwindling supply of weed.*

"Oh, there's that dangler line again!" whispered Allison to Rico Far. "Now you know why Anselm is really great."

The beauty of Pester's "Ode to the Flat-Nosed Moon" had apparently sent a shiver up the Minter girl's spine. She looked eagerly toward Pester, waiting for him to begin another poem. But he was busy adjusting his wrist knives. One had come loose on his wrist and he was afraid to make a hurried move. He horsed around with the knives for a full five minutes. Allison grew impatient. She leaned into Far. "Charles," she whispered, "let's go up to your studio this very minute. I want to see your studio. I want to see what *you* are doing as an artist." So up to the studio Allison and Rico went.

But the painting Rico had just completed did not really impress her. It was the first of what he hoped would be a series to make his mother proud. It was a picture almost nine feet long, in acrylics, of a recumbent carrot. The ten-inch carrot that posed for the painting had come from Sara's garden, and Pooch had brought it up to the studio to impress Rico with what a vegetable garden in Milwaukee could grow. The artist had painted the carrot in an outpouring of emotion in about twenty minutes. So the painting retained that vigorous, informal quality so characteristic of the "new expressionist" movement that was given up for dead in the 1980s. Rico had intended to do ten works in his recumbent-carrot series and to hang them outside from the windows of the apartment tower, a kind of frieze. He was also intent on catching the eye of local dealers.

The carrot painting did make a hit, in a manner of speaking. A dozen people trooped up from the bar to see the painting, including a newspaper art critic. And after the viewing, the critic got Pooch aside to give him some advice that he might pass on to the artist "in a friendly, constructive vein." "The work lacks emotional focus," he told Pooch. "Though it is, to be sure, a cry from the heart." He also told Pooch that if young Far had any designs on a major gallery in Chicago or New York he would have to make his carrots "far more sexually explicit than they are. A few root hairlets will not do. We tend to see a carrot as if it were a carrot. Or to imagine it sliced and floating about in soup. Such prosaics will not do on the outside."

When Rico realized that Allison was not taken with his painting of the carrot he began to sputter, to explain, to make excuses. "You might like the work I have done on the ceiling of the tower. It's different."

The painting was different, in several respects. For one thing it was called "Untitled," so that no demands were made on the viewer to see something he could not see. For another, it was painted in primary colors, perhaps a sign of the still-innocent side of Rico's mind or his consuming love for Allison. It might also have been triggered somehow in Rico's subconscious mind by his experiences in Mexico. It was a giant black cross lying in a field of yellow, with blue swirls cutting across its edges and down the sides of the tower, with bold slashes of red here and there.

But what impressed Allison was not just the ceiling mural in the tower but the whole layout of the bedroom. It was entered on a steel ladder that curled up through a hole in the ceiling at the east end of the studio. A row of small hexagonal windows circled the tower and made the room seem to float, like some surreal chamber where Romeo and Juliet might meet in a romantic nineteenth-century opera, high above the city below. The great bridge swept out toward the east toward the cream colored, antique stone watertower that stood on the bluffs of Lake Michigan. The lake swept over the horizon, a gigantic flat stretch of water that seemed to slumber under a layer of dark blue glass. And in the direction of Canada, near Sault Ste. Marie, a land of romance, the moon was rising. It hung in lovely silence over that land of French traders, birchbark canoes and spruce-fringed rivers, a land of voyageurs, Indian maidens, and as the British often said of the French, "ruddy voyeurs, too."

In the center of the bedroom was an enormous circular bed. The bed was built by the former tenant of the third-floor studio, a retired naval ordinance engineer who had also decided to turn artist after he had retired and then his wife had died. The bed rotated on a large gear ring and was powered by a small electric motor. It moved on the same principle as a heavy naval gun. And on the opposite side of the bed, opposite the hole in the floor where the ladder thrust upward, was another hole of about the same size, but with a brass fireman's pole passing through it instead of a ladder.

The fire pole had been put into the tower bedroom by the engineer as an afterthought. The man had moved into the tower and constructed the bed to impress his young woman, a red-haired girl from Dusseldorf. She had a violent temper. Some said it was because the drinking water of Dusseldorf had been polluted for many years with red dye from a printing plant. Dusseldorfers had begun to earn a reputation all over Europe as volatile and dangerous people who flew off the handle for the slightest of reasons. In any case, the girl loved the engineer's bed. But she often attacked her lover in vicious and unpredictable ways, with bites and nail gouges, sometimes when they were submerged in the tenderest of love scenes. The fire pole was put in so that the engineer could make his escape at short notice, at the least sign of her displeasure with some small, unspoken infraction of their sexual rites. But the strain caught up with the engineer. He died of a coronary thrombosis, evidently after a weekend of wild erotic experimentation by the girl from Dusseldorf on the principle of a rotating gun turret.

Just what precise anatomical or physiological extremity had been breached on the fateful weekend was never determined, though Louie had sent a "task force" of five patrons of his bar up to the tower to try to figure out what had gone wrong. Nothing was ever found in the way of incriminating devices, guidebooks, or erotic TV tapes. The secret was to leave Milwaukee buried in the heart of the red-haired girl from Dusseldorf when she moved back to Germany a year later.

Allison Minter had no more than set eyes on the great bed in the tower, with the zebra-striped sheets that Rico had bought for it, than she decided to invent a game of love that would involve all of the resources of the studio, the bed, the pole and Rico. She abruptly stripped her clothes off on the spot, let down her hair, and with a "Bet you can't catch Allison!" she ran up to Rico, embraced him, kissed him deeply, tore loose from his arms, already eager, and went whistling down the fire pole, her hair flying up behind her as she disappeared through the hole in the floor. Rico also stripped on the spot. He was after her like a shot, around the studio, behind the easel, first this way, then that, up the circular stairs again, and just as he got within reach of her again, she went down the fire pole with a great joyous "Wheee" and another taunt, "Bet you can't catch Allison."

And then they took turns chasing each other, "the pole game" as they dubbed it. And she would make suggestive remarks to Rico as she whizzed past him. And Rico, fired up, eager as a spring billygoat, in a high state of what psychologists still called "learning readiness," would make jesting "Grrrr" sounds and pretend to stalk his prey like a kind of giant ostrich as he put one foot out slowly in front of the other and moved toward Allison, and she would pretend to hide as the hot-blooded animal making "Grrrr" sounds tried to corner her. Until finally, after ten or fifteen minutes of this tearing about, both pretended to tire. And tickling, kissing and fondling began, then a race for the bed, and Rico switched on the gun turret's little, purring electric motor, and they made love, proud as punch of each new wrinkle they were able to give the venerable and ancient procedure. The tower seemed to sway in the moonlight and the world melted into soft sounds and mysterious tempos, as Allison, remembering the sound of the oboe she played years ago at the Conservatory of Music on Prospect Avenue, sighed, "agitato," "fugue," "presto," and a moment later whispered in Rico's ear, "Well, all right!"

The lovers ended their sojourn into the land of bliss and blessedness lying on their backs. A warm breeze moved through the open windows. They stared at the moon as it seemed about to enter Rico's mural on the ceiling. "Do you see the moon, my darling Charles?" she asked. "That's the Sea of Tranquility, that lovely smooth gray-golden patch."

And he answered, "Yes, I see it, my love. You need a rocket to get there."

"Yes, I know, she said softly, her eyelids closing.

WHAT HONORABLE MENTION CAN DO FOR MAN

HAD OLD PROFESSOR Fechner made love to his wife with the ardor and unabashed invention that Charles Far lavished on Allison Minter in the tower, the rewards that would have come his way would have probably changed the great thinker's life. He would not have had to boil a cat to try to find out what would make a noticeable difference.

Just what precise magic Rico worked on Allison will never, of course, be fully known. But it is certain that he was not a virgin at the time of his encounter in the tower. He had spent a lot of time between school terms and on weekends helping out in his father's boom-box stores in Mexico. So he had considerable experience running with or trying to avoid being killed by one of the boom-box youth gangs. This meant inevitably that he shared in the fruits of gang life, especially the opportunity to make love to young women of the gangs, quickly, furtively and often

under ridiculous circumstances. He made love in doorways, alcoves, behind parked cars—if no one could pick
the lock on the machines. He was a kind of sexual kan-
garoo, hopping in and out of the lives of women of all
kinds, beautiful, small, large, attractive, or not quite repulsive enough to be out of bounds.

But Rico found this sort of thing generally distasteful.
Something inside him, a natural good taste or refinement,
told him there ought to be more to sex than having one's
ashes hauled within earshot of an unkempt thug with a
boom-box. It was Allison's beauty and grooming, and the
fact that she was very rich, and in some sense cultivated
in spite of a coarseness that came easily to her, that made
him feel for the first time, in the tower, that love could be
more than sweat and vulgar, unwelcome after-images.
Allison's body was designed, for one thing, to absorb kisses,
thousands of them. The lovely, faint, soft baby-fat line that
had formed under her chin in the last few years was one
of his favorite targets for his kisses. Rico rained them on
that spot, and elsewhere of course, with a fervor that she
assumed was peculiar to men from Yucatán. But that was
not so. He merely desired to kiss her until he was sated.

For Allison it all seemed even more remarkable, given
the fact that she was four or five years older than he was.
The first, almost imperceptible evidences of her body's
drift toward the overripe had already begun to appear.
Even though others did not notice these changes, she did.
They seemed to appear in particular behind her knees and
on the backside of her upper arms. But with Rico in her
arms she began to sense how easy it would be to forget
about such subtle ravages by time, at least for the moment,
and to fall in love completely, nuttily, helplessly, even as
she resented her sense of helplessness. She had been in
love before, she thought, and many times, but this was
different. For the first time what she wanted seemed to lie
just beyond her emotional reach. Not beyond her finger-
tips, to be sure. She had long ago mastered that side of

143

love. It was the new feeling that mixed joy and jealousy and possessiveness (never in equal parts from one moment to the next, but always varied and unpredictably mixed) that left her feeling so strange, somewhat tormented, sometimes overcome by a sweet feeling she wanted to share with the entire world. At other times she was furious at the idea that she could not fall asleep but could only stare at the ceiling of her bedroom and imagine herself next to that handsome young man in the tower staring at the Sea of Tranquility. She found herself resenting any woman who even talked to Rico, even Sara Steinberger, for heaven's sake, a frump who used no makeup but who wore a damn ankle bracelet. If some woman touched Rico in Smudge's, even in a casual or playful way—which every woman in the place seemed intent on doing, sneaking around like little thieves in a Fanny Farmer store, copping a feel—she could feel a tautness come across her chest. She could feel her body juices turning green and acidic. It was all, she told herself, just too utterly damned absurd. But it was real, present, a grim ineluctable force festering on the back side of her heart somewhere. And hanging one on only made it worse. Then she would call Rico and make an absolute fool of herself over the phone, as if she were back in high school and had lost the last shred of common sense. Throwing a piece of bric-a-brac against the wall in her bedroom didn't help either. About all that helped was a cocktail with Dádi and perhaps a swim. Allison was, in a nutshell, in a bad way.

As for Rico, during the long days when he was shoveling sand, moving gravel about, shirtless, getting a tan—which would only make Allison's desperation more severe, because she knew his tan was earned by hard work and that under it there was honest-to-God muscle of the kind rail splitters and lumberjacks sported—he would think constantly about the beautiful woman he had just met. She was gorgeous, in fact, not just beautiful. There wasn't a blemish on her anywhere and her hair always smelled sweet from a shampoo scented with honey and coconut, something she had learned about, she said, on a trip with Dádi to Kapalua Bay on Maui. But God, was she possessive. And reluctantly Rico admitted to himself that Pooch might be right. She could be a spoiled brat, a cannibal brat. Perhaps he loved her, he said to himself. But after a year of love like that, Pooch had said casually, there would be nothing left of Rico to lick but his bones. What if Pooch was right? What if his friend was right? And Rico would heave a bag of cement onto a truck. And each time he worried about the woman, the cement sack seemed to behave more obstreperously than ever, or it would split as it fell off the stupid truck and a demon would grin out at him through the split in the bag. "Bet you can't catch Allison." He vowed to love her that night until she said "uncle," and she'd back off her damned possessive ways.

"I'll be goddamned, Pooch," Rico had said in a typical display of helplessness and fascination, "she's impossible. It's not that she wants to do it all the time. She's like I am. A half-dozen times or so and she wants to take it easy for a while. But she's impossible! She calls Mabel every day to find out when I get home. Mabel just shrugs. But I know she doesn't like to be pestered. I haven't been able to do any damn painting for weeks. My carrot series is stalled. I got about ten of them. I wanted to do twenty, all big fellows, something that the critics couldn't ignore. Now she wants to take me out on her dad's yacht for the weekend. I'd like that. Who wouldn't. Never been on one of those really big boats. But the creeps she hangs around with at the yacht club! My god, I thought disease had wiped out all of that kind, years ago."

Allison, meanwhile of course, would be sprawling in a deck chair on her father's huge boat just offshore of Milwaukee. She kept a ship-to-shore phone handy so she could find out if Rico happened to get off work early. "He works so hard," she would say to one of her polo-playing boyfriends.

145

He would fuss over a new batch of bloody marys at the boat's bar. And he would answer, "You must get hold of your feelings Allison. He works in a sand and gravel yard, for Pete's sake. I've seen him. I would admit he's good looking. But so are others of us." And he'd smile as he playfully adjusted the bright yellow scarf that had blown out from under his blazer, exposing a hairless chest, or a chest that had been, apparently, shaved.

"Well, he's not just a workman you know," Allison protested. "He's a painter. A very good one too." She threw her head back and stared at the sky. "I think he's a genius ...in more ways than one."

Allison sipped the bloody mary, then slumped deep into the deck chair. She thought of all those times she had traveled to such wonderful places as Nice and Monte Carlo, or those long days tied up at the docks of Dádi's rich friends' estates on the northern shores of Lake Huron. There had been erotic encounters and love affairs there too, and even in India. In fact, India had left a permanent mark on her. At first Allison was merely impressed by the subcontinent's obvious charms, its profusion of flowers and strange birdcalls, its processions of beautiful erect women in saris fringed with gold and with the great white cows that wandered about on the sidewalks of Delhi, cadging a meal at a fruit vendor's stand. She was also impressed by the advantages of being an American in India. For a dollar, gypsies with dancing bears would perform along the road to Agra. The bazaars impressed her too, even the third-world aroma of perspiring men, the smell of the salty, well-cured, multilayered residue of weeks of sweat that had accumulated between downpours of rain. And it was fun to dicker with jewelers who sold precious stones the size of a quarter for ten dollars, even if, usually, they were just glass. Wisemen squatting in the dust impressed her too, as did the swarms of beggars with missing or oddly deformed limbs, something right out of her *National Geographic* magazine, where it was always made clear that there was some mysterious, but natural, connection between American good fortune and American virtue.

But beyond all of that, Allison quickly became a student of the Vedas, at least in the sense that she learned that she should praise such things once she was back home in River Hills, Wisconsin. Because Indian literature contained some of the most majestic epic poetry in existence. You did not need really to read it, for it was always assumed at dinner parties that if you mentioned things like the "Bhagavad Gita," you had.

Ancient temple sites and stupas ringed with marvelous carvings also moved her deeply. The erotic carvings at Khajurāho had actually left her giddy. They were a virtual aerobics catalogue for the sexual acrobat. About the only thing an American might add would be a Dewey decimal system in tourist guidebooks, a quick and ready reference for those set on fire by the sculptors' liberated approaches to love.

Staring up at the figures at Khajurāho, Allison's traveling companion at the time, a very proper, plain young lady with a great deal of money but few charms and boyfriends who were mostly dull fellows committed to nothing but making enough money of their own to match hers, found herself talking out-loud to Allison. "It has taken our civilization a thousand years simply to invent the missionary position." And she went on to reflect on the melancholy fact that her ancestors living in Sweden and Finland—in climates so cold and sleet-lashed that nakedness was an oddity when first discovered and promptly perverted into a rite in which an individual sweats in a sauna only to prepare himself for a beating with birch boughs and a roll in the snowbank—were a sorry lot indeed. Her boyfriends, she told Allison bitterly, were typical products of capitalism. All they did was talk about things like debentures and tax-shelters. They were clumsy, prosaic jerks, as emotionally penurious as white bibs on Plymouth Rock puritans. "At least these people knew how to screw," she

147

said disconsolately as she and Allison drifted back to their waiting limousine.

Rico did not know it at the time, of course, but it was Allison's scholarly interest in Asian sculpture, especially the erotic carvings at Khajurāho, in combination with his skills as a lover in the no-holds-barred school of the boombox gangs of Mexico City that had made Allison's love for him such an awesome thing. Plus that somewhat shy, slightly withdrawn quality in Rico which made it impossible for the Minter woman to possess him fully.

It was during one of Rico's and Pooch's conversations in the sand and gravel yard during a break, when they tossed off a Seven-Up as they lay on the warm side of a pile of sand, that Pooch broke the news to his young friend that he had received a letter, misdirected to him and opened by someone else before it got to him, informing Rico that he had not won the contest for the design of a new flag for the State of Milwaukee. Rico had won an Honorable Mention.

Rico was strangely unmoved, Pooch thought, by the bad news. He knew what the young artist had gone through to try to win. Rico had determined, first of all, that the governor's surname was Monkopf, evidence, he assumed, of German ancestry. Then Rico went to the library and found a book that alluded to an obscure monarch by the name of Monkopf who had ruled, it was said, the principality of Schwarzburg-Sondershausen in the seventeen hundreds. Rico used the principality's coat of arms as his inspiration, assuming, of course, that the governor, with his notorious interest in flags, would recognize just enough in Rico's design to assure capture of the prize. The flag that the young artist came up with contained all the necessary ingredients, a "pavilion," a decorative background for the coat of arms, medievel helmets and "mantlings," decorative cloths attached to helmets. He drew a nude man with a large fig leaf on the left or "dexter" side of the display, and a nude woman with a tiny fig leaf, on the right, the "sinister" side. Both figures were copied, more or less, from the Schwarzburg-Sondershausen coat of arms. He set it all against a blue "pall," a broad Y-shaped stripe, and that, in turn, was placed on a green field.

"It was a masterpiece, Rico, a masterpiece," said Pooch. "I cannot understand why you did not win hands down." He was trying to be nice.

Rico smiled. "No bullshit, remember, Pooch. Or I get out the machete. We both know why I didn't win. I missed the whole point of this state. At least its main idea. My flag had no idea."

Pooch shrugged. "I hate to say it, my friend, but I think you got that right."

The governor was not of Schwarzburg-Sondershausen ancestry. And perhaps would not have given a damn if he had. He just liked flags. His name was, in fact, some kind of shortened version of Monkovyetski, a Russian name. Which accounted, said his detractors on the outside, a few of whom lived in Illinois, for the old man's interest in Schumacher and the appeal of socialist founding fathers in the city's early history. They said it accounted for the governor's preference for being called just Governor, rather than Governor Monkopf. One editorial in a Chicago paper said that there was a skeleton in the Milwaukee State house. It was not the governor. He was too fat to be a skeleton. The real skeleton was the Bolshevik sound of his real name.

Interestingly enough, the new state flag was designed by a bright young black artist called Frugal Jones, from Milwaukee's Capitol Drive area. Frugal had grown up in a very poor family and the idea of thrift had been burned into his soul. "A stitch in time saves nine!" his mother would tell their children at the dinner table. His father would chime in, "Waste not, want not!" Then the mother would top the father, "A penny saved is a penny earned!" Not to be outdone, he would announce solemnly, "It is easier for a camel to pass through the eye of a needle than for a rich man to enter the kingdom of God!" which was not altogether relevant. From where his wife sat, it was his excuse for turning down the chance to work overtime at his job. But Frugal grew up with a realization that parsimony was a virtue, perhaps the grandest of them all, despite the fact that his church's pastor drove an ancient Cadillac that cost a fortune to maintain rather than a sensible Shikel.

The winning flag was the soul of simplicity. It left the state flag as it was, a green hoist section and a blue fly section. But across the top of the flag in black it had printed, in bold letters big enough to cover the top third of the flag, "THERE ARE LIMITS."

The jury knew that the governor would love it. It sounded like pure Schumacher and it did not require changing the state flag, merely adding to it.

"Now, that man understands what this state is all about!" shouted the governor as he came barreling out of his office into the news conference that was to announce the winner of the contest. "Get that brilliant young artist in here and get him in here fast. Let's not make our friends from the press wait on this one."

The press conference was brief. The governor began by quoting some Fritzland wisdom from *Small is Beautiful*. "Where is the rich society that says: 'Halt! We have enough!' There is none." And, "The stupid man who says, 'Something is better than nothing,' is more intelligent than the clever chap who will not touch anything unless it is optimal!"

The first quotation made a lot of sense to the reporters. The second did not. But the newspeople quoted both and ran long commentaries on their meaning. Then the governor read the list of all seventy-five of the Honorable Mentions. He read the names slowly, so that no one in the state who knew an Honorable Mention would miss the name in the newspapers.

After the press conference the governor explained with a wink to his aide why he wanted so many Honorable

Mentions. "Took the idea from Napoleon," he said. "Give me enough Honorable Mentions and I'll conquer the world."

Why did the governor actually insist on so many Honorable Mentions? Actually he was old enough, and wise enough also, to take a lead from Machiavelli. People have short memories, so when you reward them make the rewards plentiful. The fact that they have short memories assures that you will not cheapen the coin, provided you leave a little time in between so that they can forget.

It sounded cynical, to be sure, but the governor was not a cynic. He had merely become convinced, in living a hundred and five years, that people would rather have an inexpensive plaque on the wall that toots their horn a bit than an expensive award that is invisible to others, such as a free trip to Rio de Janeiro that the neighbors will never get and secretly resent anyway.

The prize for the flag design contest was, therefore, as ostentatious as Fritzland principles would allow. It was a handsome new Shikel touring sedan, complete with roll-down canvas sides equipped with small plexiglass windows, and a first-class, ten-layered paint job in blue with green trim. Around the trim line of the big square car, across the doors and fenders, meticulously lettered in red, were sayings from Fritzland literature. And from the radio antenna, a stout affair as thick as a finger, a small elegant copy of the new state flag fluttered.

Rico did not go into a funk following the flag contest. Nor did he blame Allison for lack of clout with the governor. He acted down about it, though, when he was around Allison Minter, but seemed positively cheerful when he was with Pooch alone at the sand and gravel yard.

But then he did something that made even Pooch wonder if the debacle with his great Schwarzburg-Sondershausen tour de force hadn't unhinged his young friend. Perhaps the grief had gone so deep that it did not surface until weeks after Rico had accepted his Honorable Mention. But all of a sudden one evening, when Allison wasn't with him—another charity fundraiser demanded Dádi's and her time—Rico carted all of his giant recumbent carrot series paintings down the apartment's back steps and out into the street in front of Smudge's, doused them with a bottle of cheap brandy that a drunk and gleeful Clement Jensen provided and set the lot on fire.

"Free spirit flambeau!" Jensen shouted as a small crowd gathered to watch the immolation.

Pester had also come out to see what was going on. He mourned the event but praised it too, as a poet might be expected to do. "A moment of total abnegation," he exclaimed to the first policeman who showed up in his squad car.

Rico told the police that it was their duty to arrest him, that he would be proud to go to jail, and that they would not have understood Van Gogh's rages either. Then he called them "philistines." They still refused to haul him in.

Then Mabel came running out of the tavern. Rico told her that the artist must cultivate cold indifference toward his work. "Once torn from the womb of holy imagination, they must be objects of contempt," he said.

Words like "holy imagination" were not at all like Rico. "Have you been working on this kid?" she demanded of Pester. Pester shook his head, denying any such thing.

Mabel ran up to the fire and rescued two of the carrot paintings. She cuffed Rico on the side of the head, a whack so hard it could be heard above the ruckus of the chattering onlookers. "Now you help me carry these into the tavern! Have you gone crazy or something? Rico Far, you deserve a thrashing! And I'll give it to you if you pull anything like this again."

As the bonfire subsided, the police gave Rico a rake and told him to clean up the mess and throw the remains into the garbage cans behind Smudge's.

"You from Madison?" the officer demanded of Rico. Rico

insisted he was not. "This sort of thing doesn't make sense," the officer repeated. "Are you damn sure you're not from Madison?" Rico denied it again. "Well, whatever you say will be held against you in a court of law if this thing goes to a judge. Disturbing the peace in a damn fool way like this!" Rico meekly cleaned up the mess as the officer ordered. Pooch showed up at about that time too, with Sara. They were concerned, deeply concerned. Rico was having some kind of breakdown. It was the only explanation that made sense.

The two paintings went into Smudge's. The yellowing prints of Louie's photographs of Old Faithful that hung on the south side of the room above the row of booths were taken down. One of the carrot paintings was hoisted into place to await the admiring comment of tavern regulars. The other painting went up to Steinberger's apartment. Wilhelm would not tolerate it in their living room so Pooch mounted it in Sara's bedroom, bending it at midpoint around the corner of her room.

Wilhelm told his daughter he thought the thing looked ridiculous. "No more ridiculous than what you are doing with the club!" she said defiantly. It was the first time she had ever talked to her father that way. And he took silent but serious note of it. Diego Grenada was obviously at work, he said to himself, undermining a loving daughter's affection for a loving father.

What impressed Pooch about Rico's curious alterations in mood, one minute shrugging off the humiliation of having his flag design given nothing more than one of the seventy-five Honorable Mentions, the next building a bonfire of his paintings and proclaiming his indifference to his creations "once torn from the womb of holy imagination," was that his appetite remained as robust as ever.

In the evening, when Pooch and Rico frequently cooked together in Pooch's room because Pooch had a full-sized stove in his place and Rico only had a hotplate, Rico ate anything in sight and double portions at that. Pooch found himself playing friend, counselor and dietician to young Far. They would finish eating about seven o'clock and then Allison would show up and drag Rico off again on some date or other, or straight up to the tower. She insisted that Rico launch another series of giant paintings, perhaps of something else from the Steinberger garden.

Rico loved the attention he was getting from a beautiful woman. Anyone would have. But there was that possessive side, that ravenous element, in Allison that he was still having trouble handling. He told Pooch he cared deeply for the Minter girl, that he might actually be in love with her, "but really, Pooch," he'd say, sometimes wistfully, sometimes with a wan, helpless smile on his face, "don't you think she is more demanding than she has to be. I do love . . . I do love her. But I'm beginning to think she wants to make me into a pet."

The idea for Rico's rehabilitation by way of another series of monumental paintings got underway when Sara presented Pooch with a paper bag full of beets. They were fine, plump beauties—as beautiful, Pooch said, as he held them up before Rico, as the domes of St. Basil's. "We shall dine in style tonight," he announced. And they did.

Pooch steamed a half-dozen beets slowly in a lidded pot until the skins could be slipped off with the slightest squeeze of the fingers. Then he sliced them and drowned them in butter. He set a plate of spaghetti on the side. It was an inviting sight. But the beets drowned in butter were the hit of the show. The butter glistened and fluttered, mixing slowly with the beet juice. Pooch regaled his young artist friend with quotations from the butter carton. He quoted sections of the law that had outlawed margarine. It alluded to the "suspicious odor" of melted margarine and noted that "butter is the product of our soft-eyed holstein cattle, well mannered and heavy uddered, turning the sweet green grass of our state into liquid gold, a philosopher's stone for chef or homemaker."

The result was that Pooch and Rico overate, and not just marginally. To get his mind off all the butter, Pooch had to take a long walk that lasted well into the night.

Rico did not fare any better. He tried to paint, tried to exercise, first in the studio and then by jogging around the block outside Smudge's. He tried putting away a stein of Schumie's with Anselm Pester. That did not help at all. Pester said he thought Rico looked "unaccountably jaundiced." Rico found himself retiring early, lying on his back, staring for hours at his ceiling mural as his stomach growled and he wondered uneasily what he could do with Allison Minter's growing demands on his time.

Allison was not with Rico that night for a reason somewhat like that which had kept her away on the night he burned his carrot paintings. She and Dádi were hosting a black-tie dinner party for some out-of-state businessmen who were trying to get Minter to begin selling the Shikel outside the State of Milwaukee, in violation of state law, by some black-market arrangement or other that no one at the party would be very forthright about. For some reason the big, square, superbly painted and finished Shikels, odd as they at first seemed, now began to seem elegant to wealthy people on the outside who could not get hold of one. Several Shikels showed up in Hollywood. Their owners took enormous pride in being able to roll up to the porte-cochere in front of their five-million-dollar mansions and have a doorman help them descend from a Shikel.

The idea of exporting much of anything outside the state ran counter, of course, to one of the main tenets of Fritzland economics, which was that local production for local use, with labor-intensive love and devotion, was the only sensible way for industry to go. The governor realized that the minute an upward soaring production curve began to glisten on the surface of an industrialist's eyeballs things were about to go wrong. Scale and common sense, he had said often, were always related. With few exceptions, big meant stupid, overgrown meant miserable and colossal meant egomaniacal foolishness.

The governor had confronted the same thing in the agricultural area when the state first seceded from Wisconsin. The hinterland of the capital city was enormously rich and productive. As soon as a few surpluses began to appear, farmers began standing around their smalltown banks, leaning against the corinthian columns on either side of the entrance, spouting off to one another about "export-import balances," "overseas markets" and "amortization schedules" that would allow them to sell their horses, or old tried and true John Deeres, for fancy new machinery that would do for their soil what it had done for Iowa's once rich land. Iowans had pumped their soils full of fertilizers, pesticides, herbicides and fantasies taken from television programs about the rich and famous. Then they harvested everything that grew at such a pace that farming became a mining industry. The rich soil was suddenly all but gone. The governor had toured the State of Milwaukee and talked all its farmers with those kinds of ideas in their heads back down to earth. The answer to having surplus on hand was not to work harder to make the problem worse but to increase the time the farmer spent with the wife and kids and dog on the front porch listening to music and stories about what happened last Saturday at the dancehall two miles down the road. After all, a life of ease, good times and an occasional serious prayer was what they all said made them work hard in the first place.

The real shock, however, of Rico's orgy with Pooch's beautifully cooked beets did not come home to him until the next day. He found blood, lots of it, in the toilet bowl. He was terror-stricken. He flushed the toilet, then found himself staring into the mirror. So this is how the end can come, he said to himself, without warning, from some wretched parasite eating your insides out.

"Goddamned gringo bastards! Too proud to tell a guest

from a foreign land not to drink their filthy water!" The pollution that was ruining Mexico and most states in America was also at work in this "utopian" State of Milwaukee! Moreover, the governor was a liar. It was good that he did not win the damn contest for the new state flag after all. In a cold sweat he went down to the second floor where he shared a shower stall with Pooch. He bathed and went up to the tower and crawled into bed. He tried to sleep. It was no good. He would write his mother when he was strong enough to get out of bed. She would be all alone in the world now. Her relatives were worse than none. "Well," he said aloud, bitterly, "everyone is born alone, everyone lives alone, everyone dies alone."

When Rico did not show up for work that day, Pooch assumed that he had spent the previous night in the tower with Allison, sipping Schumie's, rotating on the great circular bed, and was pretty well wrung out. Pooch made excuses to their employer for Rico and little more came of it until that evening. Then Allison showed up, knocked at the door repeatedly and when she got no answer went to find Pooch. But Pooch was at a loss, too. They both went to Mabel.

"The boy has been acting goofy as hell lately," she said. "We'll get to the bottom of this here and now."

Mabel took the passkey for his apartment door and followed by Pooch went up to the door, unlocked it and knocked timorously. "Son? Son? Are you alright, Rico?" They heard no response. "Do you suppose the kid has gone and done something really foolish?" asked Mabel. That meant "suicide" to both Mabel and Pooch.

Pooch tried to pass it off with a joke. "He's young. You can count on something foolish."

Mabel said "Hush!" and pushed the door open. "You better go up and look," she said to Pooch.

During his lifetime Pooch had seen a lot more grisly sights than a hanging. But he was terrified. He might be losing a best friend, almost a son now, and an artist, perhaps not a great artist but an artist nonetheless. He went to the foot of the ladder, called again and then crept up the ladder into the tower. He found Rico lying on his side, shivering. "Why didn't you answer us, for God's sake, Rico?" he said impatiently.

"I've had it, Pooch," was the quiet response. "It's really bad. I'm hemorrhaging."

"Hemorrhaging? I don't see any, blood. What the hell are you talking about?"

"From the back end, Pooch."

"Are you kidding me?"

"I'm not kidding you."

"Perhaps you are atoning." Pooch was trying to divert him with a joke.

"I have nothing to atone for."

"We all have, my friend. Your fear and pain are atonements."

"I haven't any pain. But I am concerned that Mother will be left alone."

Pooch reached up and touched Rico's forehead. "No fever. Cool as a stein of Schumie's."

Mabel called up from the studio. She had heard their talking but could not make sense of it. "Is he *all right*, Pooch?" she shouted.

"Come on up," Pooch called back.

Allison climbed the ladder. Then Mabel heaved herself up the ladder. There was just enough room for her to wiggle through the hole. "God, I'm getting fat," she grumbled. As she stood next to the bed she said, "Now what's wrong with this boy?"

"He's hemorrhaging. Claims he's dying," said Pooch.

Allison Minter gasped, stifled a scream and went running down the stairs, crying, "Get an ambulance! Get an ambulance! My darling Rico is dying!" Louie called an ambulance and then tried to comfort Allison. She stood for a minute with Louie, then went tearing up the stairs again to the studio.

Mabel was the picture of the unflappable lady of the house. "Oh come on, for *Pete's* sake!" she was telling Rico. Allison had arrived back at the bedside. "Let me look at you! You men. Sometimes I wonder if you're worth it. Worth anything."

Allison was now in tears.

Mabel rolled Rico over. His shivering eased a bit. "Now what's this about hemorrhaging. Where from?"

He told her, in a half-whisper, frightened, embarrassed.

"You got the runs?" she asked.

"More than that," he said, again very quietly.

"What have you been eating, for Pete's sake?"

"Pooch and I had dinner together up here last night, or the night before. I have lost track of time. The days grow short as we near the end."

"What did you *eat*, for heaven's sake?"

"Beets mostly." Rico turned his face toward the wall again. The thought of his dinner with Pooch left him nauseated.

"You poor dumb bunny, Rico Far! Haven't you ever eaten beets before?"

"Not like these. But it must be something in the water. Perhaps we did not boil the water long enough."

"Well, you aren't sick!" Mabel hit her forehead with the palm of her hand. "You're just shittin' beet juice."

"Are you sure?" Rico asked weakly.

"Course I'm sure."

Allison was smothering Rico in kisses. "Everything's all right now, dear, everything is all right."

Louie was at the foot of the tower ladder. "Ambulance guys are here. Let's you all get out of there so they can get him down quick."

"Tell them they ain't needed!" shouted Mabel. "Tell them the problem has gone into total remission. Tell them anything."

Louie told the ambulance people anything.

Rico was abashed, to put it mildly. He eased Allison

back, gently pulled her arms from around his neck, then turned to Mabel and Pooch. But there was that strange, curiously untroubled look on his face again, the same one that had been there after he had burned the great recumbent carrot series.

He sat up slowly on the side of the bed. "Oh my God!" he said. "This on top of Honorable Mention." He would say nothing more. He insisted that the ordeal had been almost too much for him, that what he needed was sleep and to be by himself, to be alone, totally alone, which meant without Allison as well as the others.

Mabel wiggled down the stairs. "Snooze as long as you feel like, kid," she said. "One excuse for a little shut-eye is as good as another."

Pooch, his eyebrows knit, puzzled, helped Allison down the ladder. "See you later, my friend," he said to Rico. "We'll get together later. Let me know when you are shipshape again." He knew that Rico was faking. He would wring the truth out of the kid later.

"What's come over Charles, Diego?" Allison asked him as he saw her to the door of Smudge's.

"Beats me," he said, "no pun intended."

"But he seems worse off than ever, somehow," said Allison.

"That is a blessed state for all great artists," said Pooch, trying to be pleasant and funny at the same time.

Rico was worse off than ever, in a way. Though Mabel and Pooch swore never to divulge how Rico had cheated the grim reaper, Pooch kidded him now and again in the sand and gravel yard, calling him "Bloody Rico" and "the beet juice kid." He did not realize for several days that Rico seemed too indifferent to his jibes.

In the meantime, Rico had written his mother again.

Dear Mother,

I must leave this place and continue on to Europe. It is a wonderful city and I have met a beautiful and very rich

160

girl. But she is more than I need right now. In fact, she won't let me live my life the way I know I want to. She wants to arrange everything for me, down to the smallest detail. She insists that I go out with her rich friends, even though I don't have the money. She is always slipping money to me under the table to pay for things. She says she only does it for my own good. But she likes to show me off as a "painter" even though I haven't been able to do much that is very good. I am not sure, in fact, that I "have what it takes," as they say. She does not know yet but I am going to Paris. I will find the money somehow, but I will not take it from her. *Do not even think* of trying to send me any of your money. I will just send it back to you. I know you need every peso you have.

Thank you for your long letter of a few weeks ago. It is good to know you are safe and well even if things are bad. The riots at the Corumba Rope Company sounded very bad. Such gentle people, León and Gomel and the others. It is hard to believe that they would become so angry that they would chop up their foreman with their machetes. I am glad to hear that they have escaped.

The owners of the company have always cheated the workers, so I am not surprised that they left in a hurry when the riots started. But it makes me very angry to think that they will be able to live in those beautiful houses in Miami and tell their own country to go to hell. If it was not for the army general living in Florida, I don't think they could have escaped.

I did not win a contest I entered here, to design a new flag for this beautiful state. But I did not deserve to. I cooked up a beautiful, very fancy design, very "Mexican" in some respects, although I took my ideas from a place in Europe. But it was not what this state needed. The new flag is very simple. It uses the old flag (blue and green) with a saying printed on it which says "There are limits!" The saying has to do with the way the government here sees things. It thinks people should spend less time trying to make everything in America bigger and more expensive, or bigger and cheaper (sometimes you can't tell which they want), and just live. Sometimes I am reminded of what your mother

161

used to tell you when grandpa made speeches about revolution. I can remember how she told us that "anybody who wants a lot is owned by what he has." I was little but I still remember it because I knew that Dad did not agree with such ideas and would get annoyed whenever she came to our house and talked like that. But in most of America that is all everybody seems to want, to be owned by whatever they own. (Do I sound like a philosopher? Be patient.)

There is so much for me to learn about art. So I go to the library now and read what critics write about what artists are doing all over the world. One local critic told me (I showed him some big still lifes I did) that I am "unwilling to enclose my art in its own processing." God only knows what that means. Pooch says it is all rubbish and that I should just paint. He does not know yet that I am determined to go to Paris to study art. I will let him know when I am ready to leave. I know he will not want me to go. He loves it here very much. And I think he has fallen in love with a woman that lives with her father in our apartment building. The father is a mean fellow but the daughter is very sweet. She doesn't say much but she has a heart as big as a suitcase and she adores Pooch. She is trying to get him to begin writing again. She has at least gotten his mind off (a little) the wife and children that died last year in Mexico.

As soon as I am in Paris I will write you again. It is the most important thing in the world that I go there. I love you with all my heart, and Pooch and his woman friend Sara send their love too, even though they do not know you. I send twice as much love as ever. I am in good health. I never felt better. God bless everything you do. Say hello to all of my neighbors in Villa Rito.

Love from you son,
Rico

Rico did not tell Pooch that he intended to leave for Paris until ten days after the incident with the beets. At first Pooch thought it was a matter of pride, because he could not stand the humiliation of losing the flag contest and then being laughed at for burning his paintings. He also suspected someone might have said something to people in Smudge's about the beet-eating orgy.

Or perhaps it was Allison. She had been more attentive to every detail of Rico's life than ever and Rico would sometimes lose his temper and tell her to stop treating him as if he were a "dumb kid from Mexico." But he did not scream at her or make a scene. He would just do a slow burn, which left her bewildered and in a pout. But judging by the time she spent in his studio in the evening, and how little painting Rico had managed to do, Pooch knew something had to give.

Then Rico dropped the Paris business on Pooch, one evening when they were walking on the downtown river-walk. Rico was bound and determined to leave. And he would not tell Pooch where he got the money to fly to Europe. The question troubled the old writer. He did not like to think his young friend had fallen into the hands of some miserable loan shark who had entered the state through the sewers from Chicago to prey on the innocent people of the state. There were still a few simple souls about who resented the state's preoccupation with frugality. The number of sharks loose in the state was small but one was enough. State authorities could not keep every last manhole padlocked.

The night before Rico left for Europe, he and Pooch went for a long, rambling, late night walk through the city. It was Pooch's last hope of talking sense into the kid. Things "on the outside" had grown more ludicrous by the day. In fact, in Paris itself one of the "Begin again" cults had begun meeting in the great plaza of the Louvre every three days to dance around the glass pyramid designed in 1983 and finished by the Mitterand government six years later, a bit later than scheduled, but better late than never, said the sang-froid French. The Pyramide de Pei was one of four massive public projects that the socialists had been bent on completing in the final decades of the twentieth century as evidence of the government's patronage of democratic culture. One was Johan von Spreckelsen's giant, hollow, cube-shaped building at the terminus of the Louvre—Champs Élysées axis. Another was Ott's Opera de la Bastille and a fourth was Tschumi's Parc de la Villette.

But at the Pyramide de Pei cultists in body paint and scuba diving gear had begun to invent strange, sometimes frightening, divination ceremonials. At times almost a quarter of a million people gathered around the glass pyramid. Those in diving gear, in a way, were the least impressive. Others used haute-couture body and face paint to push the "Begin again Very-new Wave" as far as it could go. Some decorated themselves to look like people of the Sepic River in New Guinea. Others looked like Laplanders who had turned into punk rockers. Others resembled thoroughly ruined rock stars of the nineteen eighties, their faces held together with make-up and varieties of glaze.

The cultists writhed about on the ground, "spoke in tongues" and snake-danced about the pyramid. They chanted "Begin again!" by the hour, until some fell exhausted to the ground only to be revived by their fellows with drugs and cheap wine. Many spilled into the underground arcades, bookstores and museum shops below Louvre ground-level where they milled about in a daze, gumming up subway schedules and the lives of gallery goers trying to put the "Begin again!" hysteria behind themselves for at least a day.

Government officials were caught with their political pants down. The chief of police wanted simply to clear the area with mounted policemen. The mayor waved that idea aside impatiently. *"Ils sont aussi les êtres humanes!"* he shouted. Or: "For Pete's sake, Chief, they're human beings too!" and he added as he stared out the window, his hands held behind his back, *"Vive les peuples."*

The focal point of the rites at the Pyramide de Pei, the raising of the monstrance as it were, involved the tossing of a tennis ball that had been dipped in red latex paint, while still wet, by an old, very wrinkled naked woman who claimed to be a virgin, toward the top of the pyramid. The tracing of the red ball's wobbly descent to the ground was read by leaders of the cult as a mystic clue to the direction in the sky from which space vehicles would first arrive in the heavens. A variety of Pharaonic associations were added to the divination rites. And each day French television commentators broadcast to the nation, with a mixture of amusement, lofty commentary by anthropologists and their own hypnotic interest, what cult leaders made that day of *"la signification de traject de la balle de tennis rouge."*

Pooch was more than a little curious about the mysterious things going on in Paris. "The world is truly a magical place," he told Rico. "But it is not the place for you, my friend." He feared, of course, that Rico, almost a son to him, some small compensation for the loss of his own family and still young and impressionable, would get caught up in the cult, or fall in love with some beautiful member of it. He had seen beautiful young French girls on television around the pyramid. In their bodystockings and flopping their scuba flippers across the Louvre plaza, they had a far-out erotic quality, certainly something that Rico was unlikely to encounter in Milwaukee. The young friend of Pooch's might never return to the state. While there were no Pei pyramids in the State of Milwaukee, there were other beautiful places, and some strange people as well. As he maneuvered Rico around and among some of Milwaukee's more beautiful spots, he still hoped that he might get him to change his mind.

As they settled in at a sidewalk table at Contetti's bar and restaurant in the Little Italy section of Milwaukee just across the bridge from Smudge's, and the smells of wine and garlic-butter bread moved among the tables, Pooch suddenly asked Rico, "Did Allison give you the money to go to Paris?"

"No, I have not seen her in a week. I have refused to.

She's smothering me, Pooch. She wants me, all of me, lock, stock and barrel."

"Lock, cock, stock and barrel. So I've noticed."

It was a cool, sweet, quiet evening. At other tables on the sidewalk couples billed and cooed, touching fingers gently between sips of wine. An old couple at the table next to Pooch and Rico, both fat and jovial looking, he bald and potbellied, she full-bosomed and heavy waisted, laughed quietly when one or the other said something. And then they would playfully rub noses as if imitating Eskimos in love. Rico smiled as he watched them, then turned sternly toward Pooch. "I cannot be bought," he said.

Pooch ordered Cavallo red and some garlic-butter bread. "But why must you leave? Was losing the flag contest such a blow, really?"

"Of course not. But I let her think so." Rico grinned.

"And burning your paintings? That act out in the street?"

"A man must do what he must do," said Rico, the grin now a self-satisfied smile.

"Why you deceitful bastard," said Pooch. "You, Charles Far, handsome, clean-cut, always with the ready smile! I should have figured as much."

"I had to. The woman is a beautiful maneater, a blonde shark, and she knows more about love than I could describe if we sat here for the rest of our lives."

"Try me," said Pooch, leaning forward.

"Gentlemen don't discuss their loves."

"Gentlemen are extinct. There's been an information revolution, or haven't you heard."

Rico turned serious. "I'm going to Paris to walk in the footsteps of men like Delacroix. Nothing can stop me now."

"The money hasn't," said Pooch. He wanted Rico to flare up, to tell him how he could afford to fly to Paris.

Rico did not rise to the bait. "I will visit Giverny. I will walk in the footsteps of the great Monet."

They sipped their wine slowly. As they finished it, Pooch said, "Let's move along. It is a wonderful night in this City of Palms. The moon is more beautiful than ever. It is a golden lamp above a city of gold." He was hinting. He had picked up gossip to the effect that someone had tried to waylay Wilhelm Steinberger again. Much as he hated to consider the possibility, the thought nagged him that Rico might somehow have gotten hold of some of the Steinberger club's hoard of gold. It was possible that Sara had inadvertently let the cat out of the bag and that Rico had been desperate enough for money to try to get some of the gold.

They continued their walk south on Prospect Avenue, past the great old mansions that had been converted to law offices, eye clinics and condominiums. They walked across Prospect Park and stood briefly in front of the great statue of Solomon Juneau.

"Know who this guy is, Rico?" Pooch asked.

"A little. They almost named this city after him, way back. They told me that at Smudge's."

"They almost had a war here too. Do you know that? Over which side of the river was more important. Lined cannon up at the bridges. God's truth, Rico. This city has a history to rival—"

"Durango's?"

"No. I was going to say Villa Rito's." The joshing went on.

"It's also the reason the streets don't line up at the river, because they couldn't agree which side was most important."

"The governor has ironed all of that out. 'There are limits!' So he put in these beautiful bridges to make his point." There was a touch of sarcasm in Rico's voice.

"Don't take it out on the old man because some female has got you by the balls." Pooch did not like Rico's taking shots at his City of Palms just because the Minter woman was swarming all over him. "You didn't exactly discourage Allison when your little affair was on the runway and picking up air-speed."

"Paris is something else, Pooch. Something else entirely. I want to find out just how much beauty is left in this world. I intend to do so."

"Beginning with Paris?"

"You have to start somewhere."

"Why not here?"

"I can't work in that sand and gravel place all day long and then—"

"Work all night too? Most men would envy you. Every guy in Smudge's would give his eye teeth to be in your spot. His balls, too."

"Lay off, Pooch. You know damn well why I'm leaving Milwaukee. At least for a while."

"Do you think she will cool down?" Pooch wouldn't let up. "You'll never own an automobile factory at this rate, my friend."

"Let's walk. More walk, less talk, okay?"

They walked across the park toward the south. Pooch said, "The lake is beautiful in the moonlight. Especially when you look down from here. The art museum looks like a temple there on the other side of the drive, with the flags all lit up along the approach. In the moonlight I even like that sculpture on the lawn."

"The woman that sunk all the money into the big addition there on the left liked that stuff. They're minimalist works," said Rico, quite seriously.

"You can say that again," said Pooch, chuckling. "I like what the governor did with the big one at the end of Wisconsin Avenue ... the ... I forget the sculptor's name."

"It's a Di Suvero," said Rico, pleased to let Pooch know he had been taking in the art scene in Milwaukee, "from the nineteen eighties."

"Must have been pretty plain before the governor had

168

the little bells hung all over it. Makes a pleasant sound in the wind now."

"You can be sure the sculptor would not be too happy about that. Minimalists like to stay minimal."

"The lake is a wonderful sea," said Pooch, changing the subject.

"It is not really a sea you know."

"Yes, I know."

"There is no salt in it."

"There was no salt in our wine. It was still wine."

A conversation stopper. They walked down Kilbourn Boulevard. "Look at the way the palms march westward on the boulevard toward the courthouse. Standing on that low hillside, the courthouse looks like it was in the Roman Forum. That is magnificent." Pooch and Rico stood for a few minutes in silence looking down the boulevard. The big flower beds gave off a strong, perfumed smell in the night.

"And the theater district buildings. The bratwurst trucker ought to see them in the moonlight," Pooch said.

"I feel like another drink," said Rico.

They veered off to the right and ended up in the old John Ernst restaurant. The place was quite full, even though it was well past midnight. They were seated at one of the circular oak tables near the famous Ernst fireplace. There was no fire in it, of course. There had been no need for that for some years. But the logs were carefully piled in it and a small red light lit them from the rear. Above Rico and Pooch, in the center of the main chamber of the restaurant, hung the massive wrought-iron chandelier that the founder of the restaurant had fashioned for his establishment back near the turn of the twentieth century. It was ringed with burning candles, virtually the only light in the room except for candles on the tables. A giant beer cask hanging from chains was dimly outlined high above the bar. That too had been in place for over a century, along with a collection of antique steins above the bar mirrors.

A waiter in black lederhosen and red vest took their order for large steins of Schumie's. "Put this on top of that red wine, my friend, and we will know tomorrow that this was a special occasion. Your going away tomorrow, I mean, leaving all your friends," said Pooch.

In front of them, seated in a musicians' box surrounded by a hand-carved low oak railing, a violin and cello trio played. It was something from Strauss. But neither Rico nor Pooch knew what it was called. "It's a waltz," said Rico.

"Not something you'd pick up on a boom-box very often," said Pooch. He asked the waiter what the music was called. "I didn't understand him, but it sounded like 'Vienna Moods,'" he reported to Rico. They said little for a while, then Pooch said, "You are lucky to be able to afford the trip to Paris. Such trips cost a great deal."

Rico was uneasy. He could not bring himself to tell his friend where he had gotten the money.

"Allison has told me you could get a commission if you wanted it, for a thirty-foot piece of sculpture. Did you know that, Rico? I have talked to her privately about your going away."

"Did you tell her why I must leave?"

"Of course not. That's none of my business."

"Do you know what the sculpture would be?"

"In a way."

"Good God, Pooch. It's supposed to be a big statue of her father. It's to be called 'Dádi Honored.' Because he gave a wad to the art museum. Can you imagine? She'd own me for the rest of my life."

"You don't love her then, I take it?" Pooch said, rubbing it in a bit.

"She's a magnificent barracuda, Pooch."

"I can think of worse ways to go."

"If Sara was like that, you wouldn't be so damn smug."

Rico's comeback got Pooch back to being serious again.

"I wish I knew what love is," said Rico, sighing. "Shit, if it isn't one thing it's another."

"Now that's what I call using the machete," said Pooch. Rico laughed. He had heard Pooch's line about a machete cutting through bullshit many times.

There was a long silence. Two more pieces of music were performed. Then the musicians left the stage for a break. There was a round of applause. Here and there about the big room, steins were being hoisted in toasts.

Pooch and Rico ended their drinking that night at the sidewalk tables in front of the old Pfister Hotel. Some kind of dance was taking place across the street near the Emil Seidel fountains. The fountains were great, ornate, Victorian-looking affairs, replete with goddesses, seagulls and gushing urns. They were installed by the governor and named in honor of a German woodcarver who had become the city's first socialist mayor in 1910. Seidel was a remarkable fellow. He cleaned house in city hall and ended cronyism. He undertook America's first municipal government efficiency study. The cost of the city's asphalt paving bill dropped from $1.75 a square yard to 40¢. A socialist sheriff, Bob Buech, drove drunken sailors and whores out of town. Eastern seaboard Reds derisively called the Milwaukee reformers "Sewer Socialists." They were, indeed, long on common sense, short on philosophic ornamentation. But the old woodcarver got things done. He laid the foundations for the good life in the City of Palms. He was the governor's kind of man.

Pooch and Rico ordered Schumie's Weisbier.

"The drink of kings," said Pooch. "To your stay in Paris."

"You said you would explain love," said Rico.

"I will, my friend, I will," said Pooch, voluble now from the wine and beer, a potent combination in Milwaukee as well as on the outside. He called the waiter to their table

171

and asked for a small sheet of paper. The waiter gave him a blank dinner check. Pooch carefully folded an inch-wide strip and then tore the strip off. "You see this?"

Rico nodded, sipping his weisbier.

"This strip of paper, which has two sides, can, in fact, have but one."

"Prove it."

"I shall do so," said Pooch, "as many a mathematician has before me." He took one end of the paper strip and twisted it in a half-turn, so that the front side of one end lay against the backside of the other end, joining the ends. "Now there is only one side. You may trace your finger along the paper. You will see I am correct."

Rico followed the curve of the paper with his finger. "You're right. So?"

"So that is what love is like. It is a force in nature that seeks to make opposite things into things that are not opposite. That is why we feel as we do when we are in love, why we want to lose ourselves in the woman we love. It's the Big Mathematician's greatest trick of all." Pooch pointed his thumb toward heaven.

"Do you feel that way about Sara?"

"Much too soon to know."

"Well, when all is said and done, Allison and I don't end up on the same side of that strip of paper," said Rico. "And I'm not about to stick around to see if she can make it happen. Tomorrow, I'm out of here, Honorable Mention and all."

Pooch wanted to continue the sermon. He was pleased with the way his paper demonstration on love had gone. "Consider nature, my friend. It can be an ugly thing, can it not? Everything devouring everything else. Insects eating leaves, birds eating insects, other birds eating other birds, hunters eating birds..."

"Cannibals eating hunters," said Rico, laughing now and urging Pooch on.

"But it is true, is it not? All of nature is trying to envelop itself. That is my point. Have you not often heard women say of a beautiful little child, 'Why that child is so darling I could just eat it up.' What do you think that means? That they are cannibals? No, it merely means that the force of love is at work in what they say."

"Which is why I feel as if I could be happy if only Allison Minter were *truly* mine?" There was a touch of sarcasm in Rico's voice.

"Exactly. Love is a force that is forever trying to make all the differences in the universe disappear. *But,* and this is the mystery, Rico, love cannot exist without differences—such as those between men and women. That is why love is such a longing. That is why it must remain incomplete if it is to remain at all. And that is why everything is as it is. You can only understand it as a mystery."

Pooch's demonstration that love had the same effect on differences as a twisted piece of paper was the kind of mystery that old Dr. Fechner would have probably enjoyed. But it did not move Rico to consider staying in Milwaukee instead of heading out for Paris. With that mystery tucked firmly in his mind, or sticking out of it like a sore thumb, since Allison's love had damned near reduced him to a twisted piece of paper, Rico took a bus to Chicago the next evening, then a direct night flight to Paris.

173

IN THE FOOTSTEPS
OF
DELACROIX

CHARLES FAR LEFT Chicago for Paris at eleven o'clock at night on one of the huge six-engine jets that began plying the international skies at the turn of the twenty-first century. It was a great lumbering machine shaped like a watermelon. It was not supersonic. All the grand plans that had been laid in the twentieth century for supersonic commercial jet travel had fallen through. The reasons were not difficult to identify. As oil supplies petered out, as everyone knew they inevitably would, the price of fuel went up, and up, and up again. Supersonic machines such as the Concorde had been subsidized by France and Britain as symbols of national pride. But pride became as expensive as everything else and the Concordes soon were hauled off to museums where they stood alongside America's famed SST, another egg that refused to hatch. The only place that supersonic planes still flew was in the military. The leaders remained convinced that in time of war it was essential to kill as many people as possible without delay, regardless of cost.

So the idea of twenty-first century airlines was to bring the basic principle of the cattlecar into the high-tech era. That meant airplanes that were shaped like watermelons and crammed with as many cubic centimeters of warm human flesh as possible, as long as that flesh did not suffocate and nullify credit card commitments.

The whole thing had been left to computers, naturally enough. Which meant the total triumph of quantification over compassion. In seat design, for instance, the computers resolutely ignored the possibility of an irregularly shaped homo sapiens, an odd-shaped torso, for instance, in which the fat had settled into all the wrong places. Or a rheumatic elbow that no longer unfolded the way it had thirty years earlier, or a gimpy knee that resulted when its owner stumbled over a fallen "Street Under Repair" sign at the intersection in front of the office.

The big main concept that had been bolted and screwed into the center of the computer's brain was that airline companies were to make a great deal of money, tons of it, a large mountain of it, if at all possible. The principle was to assure that suspenders snapped in corporate boardrooms, that byzantine hostile takeovers were nipped in the bud and that at the end of the fiscal year, stockholders would be bowled over by a slick, multicolored report, complete with bargraphs simple enough for a chimpanzee to comprehend.

About an hour into the flight most passengers reclined their seats, the idea being to sleep. The computerized result was that most people seemed to end up lying on a pallet in the lap of the passengers behind them. Enough room was left to breathe, of course, provided the passenger did not try to fill his lungs with more air than was known to be necessary—according to tons of computer-generated data from hospitals—to survive. And because the planes were so wide, any passenger who had to get to the toilet on short notice, because they had been plied with drinks of every kind earlier (this tactical contradiction was known in the airplane design industry as "subsystem codeflection") had to squirm over the shoes, knees and laps of twenty or thirty passengers who were by then as surly as mistreated curs in a dog pound.

Efficiency computations dictated that it was costly to fly the big machines up where the air was too thin. So the great melonlike craft did not attempt to fly above cantankerous weather cells that might rise to fifty thousand feet. They simply plowed through them, shuddering and bucking as they moved along. So there were usually a lot of upset stomachs onboard one of the big machines. But designers had, of course, anticipated this possibility. Research on the olfactory senses of laboratory animals, usually dogs, kidnapped pets as a rule, had shown that a machine sensor that was almost as good as a dog's nose could be wired into the cabin of the airliner so that the first whiff of someone's panicky use of an airbag would flood the cabin with a harmless derivative of laughing gas and smells of a gourmet cook's kitchen. When that happened, of course, the seats would all be moved slightly toward the upright position. Too much laughing in the supine position could severely strain the ribcage of the elderly, a condition that the hyperrationalist designers of aircraft referred to as the "intercostal muscle merriment injury syndrome" or IMMIS, IMS for short.

Rico was too excited to sleep or pay much attention to what was happening around him as the plane bounced around, people got sick or were gassed back to a condition of bliss. So he tried to read. He had bought two sophisticated monthly art criticism magazines in the airport bookstore in Chicago. They were the kind of thing his friend Pooch had warned him about. Pooch had told him that "too much of that stuff will start warts growing on your eyeballs."

But Rico was heading for one of the great art capitals of

the world and he needed to be able to talk, at least now and then, like an art critic. So from one magazine he learned that to "construct a self is to construct a universe." All well and good, he said to himself. No particular harm in that one. Everybody was pretty well penned up in their own universe. There really wasn't much choice. Old guys like Pester were stuck with their universe, so was Allison for that matter. One couldn't very well live in someone else's universe, especially if your self and its universe were the same thing as the critic claimed.

Rico looked up at the ceiling and smiled. He dived into another essay. From it he learned that in painting "prohibited qualities can have an implied presence." These "prohibited qualities" were evidently what made the artists he was reading about famous. Which meant that for some painters the best thing would be to surrender to implied presence, that is, not to paint at all. Rico closed the magazine and let it lie on his lap. He would have to think that one over.

But he was restless. The plane had been booming along nicely in the last hour or so. Nobody had thrown up, there had been no need for gas. He reached into the seat pocket in front of him and drew out its reading material. One item was a magazine that advertised trips to islands of the world where the most impressive monuments to extinct species of birds were to be found. The other was a large plastic card that told passengers what they could expect to experience if the plane lost power and decided to crash. He put both pieces back in the pocket and took out his art criticism magazine again. This time he learned about an artist who "a bit closer to Groucho Marx in spirit . . . abuses both the exaggerated self-pity behind the impoverished imagery certain painters derive from mass media and the academic flavor that our newly installed expressionist avant-garde carries with it." Rico stared at the ceiling. Well, this guy at least covers the bases, he thought, and put the magazine into the seat pocket in front of him.

177

He tried to sleep again but couldn't. As it turned out, diversion from the pummeling he had been taking from art critics came from a small boy sitting behind the passenger on Rico's left. Every few minutes the boy would deliver a solid kick to the backside of the seat in front of him and the blow would pass through the seat back, at the approximate speed of sound, and slam into the passenger's kidneys, first on one side, then on the other, sometimes from both feet to both kidneys at the same time.

Rico's neighbor, a big gangly fellow with a craggy, Lincolnesque face, would startle, sit up as best he could, wipe his forehead and then settle back. "Kids will be kids," he said with a faint, saintly smile.

A few minutes later his kidneys took another punch, playful perhaps, but firm enough to remove the saintly smile. "That little jerk behind me," he said to Rico, "should have been stowed with the luggage, along with the unconscious bitch who looks like his mother. I'll have ruptured kidneys before we reach Europe. Being hauled out of here on a stretcher and put on a dialysis machine is not my idea of the good life in Paris."

Rico tried to be reassuring. "The kid's restless, I suppose. He should drop off to sleep soon."

No such luck for the big man. Finally he turned, looked over the top of the seat back and said to the little boy, "If you kick me in the back just one more time, kid, I'm going to put your lights out."

The boy's mother was suddenly awake. She had been dozing. "That's *no way* to talk to a little boy!" she said. Then to the little boy she said, "Now sit still, Marvin. Let the nice man sleep." And to distract Marvin from his kidney-rupturing game she fished a golf ball out of her flight bag and gave it to him. Marvin promptly began bouncing the ball off the ceiling fixtures above him. He missed a catch. The ball went skittering under the seats. Marvin went tunneling after it under the feet of the other passengers.

Marvin recovered the ball and squirmed back into his seat. He sent the ball flying toward the side of the cabin. It smacked smartly against one of the small windows of the big plane's cabin. A passenger punched the hostess call-button. The hostess came over. To Marvin's mother she said, "Our nice big plane might crash into the ocean if the windows are broken." Marvin's mother glowered at her, took the ball from the boy and returned it to the flight bag. Some people never seemed to like children, she reminded herself. The bitch was probably childless and bitter. And she had pimply skin on the forehead, which accounted for her being so snotty to a little boy at this time of the month. Then Marvin and his mom apparently fell asleep.

But only apparently for Marvin. The kidney rupture game began again.

"I'll fix his little red wagon!" said the big man next to Rico, as he stood up, patiently threaded his way over and through his fellow passengers until he got to the aisle. He went to the bar area, ordered a double vodka with sweet soda and a tablespoon of sugar, stirred it in carefully as he came down the aisle and returned to his seat. Over the top of the back of his seat he propositioned Marvin. "Want to taste my nice drink? Tastes *just* like candy." Marvin downed two or three hefty swallows, then sank back into his seat. A few minutes later Marvin was asleep in his mother's lap, a ragdoll.

The big man settled into his seat and plugged in the earphones he had bought from the hostess for a dollar. He stared, smiling, at the reading light above his seat.

Rico began to count the hours, his wristwatch turned around, its face in the palm of his hand. Paris was only six hours and thirty minutes away.

The big man turned to Rico, the headset still in place. "The worst thing you can do on one of these flights is to watch your watch."

Rico smiled embarrassedly. He had not thought that anyone could tell that this was his first flight to Europe.

"Take the damn thing off and put it in your pocket. You won't survive these long flights if you know what time it is. The idea is to forget time, not remember it."

"Well, I—"

"Just pull the sonofabitch off and stuff it in your pocket. I know. I've been on this damn machine ten times in the last month. Here, want to listen to the music?" He offered his headset to Rico.

Rico hesitated. The idea of plugging someone's used earplugs into his ears put him off. He thought he could detect the faint brown stain of earwax on the little white plugs of the headset. "No, I guess I don't feel like music," he said. "Thanks."

"Well, there isn't much on these damn things anyway. Stale jokes from some standup comedian, or smaltzy damn music you get free on the elevator. 'Elevator music,' they call it. 'Cause that's where the damn stuff was composed. I figure it was played and recorded in an elevator, too, a big damn elevator in some warehouse. If it wasn't recorded there it wouldn't sound so true to life. This stuff is genuine, honest to God 'elevator music.' High fidelity whiffle dust."

"Whiffle dust?" asked Rico. That was a new one to him.

"Don't you know what a whiffle is, my friend?"

"Can't say that I do."

"Well, it's part of the harness that goes on a horse, the bar across the back, you know, just under the tail. The whiffletree."

"New idea for me."

"Nothing new. A whiffletree is that swinging bar that the traces of a horse's harness are fastened to."

"Very interesting."

"Whiffle dust just means horseshit. But it has a classier sound. I like class. Too many people talk like they were raised in a whorehouse. And proud of it. But I don't really give a damn. Used to, no more."

"Where are you from?"

"Nowhere and everywhere, as they say. Terre Haute. You?"

"From Milwaukee."

"The state or the city?"

"Both."

"Guess you couldn't be from the city if you weren't from the state, right?"

"Right."

"I hear a lot about that place. People there have got it made, the way I hear it. State's hard to get into."

"You have to be invited by our governor."

"Makes sense. If Indiana had a governor like that we wouldn't have so damn many refugees swarming in. Christ, in Terre Haute you can hardly find anyone to talk English with nowadays. If you can't use Spanish, you are up the whiffle-dust creek without a paddle." He winked at Rico.

"They have it tough in Central American now."

"Oh, I know that. And I sympathize with those poor bastards. Our state's taken in a million in just this last year or so. But Christ only knows where it will end. Border patrols can't keep people out."

"We have a fence around our state. Patrolled, too. The governor says it's cheaper to patrol the borders of the state than it is to try to pay for the new people coming in." Rico was pretending that he was a longstanding resident of Milwaukee. "We call it the City of Palms."

"Never heard that one. But I know you got palm trees. Odd as hell. No palms in places like Gary or Toledo. They're on the lake, too."

"It's because of a high-pressure weather system that sits over Canada, or something like that."

"I know. The weathermen talk about it a lot. Not as much as they used to. Tell the truth, the rest of the country is jealous as hell of the nice climate you get in that new state."

"It is nice."

"Why are you leaving? Relatives in France? I notice you got a little accent? French?"

"No, no relatives. I'm going to Paris to study art."

"That ought to be something. Lot going on in Paris in the arts, all the time. Don't pay attention much myself. Never cared for art. Don't like any of it, even on birthday cards. Pain in the ass. Well, think I'll try getting some shut-eye. Won't work but it's better than nothing. Jet lag knocks me on my can. For some reason flying east is worse than flying west. Just the opposite for most people."

Toward dawn, as the sun began to light up the cabin, people began to stir about, scratching, yawning, making quiet complaints. Some got up and stumbled and twisted to the aisles, then waited in line to use the toilets. The lines were long. There had been a computer error long ago when the great aircraft was still on the engineer's drawing table. There had never been any proper research on the matter. The database was weak. For one thing the women working at the aircraft plant where the research was supposed to take place resented the whole idea of running in and out of toilets, simulating their body functions while some researcher stood around supposedly dead serious—but there were always jokes after work—clicking his stopwatch. The women had taken the whole thing to the labor union as one more evidence of sexism in the company. The female part of the database was never really completed. As for the men, their efforts to provide good solid information also got tangled up in all sorts of imponderables. Some used buttons on their overalls because zippers didn't work for blue-collar men working around greasy machines. And the white-collar staff became outraged when the time-and-motion analyst urged them to "pick up the pace." Several ended up in the company dispensary because of zipper cuts. So as things turned out it took twice as long for the average bladder to empty, and for the average pair of panties to be lowered, raised and skirts properly rearranged, or male parts to be stowed away safely and zippers zipped, as the machines had predicted.

A half hour later the hostess pushed a button on her

electronic control panel in the galley. Seats went into up-right position. Each passenger was provided breakfast, high-tech style. Small trapdoors popped open above each seat that contained a passenger—if no one was in a seat the weight-trigger belayed the computer message—and a plastic bag containing things resembling eggs with chives, pieces of toast and jiggers of prune juice descended, dangling from a plastic string in front of each passenger's nose. An eating tray swung down from the back of each seat, a sign went on above each, saying, "You may begin eating, please."

Rico found the whole situation getting more exciting. The plane was now only an hour from Paris. He only ate half of his breakfast. The "Time's up" eating sign went on. The hostess up front at the control panel pushed another button. The fold-out plastic breakfast bags, now mostly empty, were drawn up by their little plastic strings, forming small satchel-shaped bundles. The bundles disappeared into the small compartments in the ceiling. The trapdoors closed once again, eating trays swung into their recessed places against seat backs. That was that for breakfast just outside Paris.

The hostess's voice was on the intercom and passengers were told in English, French, German, Japanese, Russian, Spanish and what sounded like Faroese—the owner of the airline came from the Faroe Islands—to buckle their seatbelts in preparation for landing at DeGaulle International Airport.

Paris, the incomparable city. Aloof to many, Paris was kind to Charles Far from the moment he got there. The first baggageman he talked to at the airport told him not only where he could get lodging but where he could get a job. And the very next day he was ensconced in a museum and art research center that had been made out of Delacroix's studio on Place Furstenberg. He was given a room in the basement. It had a narrow bed, a small table, a stool to sit at the table, a small sink and a commode. It wasn't much in comparison to what he had as a studio at Smudge's, but it was in Paris and Rico had been told that Delacroix had once slept off a drunk there.

The day after that, Rico found himself walking in the footsteps of the great French Romantic artist, somewhat more literally than he had wished when he left Milwaukee. He was the museum's janitor. Each day he was expected to sweep and mop the floors of the museum, which was a backbreaking job but a lot better, he told himself, than lying awake at night in the tower at Smudge's worrying about what Allison Minter thought of his future as an employee in the sand and gravel company. He realized that someday he would have to pay back the loan he had taken to get to Paris. But for the moment that was no problem. The loan was interest free; it was secret; it was from a kind-hearted soul.

That night Rico wrote letters to his mother and to Pooch.

Rico's letter to his mother was upbeat and expansive, and out of kindness to her, and to his ego, he fudged details. He said he had gotten work in the museum, "assisting in making the setting of Monsieur Delacroix's immortal works as memorable as possible." His room, he said, was superb and its studio space just what he needed. There was excellent north light (the small window above the door) and there was plenty of space to set up an easel (he had to fold its legs and plant it on the bed). His lounge chair (the stool) was perfect for reading and he often stayed up late at night learning to think like an artist of the twenty-first century. Just down the block was a wonderful café with food that only the French understood (it was an American fast-food place called "Billy's"). He was happy and would write at least once a week. And in a P.S. he entreated his mother not to take the advice of the Chuco family and try to get into the United States. Just because there had been food riots in Merida did not mean that village life was not safe for someone like her. Her pension

184

checks would continue to arrive on time. She had nothing to worry about.

The letters to Pooch were designed for a broader audience, the folks at Smudge's and, perhaps, Allison Minter. But they were written as if Rico intended them for no one but Pooch or Mabel and Louie. The letters seemed to imply that he was making out with every woman in the French capital—short women, tall women, elegant women, women who lived only for rapture and abandonment in the arms of a man of Rico's strength and artistic authority, women with every kind of manner, blonde and ravenous, red-haired and overheated, brunettes, heavy lidded and portentous as a storm cloud. The implication was that he was putting more notches on his gun in a few weeks than poor Eugene Delacroix managed in a lifetime, in or out of his scarlet cape. To the folks at Smudge's, Rico's new life was one long glamorous saga of wine, french bread, beautiful women who would not leave him alone and intense conversation with great artists of the world.

The part of the story that was most true, perhaps, was about his conversations with great artists. For indeed a great many renowned painters came to the museum and research center to pay homage to Delacroix and to study paintings of his that had not been carted off to a major museum. As janitor, Rico not infrequently sidled up to this or that great name and, casually leaning on his push broom or mop, worked in a question or two.

But to add a little spice to the letters and to make sure that the folks at Smudge's paid attention, he also included a little dirt from the history of the Delacroix family. He mentioned Delacroix's apparent bastard birth and the singular circumstances surrounding it. Delacroix's father, Charles, at fifty-seven, could evidently not have children because of a tumor on his testicles. A series of four fearsome operations was undertaken, and all before anesthesia was in use. It was a courageous move on Charles's part. For supposedly it returned to Charles "all the advantages

185

of virility." But some said it was, in fact, a cover-up. Charles remained sterile. Eugene had been sired by no less than the aristocratic Charles Maurice de Tallyrand.

In a letter to Pooch a week later, Rico noted that he had met a girl to whom he was compulsively attracted. She was, he said, as beautiful as Delacroix's servant girl and mistress, Jenny Le Guillou. The facts of the matter were again somewhat different. Jenny Le Guillou was a plain-looking girl, to put it mildly, with a face that some called plain homely. Rico's Jenny was actually a down-at-the-heels ballet dancer named Katarina Kropotkin, a descendent of Prince Peter Kropotkin, the famed theorist of anarchism and its benefits to orderly social existence.

Katarina Kropotkin had hit her peak as a dancer ten years earlier, long before she spotted Rico inquisitively hanging about the fringes of the mobs celebrating "Begin again!" rites at the Pyramide de Pei. The first time she saw Rico she was dancing about the pyramid in her underwear, French designed and very fetching. A great many men in the ceremonies had trouble keeping their hands off her and their minds on divination. On that occasion Rico had not seen the dancer and he later went home alone.

Katarina had once danced as an extra in bread and butter ideological favorites of Soviet ballet such as "Spartacus." But she never made it big and she grew restless with the pace of her career. Finally she defected and set up a small ballet school in Alsace which touted the merits of German potato salad as a training food. She even wrote a series of pamphlets under the name of *Madame Kropotkin's Special Diet for the Ballet*, claiming that certain amino acids in potato salad had a powerful effect on the electronics of the nervous system in the long muscles of the legs. Her diet, she said, allowed dancers to leap at least two feet higher than dancers on an ordinary diet.

When business fell off, because Kropotkin's dancers actually seemed to grow more leaden when filled with German potato salad, she decided to defect back to the Soviet

Union. And then there was a spate of sensational publicity because of a scene on the Aeroflot jetliner. The KGB agent, an ugly brute without a forehead, who was assigned to escort her home insisted on sitting next to her on the plane with the armrest up between them. She was snuggled up under a large blanket, red of course, trying to sleep. The KGB man kept coming on with suggestive remarks and with one big, hairy paw under the blanket. Katarina was a vibrant, high-spirited sort of person, despite the years that had taken their toll. Finally she had enough of the KGB man. She leaned toward him, kissing him long and tenderly on the back of the ear. As he pushed his hand further up under her dress she calmly pulled his pistol from his shoulder holster and shot him in the head. She turned the gun toward others in the cabin, went forward and told the pilot to return to Paris or be drilled on the spot. She reminded them that she descended from Prince Kropotkin and that anarchy was an idea still close to her heart.

Back on the ground in Paris with the news cameras on her, Madame Kropotkin quickly became something of a celebrity on the streets of Paris. She was often seen in street cafés, caught up in animated conversation with her small but growing band of admirers. And between drinks set up for her by her fans, she began performing little impromptu bits of ballet she had once performed, her favorite being a taquette, or "pegged" step, in which she moved backward on point across the floor or the sidewalk in sharp staccato rhythm until her rear end collided with a table, a lamp post or some tourist who had happened along. In the newspapers she became known as the "little lady of the sidewalks," *la petite Femme de la Trottoir*.

As soon as the cult ceremonies had begun at the Pyramide de Pei, Kropotkin had joined the crowd and soon her long, thin, almost anorexic-looking form became a regular feature of the affair. She could still manage a brief *entrechât* and, of course, the *fondue*. And when she dressed in her bright red blouse and tutu she cut a quite impressive—many said darling—figure.

That was the way Katarina was dressed the second time she saw Rico. He was standing on the edge of the great crowd at the pyramid listening to the "Begin again! Begin again! Begin again!" chant to which someone had written music that was lifted in part from Poulenc's Organ Concerto with odd fragments of heavy-metal rock music added. Heavy-metal rock still survived as folkmusic among peasantry living in isolated mountainous areas along the Spanish border where there had been considerable inbreeding and radically reduced levels of intelligence. Cultists had gone out of their way to locate and record this music and to mix it with Poulenc's great work. The results were a kind of musical signature for the "Begin Againers" in Paris. Cultists had rolled a half-dozen small piano-sized organs—the kind that provide six lessons and a money-back guarantee that the buyer can wow his friends within thirty days—onto the terrace to play accompaniment for the chanting. Rico was standing near the organs. He was wearing a lightweight jacket with billowing sleeves, blue jeans and a large beret, tilted sharply in the Basque fashion. He looked every bit the artist. His eyes, intense as always, and long lashed, had often, as with Allison Minter, reduced women to a kind of buttery state, and when they met Katarina's eyes the same thing happened to her. She suddenly found she could not dance any more that day, that the whole rite at the pyramid had grown tedious. She pushed her way through the crowd to Rico.

Within a hour Rico and Katarina had had four glasses of wine and one small loaf of bread and had headed off to his room at the museum. There they made love, throwing everything they had into it. But it was a dispirited encounter nonetheless, a disappointment to both of them, to her because his mind was obviously on another woman, to him because she felt too gangly in his arms, as if she had joints in the wrong places.

But they stuck it out together for almost a month, meeting at lunchtime and in the evening. They even tried to make something meaningful happen between them by attending more of the convulsive affairs at the pyramid. But Rico began to seem increasingly callow to the Russian dancer and she began to seem old and skinny to him. In fact, the idea of fat began to preoccupy Rico's imagination in a constant, insinuating sort of way. He began to remember those days back in Milwaukee, where, at times, everyone seemed wonderfully fat. So he began doing a series of paintings, eight of them, of fat people. The paintings were relatively small compared to the great recumbent carrot series, but vigorous statements nonetheless. He called them "Strolling Milwaukeeans."

Rico's Russian lover found the paintings repulsive. She told him that fat people were fat because they were lazy, weak-willed creatures who should not be idealized. Fat was evil, ugly stuff to be gotten rid of by any means necessary, by swallowing balls of cotton to control one's appetite, the way famous models often did, by boiling it off in sweat baths and hot tubs, in the same way, more or less, that lard is rendered from hog flesh, so that nothing but little brown crispies are left, by any means at all short of self-immolation. Furthermore, she said, the paintings were intended to mock her because fat people often lost wrinkles and that made them look younger than they were.

In actuality, Rico's encounters with the ballet dancer in bed had sent a swarm of childhood memories boiling up from his unconscious. Most of the women he had known in Mexico inclined to fat, and so did, in a subtle premonitory sense, Allison Minter—that touch of babyfat under her chin, for instance. And the insides of Allison's thighs were not concave, as they were with Madame Kropotkin. Nor did her legs end at the top in a kind of shelf, as did the dancer's. "Shelf crotch" were the words that came to his mind when he saw women in slacks who were built like Katrina, though he never had actually voiced the words to anyone, not even in Smudge's. People could not help how they were put together. But they could help advertising the wrong things. Katarina advertised the wrong things.

One could debate, of course, just why there seemed to Rico to be so many fat people in Milwaukee as he looked back on his life there. The natural conclusion of most people, at least those who were not fat, was that eating and drinking too much made people fat. But back in the twentieth century some scientists claimed that people were fat because they had been created that way. Even if they starved themselves half to death they still remained fat. Still, there were very few fat people in societies where food was hard to come by, and Rico could remember very few fat Central Americans in the famine-racked hordes pushing up against that Rio Grande Wall. Fat was very odd, he thought, any way you looked at it.

Rico remembered standing on street corners in Milwaukee, or at the entrance to a grocery, or at some polka celebration at the lake shore, wondering at the monumental quality that pure suet can give the human form. Some fat people seemed to roll along the ground rather than walk. Others seemed to rotate within their skins as they moved.

Pooch had said that there was something very mysterious going on in Milwaukee and that some of its population might have come from another planet, perhaps as the vanguard of the "Begin again" movement. He said that if you studied them carefully, the really fat specimens, not just the plump ones, they appeared to be on the verge of budding, the way yeast cells bud, their arms or legs ready to split off to form whole new individuals. Pooch dubbed them "budders." He said that while most budders in Milwaukee seemed to be women, quite a few were men, enough to pass the mysterious genes around that kept the budding strain of people vigorous and numerous. "But that may be one of the blessings of the 'Begin again' species taking over Milwaukee," Pooch said. "After all, there can never be too many women."

Pooch always said such things with a straight face. Remembering Pooch's remarks made Rico feel nostalgic for Milwaukee. For while it was wonderful and chic to be skinny in Paris, like Katarina, it was more wonderful still to be a bit on the plump side in Milwaukee.

On the other hand, Pooch knew what the famine-ravaged people of Durango could look like and he never let Rico forget how the desiccated, cadaverous bodies of many of those in Carlsbad Caverns looked. He wanted to let Rico know, he said, that it was possible that the governor himself, a chubby specimen by any measure, might have come from outer space. Maybe the City of Palms was where it all would, in fact, "Begin again." But there was no real danger, Pooch reassured Rico, that the more rotund citizens of Milwaukee, great heavy-breathing balls of fat, would explode just because they put down another stein of Schumie's.

When Pooch talked that way about fat people, Rico realized, he was trying to forget how his wife and kids had looked in Mexico. Certainly not everyone in Milwaukee was fat. Sara was not fat, nor was her father. Louie wasn't really fat, just a bit tubby. Nor was sorry old Pester. He could have used a few pounds of fat just about anywhere on his body. Allison's father wasn't fat and she wasn't either, though she was wonderfully soft to the touch.

So just what set Rico off on a new series of paintings of fat people strolling on Wisconsin Avenue was not clear or simple. But certainly one of the things that made him reminisce so easily about what it was like to stuff one's self with bratwurst and develop a bit of an innertube as a result was his being in bed with Katarina, which sometimes reminded him of trying to climb a picket fence.

Parisian galleries were disdainful of Rico's fat people series, and more obviously and unforgivingly than Milwaukee critics had been of his monumental carrot series. But it was the shock of an encounter with one art dealer on Rue Pigalle that had shaken Rico most deeply. He had taken some of his fat people paintings to the gallery, and after a small conversation about the museum on Place Furstenberg, which Rico figured would give him a leg up but didn't, the dealer had said, "My suggestion, Monsieur Far, is that you stick with what you evidently wield with the most authority, namely the broom and mop." The next day Rico decided to visit Monet's home and gardens at Giverny. Perhaps the great impressionist could inspire him to continue painting. But that decision, too, almost proved his undoing.

Rico could scarcely find the strength to enter the grounds of Monet's estate. The moment he began walking up the path toward the house he began to tremble. In fact, one of the groundsmen thought he was sick, sick in the usual sense, that is, not in the head. Far collapsed on the pebble path, a bundle of cold sweat, a bundle of fears and soul-rending self-doubt. When he was helped to his feet and had shaken off his concerned companions, he said, "It's nothing, nothing at all. Just something I ate last night I think." He proceeded into the house.

A Monsieur Van der Kemp had restored the devastated house and gardens of Monet twenty years after the death of the old genius and they were still magnificent when Far got there, including the large daffodil-yellow dining room and the country kitchen with its ceramic-tiled walls alive with the color of bluebells and snowdrops. Monet's bedroom, with its eighteenth-century writing table and armchairs covered in buttercup-toned fabric, was magnificent. And when Far looked out the window toward the gardens, the whole thing seemed to crash on top him, the beauty, the quiet composure of the genius, the cozy clutter of a fully realized life. Far began to shake again, left the group, and hurried outside. The thought of Monet's cataracts closing down his vision, like some evil gray cloud in which the devil had wrapped himself in order to visit a kind old man on the sly, sent Far into a panic. He took the train from Vernon to Paris by himself and did not speak for a week to anyone.

The reason Rico Far almost collapsed at Giverny was that the principle of "artistic integrity" had struck him like a bolt of lightning from a cloudless sky. He had never really puzzled much about it before, nor considered the possibility that it might be bestowed on artists completely by accident, like talent and inspiration—or that he might not be one of those so visited. It was clear from what he could learn at Giverny that Monet had been shot through the heart with that magnificent golden arrow while he was still very young. The sheer accidental quality of it all stunned Rico. It was as if the gods, high on some sunlit cloud, were squabbling during a game of dice, betting which among them had the most marvelous gifts to bestow on humans below. The winner of the wager leaned over the edge of the heavenly cloud and with a casual sweep of its hand, patronizingly, conferred an incomparable gift on whomever he chose, by complete whim. It was all a question of supernatural accident.

Rico tried to remind himself that the great Monet was a mere human being too, that he probably ate his breakfast oatmeal in a hurry and dribbled the milk down his chin, that his stomach was slow to digest bacon that was under-cooked, that he probably had hair between his oversized shoulder blades, that he made embarrassing sounds in front of his wife or friends and that he perhaps grew his huge, ludicrous beard because he often felt like hiding, in the same way so many other men grow beards—to put something between themselves and the world. But Monet was a decent man and likeable, according to the guides at Giverny. So the mystery of artistic integrity remained. Attempts by scientists to figure it out were ridiculous and banal. Their search made about as much sense as trying to capture in a florence flask the memory of a gardenia's scent drifting through the venetian blind of a lover one has not yet met.

That night as Rico sat up in bed unable to sleep, the caps on his paint tubes staring across the room at him like the baleful eyes of dead fish in a market, he decided to dress again and walk the city of Paris. He would trace the famous nostalgic night-walk of Delacroix in 1859. The great artist was renowned then. He had been awarded the Grand Medal of Honor and had been elected to the all-powerful Acadamie des Beaux-Arts. And on that night in 1859 he had been feted at a grand ball. Royalty had sought him out. Young artists hung on every word. And at home there was Jenny: lover, protector, "blind devotion itself." But what struck Rico most forcefully from all of the things that the great artist was quoted as saying was this: "Real superiority admits no eccentricity. . . . The great genius is simply a being of a more highly reasonable order."

It was with that remark ringing in his ears that Rico retraced Delacroix's walk to all the places in Paris where the great artist had studied art, met famous people, loved women, wept and triumphed—from the ball at the Hotel de Ville, to Monmartre, to Rue Bleue, to the residences of Mme. de Forget and George Sand, past the Place d'Orleans, back toward the Seine, to Rue St. Honoré, past the Theatre Français, around the east end of the Louvre to the Pont des Arts, past the Ecole des Beaux-Arts and back to his studio on Place Furstenberg.

For Rico things were different. The great Romantic had Jenny; Rico had a spavined dancer who found him boyish. While Delacroix seemed to have joined the gods, drifting about among the clouds of one of his own great ceiling murals, Rico was stuck with a janitor's mop and a pail full of dirty water.

SCHEMES

THERE HAD BEEN a quiet upheaval in Pooch's life while Rico was in Paris. Wilhelm Steinberger had discovered that his daughter Sara had stolen some of the gold from "Mr. Common." She had sold it and added the cash to that which she gave to Rico so he could go to Paris. Sara had always longed to go to Paris herself and to live the bohemian life there—precisely how, she had never really thought through. But the possibility of helping a young handsome artist friend of Pooch's do it thrilled her. She had every intention of buying the gold back from the pawnbroker as soon as she got her next monthly paycheck. No one would be the wiser. Both she and Rico considered it a loan, something he would make good on as soon as "trained in Paris" showed up on his credentials and he got a commission or two. Rico did not know about Mr. Common and Sara did not tell him. Nor did she tell Pooch about the loan. She knew he would oppose any such move and that he would perhaps be the fall guy if she herself was found out, since her father was very suspicious of "this so-called writer from south of the border."

Sara's use of the gold was discovered by accident. "Mr. Common" had not been really inventoried for years. Club members were happy enough just to see the little wafers of gold tumble into the box after a melt. But one evening, out of the blue, old Geezer Mike said, "Will, why don't we spread those little devils out on the table and see how many we got. We begun at this quite a few years ago. Ain't that we don't trust your tally. We do. And it ain't even the value of this stuff that counts. But I think it would brighten our dreams a little if we know just how much Mr. C has in his tummy." Steinberger said, "Of course, of course. We should do that often. Perhaps have a little ceremony when we do it." He lifted the strongbox out of its hole and put it on the table alongside the kiln where the official melter had just finished reducing another batch of trinkets, even a wedding ring from the wife of one of the old members who found that the ring preyed on his mind ever since he had it removed before his wife's cremation. Removing it from her finger seemed sacrilegious whenever he thought about it. As if he had let his greed get the best of him. The man at the crematorium had called it common sense. "Why let a nice piece of gold go up the flue?" he had asked.

Then Steinberger got out his little black ledger book and instructed old Geezer Mike to begin the count of the thin little pieces of gold. There were supposed to be two hundred and seventy-seven of them. They were sixteen short!

"Oh my God, oh my God," Steinberger began to repeat as he stumbled toward a chair and almost fell into it. "One of us is a thief. One of us is a traitor!" He was breathing heavily and perspiration stood out on his forehead.

Mike tried to reassure his old friend. "Anyone can make a mistake. Anyone. Don't let it bother you, Will. It's our mistakes that make us look good in the long run, if they don't come very often. You haven't made any until now. So take heart."

But Mike had a slightly skeptical look on his face. It soon began to appear on the faces of other members of the club who were at the melt. Steinberger was mortified, humiliated, crushed and panicky. It was the first time in his life that anyone had even dared suggest that he would do anything dishonest. Then there were whispers among the members present, speculations about who might have been crooked or desperate enough to break their sacred oath. None of them remembered that Sara had accompanied Wilhelm to a melt several years ago and was not bound by the oath of secrecy.

That evening Steinberger could not eat dinner. He simply sat in his big rocking chair by the window and looked south across the river and toward the city skyline. Sara grew concerned and pressed him to tell her what was wrong. "It is too terrible to discuss," he said. "Just leave your crippled old father alone. He has lost the most important thing in life, his reputation as an honest man."

Sara could not make sense of his remarks. She pressed him further, and finally got him to eat something. Then he returned to his chair. She noticed tears running down his face, and she fell on her knees in front of him and pleaded to be told what had hurt him so deeply. And when he told her, she herself went into an emotional tailspin. She began to weep also, and then she confessed. She had only taken a small amount of the gold, she said, because she needed to add a few dollars to the money she wanted to give to Pooch's best friend, as a loan, strictly a loan, so that he might be able to do what she had always dreamed about, breaking her ties with her job and her city and going after life with a vengeance, all out and without looking back, perhaps even to find a good man, a man with some sense of adventure in his bones, perhaps an artist or perhaps a writer.

"Well, you got your so-called writer!" said her father,

without looking at his daughter. And those were the last words he spoke to her.

Sara's weeping, her entreaties, her offer of a check or cash to make good for the missing gold, her pleas to Mabel to intercede and Mabel's intercession, none of it would move Steinberger. Mabel's conversation with the old man the next morning while Sara was at work had no effect at all, except to harden further Steinberger's heart against his daughter "and that Mexican."

"Your daughter loves you, Wilhelm, loves you very much. Why do you think she lives with you? Why do you think she *puts up* with your cranky ways? You can be a *very* selfish man. It's time you took a good look at yourself. You won't like what you see. Just because you lost that leg, you think you have the right to take it out on the rest of the world. You're *selfish*, Will, selfish!"

Steinberger defended his reaction by saying that he had undertaken the whole gold club scheme simply to make a few old people like himself feel a bit more secure. He had done it because he was *not* selfish. "I did it to help people. And what do I get? They all think of me as a damn sneak, a con artist preying on their fears. That's what I got for my trouble. Well, I have told them all I would resign as leader of the club. And I intend to. And, I think I will have to leave this city as well. It is not the money. We all know that the gold was not worth all that much, a few thousand dollars perhaps. But it is the principle of the thing! The way things are going on the outside, this is the only kind of thing that old people can hang onto. Gold, goddamn it, Mabel, gold! Not this paper money with the picture of some longhair president on it. Not paper, for the love of God, but gold!"

"It's got nothing to do with gold. It has to do with your pride as a leader," said Mabel.

Steinberger and Mabel went at it for almost an hour until he was hoarse and the stump of his leg throbbed and Mabel threw up her hands and walked out, slamming the door behind her. "Let the old bastard go live somewhere else," she said out loud to herself. "He's a mean old man who persecutes a lovely daughter. He thinks because he pays his rent ahead of time it's a license to be an asshole."

Steinberger refused to speak to his daughter. He would communicate with her with notes that he left on her bed each day, anonymous-sounding as he could make them. "Wilhelm Steinberger wants... etc." "Sara Steinberger should immediately attend to..., etc." One of the notes he placed on her bed about a week after the discovery of the theft from Mr. Common read, "Wilhelm Steinberger absolutely refuses to allow his daughter to see Diego Grenada while his daughter is living under the same roof as he is."

Sara was defiant. She responded with a note of her own that read, "Sara Steinberger is fed up with being treated as if she was a child. She will see Diego Grenada whenever *she* pleases to see him. She has accordingly moved her clothes and personal belongings from the residence of her father. She is also moving from Smudge's. Her father should not try to reach her until he is ready to show the love and understanding toward her that any daughter has the right to expect from a father who *claims* he loves her."

Pooch was beside himself over the entire episode. He tried to talk to Steinberger. The old man would have nothing to do with him. He tried to get Mabel to help, swearing her to secrecy about the Mr. Common situation. Steinberger refused to discuss it again with Mabel. He became more surly and withdrawn than ever, and each night his peg leg thumped about the floor above Smudge's bar louder and longer than the night before. "Old Steiny's really pissed off about his daughter moving out on him," they said at the bar. "He blames it all on Pooch. But you couldn't bump into a nicer guy than Pooch Grenada," was a typical reaction. Or, "From what I know of old Steiny this should

199

have happened a long time ago. Sara is a saint to put up with that mean ol' sonofabitch. Him and his constant bitching about the governor. If he can't love this state he should leave it. Love it or leave it, I say."

Sara took a room with a lady friend who worked with her in the Grand Avenue Mall. Each evening she and Pooch would go for long walks. Several times when they were alone they made love in the small apartment Sara shared with her friend. It was the first physical love Sara had experienced since she was an eighteen-year-old girl.

It was Allison Minter who complicated things by insisting that she come to the aid of Pooch and Sara. And there is nothing quite as destructive in the long run, perhaps, as a sustained but contaminated good intention. Allison wanted to put both Sara and Pooch up in the big studio that Dádi had built for her on the River Hills estate when long ago she had hopes of becoming an artist herself. It provided commodious quarters, about as far from the kind of bohemian arrangements that Sara had imagined writers used as she could think of. The building was in half-timbered Tudor style, a two story affair with room for four of Allison's cars in the garage on the ground floor and a splendid apartment on the second floor. The floors were finished in polished oak; large Navaho rugs were scattered about before the fireplace. There were skylights on the north slope of the roof. The studio was surrounded to the rear and east side by a forest of ancient oaks. Bluejays and woodpeckers were everywhere.

Pooch, of course, resisted any such arrangement. He did not trust Allison's motives. Sara was the one that got him to go along. She told him that it was a chance to live rent-free, that it was a chance for her to prove she loved him, it was a chance for him to return to his writing. It was a chance for both of them to get away from all the gossip at Smudge's, to live their own life, to marry if he liked, and to make a generous rich girl happy at the same time. Her salary would meet all of their needs. He could quit the job in the sand and gravel yard, no place for a man of his talent to be working anyway.

Allison's agenda had been shaped to a good extent by the fact that she had learned from Sara that Pooch had begun making notes for a novel called *The Grackle* and had evidently finished several chapters. It was to be a tour de force in the Latin American magical realism genre. Allison could think of nothing nicer than including a novelist in her stable of new artists, each orbiting about her emerging role as a young, swinging and beautiful patron. She would build a kind of salon and there would be receptions every few weeks at Dádi's mansion, during which her poet Anselm Pester and her novelist Diego Rivera Garcia Lorca Grenada would mix among her rich friends as they all talked about imagists, surrealists, the cubist revolution, the role of the collector in the arts, what is criticism?, why patrons are important and on and on into the late hours of the night. And when Rico Far learned what he was missing he would come back to Milwaukee with his tail between his legs, or at least she would get even with him for the way he practically walked out on her.

There would be visiting dignitaries from the arts, too, like Gerald Angina and the Italian figurationist Giovanni Garcelli Bombastini. She and Dádi had met them both at one of Bombastini's shows in New York. Bombastini was one of the new artists who painted with rubber-gloved hands rather than with brushes and was much admired for the power and impudence of the slather that resulted.

Bombastini then left New York for Sicily without giving notice to anyone—his friends, his buyers or the galleries he hung around. Rumor said that the FBI had infiltrated some of his notorious all-night parties and that the air was so full of smoke from assorted narcotics that the case against Bombastini would have fallen through in the courts because the hidden cameras could not cut through the haze. But Bombastini found Sicily more to his liking anyway because it was warm enough there to go about barefoot.

Art journals could not resist doing cover stories on great artists in bare feet. So leaving America had been no real loss at all.

Angina was something else. Bombastini called him "that notorious fraud." But he also admired him, and he told the Minters why. "At least the sonofabitch is making it big. In this town (they were in New York at the time) that is what counts. It counted for me and it counts for him. Plus the fact that the scoundrel despises everything. That is why young artists can learn so much from him."

As Angina put it to the Minters, both of whom were interested in buying one of his new, "wonderfully outrageous" works, his basic tenet was simple. He got Allison and her father aside at the party, stood them against a wall in a corner where they could not get away even had they tried—which they did not; they were thrilled—and said, "If a man would be great, if he would *make it*, and I mean *make it big*, he must be prepared to insult something great. There is no other way. There are far too many artists in the world as it is. The only way to become a great one now, a significant one, not a goddamned two-bit dabbler— there are plenty of those in Kalamazoo—is to clear space. Knock one of the big bastards out of his niche and take it over."

Allison said to her father, "You see, Dádi, that's what I have been saying about the Shikel. The only way to make it big is to bust out of that State of Milwaukee and export the car, in a big way. Knock the Japanese, for starters, out of their damn niche."

Minter was all ears. He loved the arts. Always had, at least so he said. But there was more to this Angina fellow than met the eye. And Allison was right. The Shikel was probably what it took, at last, to get the Japanese back to bonsai trees and the hell out of automobiles. He smiled at the thought. Small is also beautiful when it applies to your competitor's profit margin.

Angina was a big man, strong as a bull. He had been

202

shaving his head since he was eighteen. No compromises, he said, of any kind, including the tufts of hair above each ear that refused to grow anywhere else. He was clean-shaven, with a powerful lower jaw, all-in-all a commanding physical presence. He leaned into Dádi as he drove home his argument. While he thought Allison beautiful, sophisticated and attractive, his instincts told him that Dádi was in charge of the kind of spending money his work commanded, seventy-five to three hundred thousand dollars at a crack. "I spent most of my early years studying great artists, like Christo for instance. Now he's good, damn good! When he built that 'Running Wall' across thirty miles of California he was brilliant. He was a goddamned genius when he wrapped those islands off Miami with pink plastic. I was there, one of the crew. Just a squirt then. But I was in on the whole thing from start to finish. And wrapping the Pont Neuf in Paris? Forty-seven thousand square feet of nylon went into that baby. The stuff of greatness, no goddamned doubt about it. Well, I've one-upped that bird Christo. Knocked him out of his niche. I wrap too, but I wrap tragedy! That's the difference. You've seen my work. You know what I mean. But while Christo wrapped the bridge in Paris, a very pretty bridge, we'd all admit, I wrapped the wreckage of that jet plane that crashed in West Virginia last year. I got the tears. I got the news. I got the commissions! And the money is in the bank. So that's why you two need a major work by Angina. You're patrons of the arts, so I'm told. Bombastini told me you were. Well, an Angina will put you in the major leagues. Out there in Milwaukee especially. From what I gather, that place could use some honest-to-God heavy-duty art. And a wrapped tragedy is just the ticket."

Minter was too shrewd a businessman to commit himself to buying a major work of art without some thought. "We'll give it some serious thought, Mr. Angina," he said.

Angina had, in fact, come a long way in the arts within a short period of time. Five or six years ago he was considered a freak. But when the critics had run out of new, unheard of freaks, he suddenly became very useful. They touted him, they began following him around. They quoted him on subjects like politics and science and religion, none of which he knew anything about at all. But he was a newsmaker, without question.

Angina would watch the news for the first report of an airplane crash. He would fly in his own plane—a hot little Osage Jetsprint—to the airport nearest the crash, then rent a car and barrel out to the site of the crash. As soon as the body fragments had been taken off and the Civil Aeronautics Disaster Investigation team had completed its investigation, he would buy the wreckage, usually for no more than the cost of hauling it away. He would have it trucked or freighted by train to the city from which most of its victims came and build his own kind of artistic "assemblage," either by sorting the litter and junk into great clear plastic boxes, or by imbedding it in enormous chunks of clear plastic or in loosely bound clear plastic bags, tough enough not to puncture. Then he would spray the entire assemblage with flat black paint, leaving "windows" at crucial points in each assemblage. The works were labeled with enigmatic titles, such as "Do Unto Others" and "Unto the Seventh Generation." Angina's assemblages found themselves in many of the great urban parks of the nation, much discussed, often fought over, always treated by local press as "controversial." Relatives of crash victims would come to the sites to weep or cry out their indignity, or to spit on "this so-called memorial to my dear son." But the sculpture almost invariably stayed where it was put, especially if a "site grant" from one of the big art-endowment organizations was brought to bear. Allison Minter intended to introduce Angina to the Milwaukee art scene soon, within the month, at a party at her father's mansion.

Allison threw herself into making arrangements for the party. It would take place in three weeks. She sent invitations to everybody that was anybody in the well-heeled part of town. To add texture to the affair she also invited some people from Smudge's—Louie and Mabel, Clement Jensen and two or three others. She added artistic class by sending formal invitations to Anselm Pester and Diego Grenada. There would be out-of-towners too, such as Gerald Angina, the New Yorker. (She attached a forged invitation to the state to Angina's invitation, plus a brief note implying that if he came to Milwaukee for the party he would be put on retainer as consultant on the "Dádi Honored" project.) Then she asked her father to do a little arm twisting, old friend to old friend, on the governor. The governor's office called later to assure Allison that he would stop by for a half hour or so. The governor's acceptance of the invitations was hedged. He did not like Allison's kind of party particularly. There was too much putting on the dog, too much waste, not enough horse-sense, too many comments behind his back about Schumacher "the grubby little British bureaucrat" and not enough polka music. There were too many snickers about how he looked in his lederhosen.

But the idea of a big party with plenty of publicity wallop made sense. After all, Allison reasoned, other wealthy people around town were taking bows and getting society-page notice for a whole lot less. Her friend, Ann Vicount, made the front page of the society section of the paper with a boring fundraiser to build a new wing for hernia patients on the St. Clematis hospital. And her friend, Agnes Bent, did the same thing with her fundraiser in Chicago. It raised money to supply old, homeless bag women with new bags. One of her relatives in Madison even had a lawn party to raise money for scientists doing exotic research on pain thresholds of vivisectioned animals. But beyond all that, lawn parties for artists and friends of art could be written off on income tax. IRS wouldn't rob Dádi blind, and both she and her father would still look like St. Francis of Assisi, from a distance at any rate, and *sans* the vow of poverty. Besides, her "salon" approach would be a way of pushing a bean or two up the nose of the fat little man in the Statehouse. The governor had taken to referring disdainfully to such fundraisers as "charity with the laughing face."

The night Allison held her party for her men of the arts she welcomed her guests absentmindedly. The fact that her father had persuaded the governor to stop by the party actually added to her distress. It was not until she had three or four drinks and her wealthy friends from around town had begun to show up and had a few cocktails as well that she began to relax. And by the time Pester, Grenada, Sara (as his date), Louie and Mabel showed up, things were rolling along nicely. Then Gerald Angina's limousine showed up, courtesy of the Minters. A bit later the governor showed up, as usual driving his own car, a twelve-year-old Shikel that looked as good as new.

Everyone was dressed in leathers, as instructed in Allison's invitations, worded according to her father's instructions, in deference to the governor. The only exception was Gerald Angina, who wore striped jeans, a black shirt with red necktie and knee-length boots.

The governor was introduced as "our beloved Governor," Angina as "our brilliant avant-garde artist from Long Island," Pooch as "our leading Latin American novelist whom we will be introducing to the American public soon" and Clement Jensen as "the bright young man (he was thirty-eight) with the brilliant future in politics ahead of him." Anselm Pester was introduced as "the incredible poet about whom you have read so much." Mabel and Louie were allowed to fend for themselves.

Some of Allison's well-heeled guests sniffed the air suspiciously when they realized that Jensen was the screwball who had made the papers a week earlier when a newspaper reporter had photographed him drunk, in polkadot leathers, at the door of the Back Stage restaurant of the Performing Arts Center following a performance of *Macbeth*. Jensen announced he was forming a "Begin Again" political party. The governor was old and over the hill, he told reporters. It was time for the Fritzland Movement to move ahead, to get in step with the times.

The next day, when asked to comment on the Jensen "campaign," the governor told reporters to be kind to Jensen, that the sweaty little politician needed compassion as much as he did support. With the arrival of the people from Smudge's, the party gathered excitement. Most of Allison's rich friends were stuffy people who had little to talk about except each other. Most were not, perhaps, really stuffy at heart. They had problems, health problems, bad stomachs, swollen ankles and such, family problems, infidelities, bigotries that corroded their generosity. But these were not the kind of things one talked about at a fine party under a big striped party tent near Minter's sumptuous swimming pool. Under such circumstances, stale humor and simulated stuffiness were staples of the conservative conscience. So they were all secretly grateful when people like Anselm Pester showed up, wearing wrist knives, and then a bull-voiced artist called Angina from Long Island.

After an hour or so people had enough to drink to assure that one of them pushed another into the swimming pool. Then Pester fell in on his own, still in Kau wrist knives and body paint. He dogpaddled to the nearest ladder and pulled himself out, looking like a very wet and annoyed ferret, leaving a slick of oily colors behind. The copy of the poem Pester had typed onto a small slip of paper and stuffed into the pocket of his lederhosen in the hope of reading it later that night to the partygoers had begun to dissolve into a useless wad of pulp.

The poem was titled "Oh Putrescent Love" and was, in fact, a poem Pester had written without taking anything at all from Casper Spent's *Book of Ruling Equations*. It began: "Oh putrescent love/ thou art the kind of love that knows no bounds/the kind of love of which only creeps do speak. . . ."

But falling into the water with his body paint and wrist knives had been a shock for the old poet. He could not swim very well to begin with and the wrist knives made dogpaddling hazardous to his health. But he reached one of the pool ladders, cautiously heaved himself out and was given a towel by one of Allison's servants. He sat slumped in one of the poolside chairs, pure despondency. He knew he would not be able to recite the whole poem, all fifty-four lines (the same number as "Kubla Khan" contained, which was no accident) without his typed copy. And he knew too that he would have to reconstruct the poem under the baleful stare of St. Jerome.

The saint had been giving Pester a hard time for months because of Pester's tendency to backslide every time he left his room. "Oh Putrescent Love" was, for one thing, a thinly veiled salute to Oscar Wilde, a figure Pester had always admired for his easy way with sin. Saint Jerome would have preferred something dedicated to a pope or John Quincy Adams or even Daniel Boone. Also, Pester had made a trip some weeks earlier through the sewers to Chicago, just to buy a few joints of pot. But as it turned out, with the paper on which the poem was written reduced to a crumbling wad of waste, it was unlikely the original poem would ever see the light of day. "Oh Putrescent Love" was a stillborn creation.

For a good part of the evening Gerald Angina was the focus of attention at the party. He held court at the end of the pool opposite to where Pester sat forlorn and wretched looking, his body paint running down his sides and down his hairless, white legs. From a distance he resembled a chick that had been hatched before its time and was then dipped into a swirl of Easter egg dye. Angina's notion of tragedy might have been put to vivid test then and there had Jensen had the bad judgement to go to Pester and pass off some bit of gratuitous ridicule. And Jensen knew that a squabble with Pester could put him in a bad light with people at the party who could do him some good.

Angina loved to hold court. He was saying to the ten or so people crowded about him, "To be postmodern is not just to recognize tragedy. To be truly postmodern is to know what to do with tragedy, what to do that is peculiarly American, in my case. That means knowing how to package tragedy, in a word, how to wrap it."

He scanned the cluster of partygoers just beyond his immediate audience, hoping for new recruits. "That, then, is the central idea of my work. I have learned how to wrap tragedy. I began small, needless to say. One must always start small in the arts. One whittles a stick, one might say, before one tackles a block of marble. My first wrapping of any significance was a Piper Cub that crashed near Cape Cod. No one was killed in the crash but one passenger was paralyzed from the waist down. It was a start. I worked up from there. I wrapped the wreckage of an old DC-3 that landed in a storm at Albany, kicked over on its back and burned. Four people died in that crash. It was the first work of mine that drew any attention worth mentioning. The press can be very stingy on things like this. The press will..."

Allison had brought the governor over to meet Angina. The sculptor loomed over the chief executive. Angina shook the governor's hand mechanically, casually including the old man in his audience. "... the press will be stingy at times, as I was saying. But one has got to seize the moment. My moment came when one of those old Lockheed Electras, a turboprop, crashed in 1992 in Ohio. Wings came off. No survivors. Scattered wreckage over a mile and a half. It took me a year to assemble the debris. I decided I would cast this piece of work in large blocks of clear, crystalline plastic, each piece nine feet square. Now it sits in Youngstown in front of their courthouse. Very wisely sited, if I do say so."

The story of how Angina got an invitation to enter the state in spite of the governor's conviction that he was a fraud was a separate side of Allison's venture into the arts.

She knew Angina would have trouble because he had gotten so much publicity all over the country and represented everything that the Fritzland Movement considered stupid and wasteful. So she had used her connections to find out where the governor kept the richly lettered, heavily embossed cache of invitations waiting for his signature. Then she squeezed a few dollars into the fist of the man in charge of supervising preparation and distribution of the invitations. She got hold of a dozen of the forms. After that she arranged to meet with Cherryman one night at Smudge's.

Cherryman was a professional at more than smuggling cherry wine from Cedarburg to Chicago. He knew cocaine pushers, stolen-car peddlers, forgers of birth certificates for blackmarket babies, as well as how to find the right man to copy the currency of nearly any country in the world.

Cherryman arranged to take the invitations to Kenosha, where he linked up with a slippery scoundrel in unlaced shoes and a ruined trenchcoat. They met on an old, unused pier south of Kenosha. Cherryman forked over half the money Allison had provided for the forger, along with a copy of a genuine signature of the governor as a model. Then the two men, speaking in whispers, settled on the day and time of their rendevous. With their collars up and their caps down over their eyes they disappeared into the night, one to the north, the other to the south.

A week later Cherryman met Allison at a bar on Oakland Avenue in the Milwaukee suburb called Shorewood and got the rest of his money. It had all gone off as smoothly as their high-priced drinks had gone down. It was the kind of caper both Cherryman and Allison loved. It mixed intrigue, contact with slippery-looking fellows who moved around in the dark and money.

While this little flashback was playing through Allison's mind at the party as she stood next to Angina and the governor, the old man listened intently to the big, loud-voiced artist who seemed to brim with confidence. He had read about Angina recently, the governor recalled, in a short piece in *Time* magazine. Seeing, in this case, was more than believing. It was also disbelief. How this big phony had ever made it as far as he had was something the governor could not imagine for the life of him.

Angina's eyes continued to rove, hoping for more recruits to his monologue. "My advice to young artists studying under me is sometimes quite simple. I tell them, for one thing, that charred wreckage is always best. Richer patina. I tell them also to get the seats. The seats are worth twice as much artistically as a damned piece of tail. People will cry over a burned-out seat. A piece of tail makes them laugh." Then he looked down at the governor and put a patronizing hand on the old man's shoulder. "There is some significant artistic work here in your state. For instance, what you have done to the large bridge, the Dan Bone bridge..."

"Dan Hoan," said the governor quietly. "One of the great mayors of the city of Milwaukee, before statehood."

"What you have done with the bridge is very fetching. The large statues. I could see them from the highway as I came in from the airport. Who are they?"

"Mostly aldermen from the city's past. Many shared my views on what a good city is supposed to be."

"I have studied your views on kitsch and cathexis, Governor," Angina said. "Your views were quoted again in *Art Newsweek*."

"I did not know that. What are my views?" There was an edge to the governor's question. He was trying to remember the invitations to the state he had signed in recent weeks. He could not remember signing one for this man.

"That abstractionists have tried to decathect the world."

"Interesting," said the governor.

Angina sensed he was walking a tightrope. "I share your views, Governor. That is why I am so excited about the "Dádi Honored" undertaking. Very exciting project."

The governor recalled Allison Minter's proposal for a

giant sculpture of her father. It was months since he had given it any thought. He assumed that Minter had put it on the back burner. It would cost close to a million dollars. It was to be a great bronze statue of Minter sitting in a Shikel. It was to represent the hundred or so Shikel convertibles that Minter had produced before the state's Automobile Manufacturing Oversight Committee, AMOC, had decided that convertibles were unsafe, as well as wasteful adolescent vehicles, and stopped further production of them. Allison had claimed that the sculpture was to immortalize a machine that had since become known as a classic and sold, amongst collectors on the outside, for twenty, even thirty times what a typical Shikel cost. Dádi was to be sitting, three times life-size, at the wheel, with the wind and the rain in his hair. The monster bronze-work was to sit on the big lawn to the north of the Bradley Art Pavilion. Minter, it was understood, would also fork over five million dollars for an addition to the Pavilion.

The governor eyed Angina without saying anything. Angina felt uneasy. "Very exciting project," he repeated.

"Did you enter our state to work with the project?" the governor asked in a mild, inquisitive tone. He had a clearer picture of Angina in mind now. There had been a story in the Chicago *Sun Times* on the famous artist, along with a picture of one of his wrapped tragedies. He had wrapped a small empty vault in burlap and put it on view in one of the better galleries on Chicago's swank Magnificent Mile. And when the art critic who had done the story had asked Angina if it was true that he (Angina) believed that to become a great artist one must learn to despise everything, Angina, knowing the question would come up, had pulled a copy of Delacroix's *A Small Dictionary of The Fine Arts* from the hip-pocket of his jeans and read a quotation.

Somewhere in the course of their career, artists must learn not merely to despise everything which is not entirely theirs, but must rid themselves of this blind fanaticism which drives us to imitate the great masters and swear only by their works.

Angina had told the critic that he was a great admirer of Delacroix, especially of his realization of how important it was for the artist to learn to despise things. "My wrapped vault expresses that principle," he told the critic.

It was a bit of double-English on the cue ball as far as the critic could determine. Angina had included the money that other artists made in the things that he had learned to despise. The only thing to be left out of reach of one's scorn was money one could get one's hands on.

It was a bold opinion boldly put, considering that Angina had taken Delacroix's comment so neatly out of its larger context, a context that included what Rico Far had found so inspiring, which was that "real superiority admits no eccentricity." Then again, as many people had said many times, beginning with Emerson, "Consistency is the hobgoblin of small minds." Delacroix's was obviously a big mind.

Angina looked the governor squarely in the face, almost defiantly, and answered his question about why he had entered the State of Milwaukee. "I am here for a fee, of course, to make money. My special interest in the arts, Governor, as you know, is tragedy. I believe an artist without money is a tragedy."

"Perhaps," said the governor. "Sometimes the more money they make the more tragic it is for their art."

"Do you enjoy the arts? I mean do you know the arts?" Angina asked, faking amiability. He did not like the governor, and the feeling was obviously mutual.

"I know a good deal about art," said the governor playfully, "but I often don't know what I like. The result can be tragic indeed."

Angina realized he was being needled. The old man with the Santa Claus look was taunting him. He moved to take the high ground. "Piet Mondrian once called the trees of

Paris 'tragic.' Refused to look at them. In cafés he would turn his back on them. He would understand our views on cathexis," he said.

"Have no doubt on that, Mr. Angina," said the governor quietly. "Piet and I were friends, briefly, back in 1943 just before he died. He was living in New York then, as you know. I met him by accident at a ballroom while I was on leave from my navy post. Piet loved to dance. But he was a lonely, monkish man. I said to him at the time, I said, 'Piet, you are a lonely, monkish man.' He said, 'Why do you think I painted my "Boogie Woogie" paintings? If you're lonely and monkish, you turn to boogie woogie.' And off he went across the ballroom floor, eight to the bar. But I will never forget how sorry I felt for the man who had tried to hide his need to dance behind all those abstract squares in his paintings. But he was Dutch, after all. The only thing dearer to a Dutch heart than a tulip is a square."

Angina had been upstaged. He had expected to meet a kindly old rube, not a knowledgable friend of Mondrian's. He decided to end his poolside seminar. "It was nice meeting you, Mr. Governor," he said, and headed for the bar. He got a double scotch and went hunting for Allison. He found her sitting near Anselm Pester. Pester was petulantly trying to rearrange his wrist knives and complaining that people at the party seemed to treat him as if he had bad breath. "That fat old bastard is going to give us a rough time with the "Dádi Honored" project," Angina said to Allison in a whisper. "I think he's a very dangerous man. He's a goddamned heretic. That's what he really is."

When the governor left the party, Allison felt relieved. He had made her feel as if the party were some kind of orgy, which of course it wasn't. And he had punctured Angina's balloon with his Mondrian aside, indeed, made Angina seem almost silly.

And then Clement Jensen got drunk and he and a rich-bitch type from Fox Point dived into the pool together and began kissing and hugging one another as if there were no one else around. They kept exchanging comments about how well he claimed to be hung and how she intended to find out. Then Allison's father showed up. He had not been around all evening. He was obviously loaded to the gills as well. He called the party to attention and told everyone that he wanted them to party all night if they wished. "Early flight out tomorrow," he said, and staggered off to go to bed. The small band that had been playing rather staid, even dreary music, themes from old Broadway hits for the most part, finally got drunk enough also to begin bashing out some old acid-rock favorites from Allison's collection of golden oldies. The party was now doing its best to become a debauch. So far it hadn't made it.

Few people who witnessed the exchange between the governor and Angina really knew much about what was going on. But Allison and Angina did, as well as the governor. She wanted to invite Angina into Milwaukee to take on the "Dádi Honored" project. Angina would be free to build public interest in it by telling everybody that it would be wrapped tragedy until it was unveiled, a forced play on words but enough to interest local art critics and give the project momentum. Then she would let Rico Far know that if he wanted to get in on the action, to the tune of a five-figure fee for doing what Angina expected of him, he had better come back to Milwaukee while he had the chance. She would not couch it as an ultimatum, of course. Knowing Rico, she knew that would just make it worse. He'd be too proud to come home.

But come what may, Allison intended "Dádi Honored" to make a splash far beyond the borders of the State of Milwaukee. She realized that it would take some deft maneuvering to get the project past some of the people sitting on the state's Art Commission. The governor had stacked the Commission with people who shared his views on the place of the arts in people's lives. It came down essentially to what he liked to call his "theory of kitsch and cathexis."

It was the governor's belief that abstract art had tried to take the emotional meaning out of art. It had "decathected" art. That was why abstract art turned sterile so quickly and soon found no place to go. It had knocked the symbolic meaning out of things and had made war on pathos and joy. It had joined science and technology in trying to deprive man of the right to celebrate the mystery of living forms. It helped rid the heavens of angels and left the so-called civilized world crawling with preening, rationalistic pagans. So that when the reaction against it came in the last couple of decades of the twentieth century, the art establishment had become a nihilistic parody of itself. If "Dádi Honored" was ever to get by state review it would either have to be built on private land, which defeated the whole idea of making Minter immortal, sitting, forever proud, at the wheel of a Shikel convertible, or it would have to meet the Commission's criteria for sculpture in a public place. It would have to draw people in emotionally. It would have to do to the populace what a bronzed baby shoe of a grandson does to a grandmother.

Allison hoped to use Angina to get past the Commission. It should not be difficult, he had assured Allison during one of their long phone conversations before he came out to her party. The governor could turn out to be the problem, with his hangup on kitsch and cathexis, "but just give me a half hour with that character," Angina had said. "After all, the whole point of my wrapped tragedies is to put feeling back into art. I'm recathecting disaster, for God's sake. Surely that old fart will be smart enough to see that. I'm packaging tragedy in a way that anyone can understand. I am making tragedy something very American." Angina now realized he had underestimated the governor.

The party at Allison's did not break up until almost dawn, though some guests, like Pooch Grenada and Sara, left just after the governor left. Pooch was a fan of the governor but found many of Allison's other guests silly and shallow. "Useless lives," he said to Sara several times. "These people lead useless lives, needless too, for that matter."

Allison did not retire until she had breakfast with Angina, her special houseguest, and Jensen, still careening about the party grounds, kissing whatever ass seemed to offer itself. He had gotten in some solid plugs for his "Begin Again Party," and, in point of fact, had managed to get several friends of Allison's who had money to promise to provide some support. "Anything, if need be, to get rid of that fat little bore in the Statehouse," one of them had told him over the sixth or seventh drink. And there were also several promises to have Jensen to their homes "for cocktails and a light snack," as it was put, "within the next ten days." Jensen, it turned out, had made some hay. The rich bitch that had fallen into the pool with him was a lonely unattractive creature who loved meanness and intrigue. Scheming came naturally to her. It was a way for her to forget what she looked like, a moment's respite from blaming the Creator for doing to her what He had. "I'll help you get wired in with the right people," she had assured Jensen.

ARTIFICIAL INTELLIGENCE

THE PARTY AT Allison Minter's was one event of many that would make that particular week noticeably different from others in Milwaukee. For one thing, at eight o'clock in the evening two days after the party the governor went on radio with a special address to the citizenry.

There had been newsbreak specials on television all afternoon. They concerned the "Begin again" message. The news community was buzzing with excitement, and newsmen were interviewing each other, as was the custom whenever important hard news was on the line. Also, government officials were making long comments that were eloquently empty. Science fiction writers, gurus to whom the whole world had been turning since the message from ME33 first came in, were being interviewed by the score, some with a copy of their latest book held in front of them without a trace of remorse. Even scientists were being asked to comment. They all insisted, of course, that more research needed to be done before anyone should think anything further about anything. The clergy was also being asked its opinion. Another layer of obfuscation and dissembling was being troweled across public opinion.

No one really knew what to do with the news. The gist of it was that the IRS computer programmer who had fed Dostoevsky's *Notes From the Underground* into the big computer that processed data from Arecibo's radio telescope in Puerto Rico had now confessed. When he had set all the mischief in motion originally, he told reporters, he had intended to sit back and watch the fun. He wanted to see what a computer with a high level of "AI," artificial intelligence, could do with one of the truly profound insights of a great writer into human nature. The insight was that humans often hug their weakness of spirit to themselves with a passion that amounts to a terrible perversion. What is more, when they realize what they are doing, when they gain insight into this curious love of their own shortcomings, they try to turn the anguish of the insight into masochistic pleasure. They give their spiritual suffering form, they manipulate it, model it, as if it were some strange muck to be shaped on the potter's wheel of their will. Their spirit begins to enjoy the shape of the outlandish thing that emerges. But there is a price. The energy that drives the wheel comes from the heart. In time the heart begins to shrivel and is no longer capable of love.

Now this was a complicated idea for even a machine of exceptional intelligence to deal with. The computer at Kansas City got some of Dostoevsky right, but not all of it. It got just enough of it right to blurt out its fake message from ME33 and to enjoy the perversity of its deceit without a second thought about the consequences.

When the "Begin again" signal came in, the programmer knew immediately what was up. At first he thought the whole thing hysterically funny, and each night as he watched the news he would giggle at the foolishness the message had triggered. But when he watched cults spring-

219

ing up around the world, some beginning to add bizarre satanist elements to their rites, he began to grow unsettled. What really triggered the confession was when his mother, a lifelong Roman Catholic who spent most of her waking hours on her knees saying the rosary in the hope that her no-good husband would mend his ways, flew off to Boston to participate in the "Begin again" rites on Bunker Hill, claiming that "Begin again" was an extension of the great truths of Vatican II. He finally broke when he saw his mother participating in rituals that imitated those of the Pei pyramid, with a great, paint-drenched beachball being hurled down Bunker Hill toward the sea. So when he appeared on television, he beat his chest like any over-enterprising young high-school computer hacker caught trying to start World War III by tinkering with the world-wide computer network.

But few people believed the confession of the IRS wunderkind. Newsmen smelled a Washington plot to cover up real problems that were worsening by the day. There had been runs on banks both in foreign countries and in America. There was talk in Congress of the need for immediate issuance of a new series of bonds, "Begin Again Bonds." Because of "Begin again" millenarian talk, foreign countries were beginning to welch on loans, in the expectation of an imminent bailout by helpful little green creatures from outer space who presumably knew more about balance-of-payment economics than they did.

"Begin again" cultists were the most outraged of all over the IRS programmer's purported confession. They called the young man a lying little rat who was intent on getting even because his promotion to head IRS in Washington was delayed until he at least had to shave.

Revolutionists were also incensed. They said the confession was designed to rob them of their lead line in the *Manifesto for Twenty-First Century Humankind*. The revolutionaries moving about among the festering hordes of miserable people penned up on the south side of the Rio

Grande Wall called the confession a transparent attempt by the Colossus of the North to continue doing what it had been doing for a hundred years, thriving in the midst of their misery. Several warned that as soon as they got into the United States, by whatever means, they would go to Kansas City and kill the lying bastard from IRS with a machete, on sight. Others said that the skinny, whey faced, runty-looking condition of the miserable little weasel from Kansas City was further proof that what America needed most was a hefty infusion of macho values. And many in America agreed. Tearing up the environment with bulldozers while you cursed a blue streak was macho, so was building a skyscraper with two hundred and fifty floors that couldn't be ventilated. Sitting at the grandstands at the Superbowl game and yelling yourself hoarse while grown men dressed in strange plastic exoskeletons tried to batter each other into unconsciousness was macho too. But not the real macho. Real macho was screwing at least five hundred different women other than your wife, sinking it to the hilt into some female whom you would never see again, so that every woman in sight stayed pregnant. *That* was real macho.

Though the whole "Begin again" business now seemed to sadden the governor, and even though he had not foreseen just how lunatic it might become and just how clearly it would represent everything the Fritzland Movement found absurd and contemptible, he thought it suited his political cause to a T. He did not hesitate to say so on his newscast.

"Citizens," said the governor, "You have all heard the news. The message that was supposed to have come from outer space came, indeed, from the inner space of the human heart. It reminds us that the solution to our problems lies within us, not in fancy machines outside us. The machines simply amplify what we are. If we are vain, they make our vanity more dangerous. If we are shallow, they make our shallowness more frightening. If we delude our-

221

selves, they make the delusions more lethal. Our new state flag says it all: 'There are limits!' The person who does not realize this in his soul is, frankly, a fool."

The governor's voice was grimmer than usual. There was no joy in it, no sound of the wise and understanding old man who had seen it all and to whom getting even made no more sense than getting mad. "Let me tell you a story," he continued, "or rather, if you will permit, share a little philosophic insight. There was once a famous thinker by the name of Pascal. He was a genius mathematician, among other things, back in the sixteen hundreds. Much of his wisdom was collected into a little book that we might call *Reflections*. He asked a question in that little book that I remember from my college days eighty-five years ago. He asked, 'How is it possible for the human race's supposed reason to recognize our blunders and evil doings?' The problem is this: If reason has difficulty accepting its own limits, how can it be used to tell us when we must put limits on what we do? Pascal's answer was that you cannot count on reason. It is flawed, he said, by a basic incompleteness, a permanent, built-in incompleteness. If such incompleteness was not built-in, it would be logical for us to aspire to know everything. We could exchange places with God, or at least ask Him to move over and share the throne with us.

"But how well Pascal put the problem, my friends. He said, 'Reason, far from finding its own limits by her own means, is averse to accepting them when those limits are presented to her.' And that is what this "Begin again" binge shows us once again. Our vanity has allowed our reason to paint itself into a corner. And vanity cannot tell us how we have let this happen, because if it did it would not be the perverse thing it is.

"We have problems in our state. We all know that. Some of you still insist our income tax should not discourage large families, as it does. Some of you, only a few I hope, do not like your governor. Some of you do not trust the nation's currency and try to hoard gold. Well, as any housewife in the state can tell you, you can stuff only so many peas into a Mason jar. You can only put so many apples into an apple barrel. And as you know, there is very little gold in this state, other than its butter and beer and ripening grain. So do not lie to yourself simply to make life seem easier. In the long run it will be much harder.

"But I must turn to another matter more significant than any of these." His voice grew very serious. It was laced with an angry tone that had not been heard before. "It is a matter of grave concern to me. There has recently been a rash of forgeries of my invitations to live in, or take extended recreation in, our state. I do not need to tell you how serious this can become. If our borders are penetrated with impunity by people who do not share our Fritzland values, if as a result we become an Illinois or California, we will surely find ourselves in the same condition they are in. That means twice as many people as there are jobs, breadlines on every corner, farmland that can feed but a few of us. We could become another Florida. That land was once lush with fruit trees and crops of every kind. Now it is a pathetic land covered with rundown trailer parks and unpainted condominiums abandoned by the rich.

"Some of you will recall, those of you who are older, how members of the so-called 'no growth' movement of the last century were treated. All were ridiculed. In the nineties, some were imprisoned. Well, I say now, let the critics of 'no growth' go to Florida!

"I have made a simple decision," the governor continued, his voice softer now, less angry. "Under the powers vested in this office I am extending the provisions of the Tar-Feather Emergency Act beyond the crimes of child-abuse or abuse of the aged. I am asking the legislature to ratify my executive action of today so that the Act covers forgeries of the governor's signatures on invitations into our beloved state. These provisions will be in place for thirty days as an executive order. If a simple majority of the legislature in combined session does not vote against the order within that time it will become law."

The troubled sound in the governor's voice did not ease as he gave, almost mechanically, his trademark sign-off: "Sleep snug tonight, citizens, with those you love, limited though their reason may be." The comment was tinged with sadness.

A part of the governor's sadness was purposeful. In a sense, an act. His aides, who had been with him over the years, realized this. It was as indispensible an element in public leadership in 2013 as it had been in the time of Cicero. The important thing, he had often said to his intimates, was to know when the curtain was up and when it was down, and when you were onstage and when you were not. When the difference was no longer noticeable to the politician, he and everyone around him, including his people, were in great danger.

The governor had no intention of actually using the Tar-Feather Act on forgers of his invitations. He suspected, in fact, that the whole idea of the invitations was probably illegal and would not make it through a Supreme Court test. But the invitations had substantively rid the state of abusers of children and the aged. It would also be political suicide for some state politician or pressure group to come out for rescinding the policy of invitations.

So after his speech on tarring and feathering forgers of his signature, the governor turned to one of his trusted aides and said, "The least we can do is throw a damn good scare into them. I hope I did."

Most people in the State of Milwaukee did not care much, one way or the other, about the "Begin again" confession. *They* had considered it mostly nonsense from the beginning. And few worried about the tarring and feathering action. Citizens of the state prized their invitations to live in the state and they displayed them proudly on the wall in their living rooms or dens at the time of secession from Wisconsin.

But Allison Minter was worried. She knew the governor was a cagy old coot. He would wait until someone panicked, until someone tried to cop a plea or until someone ratted on someone else. She was not the only one involved with forgeries, to be sure. But she was probably the only one from a really influential family in the state, certainly the only daughter of the biggest tycoon still left there. And she also knew that the governor was the kind of man who would not make an exception to a law he considered just. Sauce for the goose was sauce for the gander ... with him it had always been that way. That was why so few fat cats had stayed in the state after secession. If they got caught, white-collar or not, they went into the jails along with the more traditional pimps and prostitutes. In fact, she knew that if she was caught he would probably have to make an example of her just to prove that his relationship with her father was not as cozy as critics implied. The newspapers had been implying just such a cozy relationship for years, but they could never come up with any evidence. The fact was that the governor put up with the Shikel Automobile elite because he needed someone smart enough to make a good solid car that would last a long time. Minter could. There was nothing more to it than that. That was the reason, too, why the governor agreed to stop by to say hello at Allison's party.

But there was also the governor's suspicions of the way the Minters treated the lieutenant governor. Jenson was an untrustworthy bastard as far as the governor was concerned. He had always viewed Jensen's election as just short of an outrage. But it was understandable, perhaps, considering all of the campaign money that Jensen had managed to get hold of. And Jensen had always had enough sense not to come out in any overt way against Fritzland principles. He was no dummy; repugnant, yes; a slippery eel of a man, yes; but not a dummy. Nonetheless it was no accident as far as the governor was concerned that Gerald Angina, a man whose artistic values were about as contemptible as Jensen's political motives, would show up at the same party he had agreed to honor that evening with a brief visit to the Minter mansion.

All of which made it especially significant that Allison Minter was arrested by state police on the beautiful Sunday morning a week after the Saturday night party. The sun was well up in the sky and a cool breeze was moving in from the northeast as usual. The Minter estate on South River Road looked more impressive than ever, with Mr. Minter giving orders to several of the groundskeepers who had just returned from services at the small Pentecostal church several miles to the south. He was in his riding breeches, getting ready for his ride before breakfast. The groundskeepers had doffed their hats and were giving him their best "Yes sir, no sir, we'll get to it bright and early tomorrow" treatment.

Minter was a perfectionist and he was annoyed that several of his evergreens near the entrance drive had died. He wanted the dead trees out of there soon, and no excuses. "With our weather the way it is, I've told you men to be on the watch for this sort of thing. When the candles on the pine don't fill out in the spring you know the tree is having problems."

"Yes sir, no sir. We'll keep a weather eye on the others." The groundskeepers were used to it. As soon as Minter had gone on long enough, he would grumble something about help not being what it used to be and move to the stables where his horse would be waiting. He liked to ride alone.

The state police car pulled up the drive quietly and two officers got out, both pictures of immaculate grooming and decorum. Minter, of course, assumed that they were hand-delivering some message from the Statehouse or perhaps the Shikel plant. He had standing orders that he was to be given any such urgent message, day or night, Sunday or holidays.

"Is Miss Allison Minter here?" one of the police asked politely as he walked slowly toward Mr. Minter. The two groundskeepers had finally been dismissed, Minter's lecture on evergreens complete.

"She should be sitting on the terrace around to your left," said Minter. "Finishing her breakfast, or reading, or perhaps just dozing. Got in late." He frowned. "Can I take the message to her?"

"I would prefer that I spoke to her personally," said the policeman, standing more or less at attention, his hand on the top of his bronze-toned billy club, rubbing the nob of it slowly.

"Suit yourself, Sergeant. She's right around the corner. Me, I'm late for my ride." Minter saluted the officer with his quirt and headed toward the stables. He did not think the situation in any way serious. His daughter had often been involved in this or that minor scrape. And she had periodically helped raise money for the ballet and the repertory theatre, as well as police and firefighter causes.

The officer snapped to attention. "Thank you, sir," he said. The other policeman responded to the sergeant's prearranged signal, a nod, and got out of the car. The two went around the side of the mansion and walked along the long flagstone walk toward the terrace area.

"Where's Minter's old lady?" one officer asked the other.

"God only knows. She's a kind of weird one."

"Nuts?"

"No. I been out here two or three times, for other things, running a message from the Gov to Minter, this or that about the plant or some damn thing. His wife stays out of sight usually. Drags around in these expensive housecoats."

"So does my wife when I let her. But they aren't expensive." The other officer laughed.

"No, this Kay Minter is something else. The Gov's receptionist told me. Came from a lot of money. A real pair of jerks for parents, separated a half-dozen times before they divorced. This Kay grew up with a screw loose."

"Now she's passin' it on to Allison."

"Tough on kids, this sort of thing. All money, no love."

"Movie-star sort of thing."

The policemen had it right.

Kay Minter was seldom seen outside her home, in fact seldom seen outside her bedroom. She had devoted her life to two things, her husband and bridge. Since Minter was a hard driving, self-reliant type, he soon learned to be hard driving and self-reliant without Kay. Kay had been well-educated and came from a good family, "good family" meaning a family with an impressive portfolio of investments off which children, and their children's children often unto the seventh generation, could live carefree lives, usually as Republicans, and usually suspicious of Jews and blacks and convinced deep within their unconsciousness of their inborn superiority.

Unless, of course, they were deprived of love. Then they become wounded animals that sought comfort in anything that would make their life seem more secure. Kay had overcome her misfortune of unlimited opportunity without a compass by learning to play games. She was a checker-playing fanatic during college. She switched to Scrabble while she was carrying baby Allison. As soon as the baby was born and turned over to a bottle, she turned to bridge. She soon found that there were few things in life one could not live without if one had a well appointed bedroom in a very big house, a maid, an occasional affair—with a man, not the maid—a rack of expensive housecoats that allowed her to go through life half-dressed, savoring existence as a kind of invalid, a deck of really fine bridge cards and three female friends who had allowed themselves to be similarly decephalized by rich arrogant husbands.

Kay's daughter, Allison, was dozing in her lawn chair

in white culottes and white blouse. She was barefoot. A breakfast tray was on the small patio table next to her, sliced melon on a bed of ice, a bowl of strawberries, a pitcher of cream, a small silver coffeepot and coffee cup and saucer. She had scarcely touched any of it. One slice of melon had been cut.

"Miss Allison Minter?" the officer said.

"Yes?"

"You are under arrest, Miss Minter. Violation of Public Law 466LR concerning forgery of the governor's signature on invitations to the State of Milwaukee."

"I'm *what?*" Allison demanded.

The policeman, his alpine fur cap in his hand, its white feather carefully protected as he held it, repeated what he had said.

"Don't be ridiculous," said Allison, flushing.

She knew they were not being ridiculous. She had feared something like this ever since the night of the party, in fact more so since the governor's speech about forgeries, which she had not heard but had read. She had also heard that one of the clerks in the Statehouse office who handled invitations had been picked up, or was being questioned by police.

"Sorry, Miss," said the officer. "There has been no mistake. You will have to come with us. We are placing you under arrest." She was read her rights.

Shaken, she nonetheless kept her composure and asked if she could change "into something more comfortable, for jailhouse purposes," and was told she could. She changed clothes without letting on to anyone else in the house that she had been arrested. She left a message for her father, "Dádi! Get me out of this *silly* situation. I've been arrested. This is such *silly* business. You must call the governor right away. Talk some sense into that foolish little man!" She left the message in a sealed envelope with the head housekeeper.

"Do you mind if I drive myself to your ridiculous jail in

my own car? My *old* Mercedes. Your Shikel is such a box!"
she said as she came outside to rejoin the police. She was
trying desperately to remain very nonchalant about the
whole thing, playing to the officers, as if her arrest were
a preposterous joke. "Do I look like a criminal? Really, this
whole thing is such a damn bother. I have guests coming
over later today. Are you *sure* this won't take much time?"

The officer said, "Sorry, Miss. You will have to join us
in our police automobile. It's a rule. We are only doing our
duty."

Allison shrugged, climbed into the Shikel, *Dádi's* damn
car, and sat sullenly in the corner of the rear seat as the
doors were locked. "Well, let's get this nonsense over
quickly!" she snapped at the sergeant through the steel
grid that fenced off the police from their prey. Then she
slumped into the corner of the rear seat, pouting. "Someone will be sorry for this shit," she said under her breath.
"Really sorry."

But the whole incident had unfolded as Allison knew it
would. She was tossed into the slammer with no more or
no less ado than any other forger might have been. And
then she was allowed one phone call. She called her father,
of course, and he called everybody he thought could get
Allison out of jail, and quietly. But the governor was va-
cationing, tenting out, in the hill country near Holy Hill
monastery. It was October and the weather was superb.

Minter's other friends tried to get through to the chief
of police. One of them did. The chief, a hard-line Fritzlander, told him politely to drop dead. Then Dádi, off again
on a plane trip, called Clement Jensen and asked him to
go to the jail with Dádi's favorite lawyer to try to spring
Allison. Dádi was halfhearted about the whole thing. A
night in the cooler might help Allison settle down. Lately
she had been having one half-drunk temper tantrum after
another because Rico Far had not answered her letters or
her cables to Paris. Allison had also tried to get Pooch to

intercede with Rico, unaware that Pooch thought Rico had finally come to his senses.

Kay Minter did not take much notice of what had happened to her daughter. Someone in her bridge club had called her to tell her she had heard Allison was in trouble. Kay had difficulty focusing on Allison's problems. She had just found a new book on bridge at the bookstore in Whitefish Bay. "Tell the lawyers to get the poor child out of that dreadful place, for heaven's sake!" she told her maid to tell the butler to tell the family lawyer.

Allison was hopping mad when Jensen and the lawyer finally showed up. There would have to be some questioning before they could get her out of the jug, they said.

"Do you realize they say they could tar and feather me for this stupid nonsense?" Allison shouted at her lawyer.

"I am afraid a conviction *could* mean that," said the lawyer nervously. He knew that Allison was involved, through Cherryman. Jensen had told him as much.

"If they do that to me, *Mister* Cordiner," she said—her lawyer's name being Alexander Cordiner III—"I shall surely die. My skin simply couldn't take it. Blonde people have more sensitive skin than dark-skinned people. You *know* they do. And just think, they'll smear that foul black stuff on me and I'll look like...well...I'll look like one of our cleaning maids. And then they dump a bucket of chicken feathers on me. The jailer told me that when I asked him." She fixed Cordiner with her eyes. "Now you get me the goddamn hell out of here now!"

Jensen knew it would all wait on her being questioned. That could take hours. He tried to be helpful. "Dear sweet Allison," he said, "you have to remember that they don't tar and feather people like they used to in the old West. It's just meant to put a person down, sort of, to make them feel blue...So they spray people with a pore sealer first, so the tar isn't toxic...they—"

Glaring at him, Allison shouted. "You stupid greasy fool.

How can you? Make me feel *blue!* Very damn funny!"
Allison threw herself into the wooden chair in the corner
of the cell. She took off a shoe and threw it at Jensen.

He ducked and smiled sheepishly. He was trying to turn
"stupid, greasy fool" into a roundhouse compliment. But
it wasn't easy. His feelings were hurt.

The lawyer said, "Besides, you're not even convicted
yet, not even charged. The whole case could just fall apart."

"Like hell it will," said Allison. "They caught that jerk
that I worked with down in those awful basement offices
of the Statehouse. The little prick squealed, let it all out.
Even got quoted in the newspaper. He probably mentioned my name..." Allison was screaming again, furious.
She took off her other shoe and threw it violently against
the wall. "The little shit probably did it to get a lighter
sentence."

"The law does allow for tarring and feathering only half
the body, the upper part or the bottom part," the lawyer
said quietly. "Depends on the judge. If he's a good fellow
he may say it's okay to tar only half the criminal—"

"Really, Alex! Sometimes I wonder about you! Can you
imagine what I would look like tarred on the bottom only,
even if I settled for that." She sighed. Her shoulders
drooped. "At least it wouldn't mean getting my head
shaved, which is what I'd have to do if they were going
to tar the top of me." She began to weep again, quietly.
"This governor says he's a *friend* of my father. You know
what his wretched chief administrator said? That jerk
Phalen? When Dádi asked him to see that this whole thing
was dropped and even offered to do another bridge all in
marble and put statues up and everything? he said, 'This
might be a blessing in disguise Mr. Minter. It will help get
your daughter down to earth.' That creep! You know damn
well what he meant. He meant all those feathers! Get me
'back down to earth!'"

"The governor is a kind man," said the lawyer. "As soon

232

as we are able to reach him, this whole thing will be cleared up and quickly."

"He's a fat little radical. He wants the whole world to be like this stupid little state." She erupted in tears again.

The lawyer put his hand on her shoulder, patting her, comforting her.

"You make me sick!" she said, shaking free.

Allison's tirade continued. "Dádi is going to tell that fat little man that the whole damn Shikel factory is going to be moved out of this state. Go ahead and tar and feather Minter's daughter. They'll be back to horses and buggies in a month."

The lawyer said, "Allison, that is not a smart move. And I will tell your father that it isn't. Monkopf, the governor I mean, would like nothing better. He admires those Mennonites who live over west of Madison. He would probably have them over here setting up buggy factories like that!" He snapped his fingers.

"Well, let them. That miserable little man once told my father that if he didn't like it here he could move to Ohio or Pennsylvania. He really did. He threatened Dádi. He said we could all move to some dumb place like... like Pennsylvania. That's the kind of man he is. Our governor is a tyrant, and a radical one too. I *hate* him." The tears resumed. "He let me down and he let Dádi down, the little *jerk.*"

But the questioning by the district attorney's people lasted only twenty minutes, questions about Cherryman and Angina. There were a few questions about Wilhelm Steinberger. Then Allison was released. Jensen, ever the toady, insisted on driving Allison home in his Shikel. As he let her out of the car he said, "Now don't worry, Allison. These things happen. Mistakes do happen, you know. To err is human."

"Bullshit, Clement," she said. "An error like this is inhuman, and you know it. And if you ever want to be governor of this state, you better do something about it. If you don't, Clement Bradley Jensen, your ass will be sucking pond water!"

Jensen tried to laugh, tried to pretend that he knew she was just kidding. But, of course, she was not. In the mood she was in, Allison was the very thing Jensen feared most. She was not without resources.

INTERREGNUM

SIX WEEKS AFTER Allison was arrested and questioned, Rico Far received an airmail special-delivery letter from Pooch Grenada. Rico had had an uneventful day following Delacroix's footsteps. He had mopped most of the second floor of the museum and was tired. He went to the fast-food restaurant down the street, Billy's, for a quick cheese-burger with fried onions, a smear of mustard, no ketchup, and a glass of wine—six weeks old—on the side. When he got home he found the letter on the floor just inside his door. He recognized Pooch's handwriting. He tore the letter open eagerly. It read:

My dear friend Rico:

    This is one of the saddest letters I will ever have to write. A week ago the governor of our state died. It was very sudden. He had not been ill. In fact, he was in wonderful shape, round as a pumpkin and as cheery. He had just delivered a radio address. A great share of it was broadcast nationally, the governor has become such a unique figure in politics. He began as usual by having a little fun, quoting from *Small is Beautiful*. He said, "Remember, dear friends, as Fritz said, 'All predictions are unreliable, particularly those about the future!'"

His talk was the second in recent weeks. Some time back he addressed the people of the state concerning that fool in Kansas City who confessed to the "Begin again" hoax. I am sure the Paris newspapers were full of that whole thing. But at the time the Governor took the citizens of the state through a little exercise in moral reasoning, using the philosopher Pascal to make his points. It was very impressive even though it made a lot of the scientific community mad as hell. He showed, Rico, why it is that we have so much trouble nowadays trying to solve all our problems with the kind of "reason" that the people in science and technology constantly prate about.

But his last talk was simply supposed to be about his plans for the next five years, through the next election. There was something different in his voice this time, as if he was trying to tell us all that he was thinking of retiring. He ended in the same way he usually does, with a friendly poke in the ribs. "Sleep tight, friends, with those you love and be kind to their good intentions." Then he leaned back in his chair and said to the people in the studio, "I guess that is about all I have to contribute to this wonderful state. Keep the blue and green flying." He took a deep breath and asked for his wife. (She was the third one, you know, and died two years ago.) He leaned back a little further in his chair and closed his eyes. That was all. He was gone. After a hundred and five years the old man just decided, as it is said, to round off his life with a sleep.

How the state has mourned him. All of the flags that fly over the capital city are at half-mast. Bells in the churches chimed off and on for three days. There were special readings by some of our famous actors, also some from outside the state, in the Theater District. The funeral procession ran all the way from Twenty-seventh Street to the lake, and crowds along the way were ten and twenty deep. Many were in tears. The honor guard looked elegant in their leathers. When the catafalque reached Cathedral Square there were eulogies and prayers in name of all the different faiths in the state, by Protestants, Catholic, Jews, Native American medicine men, even Hindu and Buddhist religious leaders. Then the casket was moved to the park above the lake, above the Art Museum, where it was buried overlooking our magnificent great blue lake of freshwater. The governor's will had asked for a simple pine coffin and a ceremony "of the kind we all like," which meant for Fritzlanders, at least, something that was warm, with little ritual.

Now that the governor is gone everyone is wondering what will happen. There will be an election in ninety days (a state law). But do you know, Rico, who is a leading contender? None other than the Lieutenant Governor Jensen. I consider him the very opposite of what we have had as a state chief executive. He is a loudmouth, a shameless flatterer, a sweaty bag of conspiracy and personal ambition. He knows nothing of Fritzland ideas and what he does know he misinterprets. When someone in Smudge's quoted Schumacher, saying, "Agriculture is primary, whereas industry is secondary," he said that this meant that agriculture was to be taught in the grade schools and industrial arts in high schools. He had contempt for Governor Monkopf. He takes to every new idea as if it is good simply because it is new, which means he loves fads and hates his own memory.

Another candidate is the state's chief administrator, Wendell Phalen. He is a good pencilpusher, and keeps it sharp, cutting costs. But he is not sharp upstairs, where it counts. Our beloved state is heading into troubled waters...

We lost a wonderful man, Rico, and Milwaukee may not be as beautiful as it always has been because of it.

I am glad to hear that you have been thinking of coming home. We all miss you very much. I suppose I shouldn't complicate your life, but Allison has not lost interest in you because you have not responded to her letters. I think, in fact, my friend, that she is more in love with you than she

237

ever was. She remains very beautiful. I saw her last week at one of Pester's readings. She was gorgeous, I have to admit.

Sara and I may be married next year. (This is something we have not told anyone but you!) Her father does not know. But he accepts me now more than he has in the past. He reads a great deal, something I did not know. And a lot of what he reads is very high quality "literature." I was very surprised but pleased to learn this. He and Sara are gradually getting over their problems.

Life is good here, Rico. How I wish you could join us tonight for a good German dinner at one of the famous old places here, like Ratzsch's, with roast duck, wild rice, red cabbage. Oh, of course, and the wine, a spatlese. (You will notice what has happened to me living here! I use words like "spatlese" without a second thought.) Sara and I have also discovered a wonderful restaurant out in the country run by a famous family of cooks. You should see the Shikels parked around that place on Saturday nights.

Until I hear from you, I send all the best. Sara and I think of you as our son, Rico. You had better get used to it. But it means we care for you and hope most deeply to see you soon.

> Sara and I send our love and hope
> you are home again soon,
> Pooch

The new acting chief executive Jensen was not one to dawdle with the reins of power. Once he was in the governor's chair, waiting for the election, he moved fast on first things first. He had the case against Allison Minter dropped. Then he had the state police inform Wilhelm Steinberger that a search was on for the location of the headquarters of the gold-hoarding club. Steinberger immediately passed the word to the membership of his club that they should lie low until after the election. As soon as Jensen was defeated they would be able to begin meeting again. In the meantime it was too dangerous.

238

The next thing Jensen did was to arrange to run Anselm Pester out of the state. Pester was a kind of running sore in Jensen's consciousness and when the poet began showing up around town with wrist knives on, and the story got around that it was his way of protecting himself from the lieutenant governor, the threat to Jensen became obvious. A smug editorial in the Milwaukee morning paper had fueled Jensen's determination to drive Pester out of the state. It alluded to the "curious animus" that "the man who now wears, for the time being, the mantle of power of the state's highest office has toward the city's most prominent poet." The editorial, effusive in its praise of the good life that the Fritzland Movement had brought to the state, went on to say that our "island of civilization will be in jeopardy if we must put up with a philistine helmsman."

Jensen's move on the Pester problem was simple and effective. He met with Cherryman on the sly—as acting governor he could no longer go directly to Smudge's and just sit around drinking in the hope that Cherryman would show up—and gave him instructions. Pester was to be set up. Cherryman was to wait until Pester left Smudge's on some household chore or other, to buy something for Mabel perhaps, anything that got him out of the place. He was then to pick the lock on Pester's door, let himself in and insert a half-dozen forged invitations to live in the state into the great bundle of papers that constituted *The Book of Ruling Equations*. He should do this some early Friday evening just before Pester was due to come on stage for his readings. It was important that the old poet did not discover the invitations before he came on stage. Jensen would have a plainclothes state police officer in the audience for the poetry reading. When the poet opened the great looseleaf folder that constituted *The Book of Ruling Equations*, the invitations would fall out onto the floor.

Everyone in the place knew what an invitation looked like. There would be gasps of surprise. The cop would move up to the stage, examine one or two of the invitations, slowly, carefully, so that all eyes would be on him at that point, and then make the arrest. It would be simple, clean, and there would be no further nonsense. Pester would have the choice. .,. get the hell out and stay out of town or stand trial. Convicted, the full weight of the law would come down on him, which was to say he would be tarred and feathered. Jensen expected Pester to plead guilty after the arrest and to jump at the chance to leave Milwaukee without incident. He would know he was set up, but he would also know that his wrist knives wouldn't do much good when it came to dealing with the new acting governor.

One of the other things that Jensen did when he took over was to double the security force in the Statehouse. Pester might be old but he could still pull a trigger.

Pester was made of sterner stuff than the new governor . had figured. He refused to allow himself to be run out of the state in the middle of the night under some phony cover story about his probable escape through the sewers. So the case went to court within three weeks and Pester was found guilty, plain and simple, said the judge. And he had warned Pester that any attempt to wear wrist knives into court would amount to contempt of court.

The curious thing was that Pester seemed almost to welcome the whole thing. He would deliver small, trenchant comments, some apparently from *The Book of Ruling Equations,* to reporters who talked to him while he was out on bond—Louie had posted the bond, $235—and now and then launch into some poetic flight, some of which sounded as if it were a fragment from his "Oh Putrescent Love." Then he would read from the long list of sins that he had cataloged over the years.

The trial was brief and decisive. Pester was found guilty and sentenced to be tarred and feathered head to toe. "Anselm Pester," the judge said somberly, "did, for wanton, premeditated reasons, with mischief in mind, realizing the full extent and implications of his deed, and understanding the dangers such acts pose to the security of the people of this state, forge invitations, to wit, six in number, to the State of Milwaukee."

Two days later, in the morning, Pester was taken to the public platform that had been erected at the east end of Wisconsin Avenue, just in front of the Mark DiSuvero minimalist sculpture that had been "adjusted" by order of the previous governor. The great I-beams of ocher-painted steel were now draped with rows of small bronze bells.

Pester stood on the platform in jockey shorts and socks. He was sprayed with a pore sealer, an aerosol-canned product called Dream Scheme Skin Creme. He had asked to have the wispy hair on his head shaved. His underarms were also shaved. The pubic area was not violated. Under the law tarring and feathering the genitals was defined as cruel and unusual punishment.

As the crowd gathered about the stands, most were sympathetic to Pester. There were yells of "Hang in there, Anselm baby!" and "Use a little kerosene, Anselm. You'll be fine in a day or two, but don't use gasoline. Too irritating to the skin," and "You're our poet, no matter what, Anselm. Remember that..."

There were also shouts from people whom Governor Jensen had salted through the audience. "...And don't come back into our state, you old piss ant!" and "Where are your wrist knives when you really need them, Pester?" Several people held up placards. "P is for poet! P is for pervert!" Jensen had obviously done some homework.

Then the small electric pump with its hose connected to a barrel of tar was started. The "executioner"—so called by the newspaper people trying to hype the story for all it was worth—began spraying a smooth, even layer of tar over Anselm. The executioner, an auto mechanic who specialized in auto underbody rustproofing processes, did his duty under the law. The whole effort went along smoothly and without incident and took no more than a few moments, including removal of masking tape from the eyes, ears, mouth and navel. Then a second man, a chicken farmer whose farms were located near Racine, and who considered himself a Fritzlander to the core and a patriot, and who therefore refused to take any money for his feathers, advanced toward the criminal with a bushel basket of feathers, all carefully clipped free of quills. With his left hand he tossed the fathers onto Pester, slowly, ritualistically, from head to toe.

Pester stood absolutely still. He was reciting a list of sins, alphabetically, from A through Z, slowly: adultery . . . burglary . . . collusion . . . envy . . . fornication . . . greed . . . etc. . . . . larceny . . . etc., all the way through pederasty, usury and the rest. But what was notable perhaps was that "plagiarism" was also included, right after pederasty and before prevarication.

"Don't forget the creep's feet," shouted someone just below the stand. Another Jensen plant?

The chicken farmer ignored the shout. "I ain't gonna do your feet, Mr. Poet," he said. "I'd rather cheat a little, even if cheating is on the list you been tickin' off."

Pester looked down at the man who was demanding that he remove his socks so that his feet could be tarred and feathered too. "I forgive you, friend," he said, "for you know all too well what you do." Which, later commentary said, was a solid point on Pester's side of the case, it being much more difficult to forgive a deliberate act than an unintentional one.

As he finished his feathering, the farmer turned to descend from the platform and paused briefly to smile for the television camera. He knew his family would be watching the TV tape on the ten o'clock news. A patriot deserved recognition.

Pester the felon was now indistinguishable from one of those baseball game mascotlike figures who had been run out of the state years before, when the Tar-Feather Emergency Act applied only to child-abusers and those who were cruel to the aged. He was then asked to walk up a plank into the back of a pick-up truck that had an inch or so of sand in its bed and to sit. The tailgate was raised and locked.

Pooch Grenada was standing next to the truck with Sara Steinberger. "Anselm," he shouted, "Sara and I will pick you up at the border, help clean you up."

"Thank you, Pooch," said Pester. "Please don't. I must do this."

The remark left Pooch and Sara baffled. They were convinced Pester had been set up. The whole thing stunk to high heavens, of more than tar and chicken feathers.

"I mean it, Pooch," said Pester. "I mean it, absolutely. The blue star has told me that this would happen."

Pooch looked at Sara. "He's gone crazy. The whole thing has been too much for him."

The pick-up truck was then driven slowly around the block, exposing Pester to another round of hoots and cheerios, then driven to the state border south of Racine and the felon was let off. He was given a can of Schumie's dark beer, to lessen any shock of dehydration, and told never to show up in Milwaukee again. Wisconsin and Illinois state police were there. They ignored the whole thing. They had real criminals to worry about.

Waiting at the border to pick up Pester was none other than Gerald Angina, driving a sleek silver convertible. He had spread the seat next to the driver's side with plastic so that his passenger would not make a mess of the brushed nylon upholstery. Pester was in a daze but he held his head high.

Angina was solicitous. To prove it he immediately set out a proposition that he knew would appeal to Pester.

"You're a tragic-looking figure. Right, Anselm my friend?" he said.

"Perhaps," answered Pester, as the convertible sped

along, the wind driving his feathers toward the rear so that he seemed to be flying.

"You are a wrapped tragedy, Anselm! Don't you see? You have pulled off a big one."

"Perhaps..."

As the car moved along the freeway past Waukegan, heading south at high speed, Angina said, "So here's my proposition. I will pay you *one thousand dollars*, that's right, one thousand cool ones, to join an exhibit I am putting together at this very moment at the Peacock galleries on Michigan Avenue. My show is called, as you might expect, 'Wrapped Tragedies.' I have models of the Mexico project in it, plus the wrapped wreckage of a station wagon that was in an accident on Eden's Expressway last month. A family of four died in that one. But I have *never* had the opportunity to display a *living* wrapped tragedy. You are it! If you're interested in a thousand dollars for five hours work."

Pester stared straight ahead. He was in the hands of a great artist, he knew that. And though he did not realize it at the time, an artist who had learned part of Delacroix's lesson all too well. Angina had learned to despise everything. Still, Anselm needed the money badly, if for no other purpose than to clean up. Cleaning up would take a lot of tar solvents, lotions, and a ton of Kleenex. And there would be the cost of renting a room where he could remove his "wrapping," as Angina called it. And he *would* become a celebrity, he knew that too. The cameras would be there, everyone who was anyone in art nowadays would be there.

"All you need to do, Anselm, is to sit in one of my plastic boxes, on a stool. The stool will be padded, so don't worry about that. You have to sit there for five hours. If you sleep, that's okay too, provided you don't fall off the damn stool." Angina laughed. "But it's a hell of a break for both of us. Living wrapped tragedy! And you will be photographed through the whole thing, through the tragedy

244

and triumph, so to speak. And if you fall asleep, we'll document that too. Wrapped tragedy asleep! Top that! It's a chance of a lifetime, Anselm. As a fellow artist, I am sure you know what I mean. In fact, Anselm, this whole situation lends itself to poetry as much as it does to my kind of visual art. You could do a reading while you are in the show. In the meantime you can sleep tonight on some plastic throw-cloths in my apartment.

The chance to read some of his own poetry during the Angina show was irresistible to the old poet. There would be a whole new audience, a whole new setting. Not some dinky little bar in Milwaukee, a real honest to God bigtime gallery, with camera men, people seeking autographs. A whole new mountain to climb.

The next evening Pester was in his plastic box in Angina's show. The box was about five feet square, with no top. It was the opening of the show that evening, so that the gallery was full of people fluttering, zipping and swishing about, most in high-fashion dress, eating cheese and grapes, oily smoked oysters and paté and crackers, sipping champagne from plastic glasses with hollow stems.

The "Living Wrapped Tragedy" was the hit of the show. Clusters of people orbited slowly around the plastic cage, nodding, speaking quietly to one another as they licked their fingers clean of cheese or paté. To Pester they looked like actors in a silent movie. Some gesticulated grandly as they pointed to Pester, others thrust their chins forward as they made their pithy observations concerning the direction the visual arts were taking in the twenty-first century, comments such as, "We *are* in a new age of limitations, most assuredly, but it actually provides the arts unlimited possibilities, don't you agree?" To which someone else added, "A whole new sense of the tragic. It's really quite contemptibly beautiful, don't you agree?" And then they drifted off in pairs, or in small intense groups of four or five. There were other works in the show to be seen, and the catalog to study.

Allison Minter showed up and walked straight for Pester's plastic box. She smiled, waved, then found herself unable to move. She looked at Pester, said slowly, her words but a pantomime to the man in the box, "H...e ...l...l...o...A...n...s...e...l...m." Then she began to weep.

Pester was saying something back but she could not make out what it was. He was insistent.

Angina hovered about. He was annoyed. "This is no time for this old fool to blow it!" he said to Allison. "Photographers are setting up." Angina moved close to the box, listened, then said "Shit!" and headed for the far end of the room. There he found a chair. He brought it back to the plastic box, stood on it so that he could look down onto Pester and they could hear one another. "For Christ's sake, Anselm. You act like you're the only one in this damn show. Now what in hell do you want?"

Anselm said, "Part of the bargain was that I could do a reading."

"Well, where in hell is your manuscript?" said Angina impatiently.

"In that bag over by the wall. The one I brought down from Milwaukee with me when they turned me loose. I have some of my real poetry in there, along with *Ruling Equations*. You promised, Gerald. You promised."

"Honest to God. A damned prima donna," said Angina. He added sarcastically, "Anything *else*, Mr. Pester?"

"Yes," said Pester. "I need water. I'm thirsty."

The manuscript and the water were brought. Pester took them gratefully and settled back in his chair. He began reading his poetry solemnly, with but an occasional gesture.

Angina prepared to begin circulating among his guests again. An art critic intercepted Angina. "Brilliant, Gerald, brilliant. The fact that he is tarred and feathered is brilliant. But what is pure genius is that you have him in that box

246

and we can't hear him reading. His own poetry, I understand. It's a stroke, Gerald, a real stroke. By *God*, it is. Reminds me of Morris's work back in the sixties, his 'Box With Sound of its Own Making.'" Angina looked puzzled. He could vaguely remember Robert Morris's work, from his days in art school.

"Surely you recall," said the critic. "Morris built a foot-square box and put a recorder inside that played back the carpentry sounds of its own making. The idea was to imprison the sound, as it were. Would you say your work here is derivative in some sense? I realize you've taken the whole thing further... but... "

Angina knew there was mileage in the question. "In a sense, yes. But I would think of this rather more as a tragedy with the sound of its own making." He added a small "hrrumph" sound.

"Love it, love it," said the critic, scribbling notes, then whirling away in search of others with something equally meaningful to say. But one thing was clear. This latest show would cement in place Angina's reputation as a major figure in American art, somebody to reckon with, someone from whom the world would hear a lot more soon.

When Allison Minter realized that Angina had, in fact, scored a major victory in the art world by wrapping poor old Pester, she returned to Milwaukee and went into seclusion. She even began asking her maid about the Sermon on the Mount.

It was one of those ironies of the time. Everything had begun to take on a life of its own. Now the "Begin again" thing was stronger than ever. People, some even in Milwaukee, without the steadying hand of its former governor, simply refused to believe that the confession of the IRS computer man was genuine, even though he repeated it for the press over and over again. And Angina's career had taken on its own momentum. He was getting more ink than ever and big commissions were flowing in. His stable of studio workers on Long Island had tripled in a matter of weeks.

Jensen's momentum as a candidate for the governorship was also in motion, moving along with enough power to prevent anyone from doing much about it other than to jump on the bandwagon.

Pooch and Sara were appalled at the prospect of Jensen becoming governor. And when Jensen had a news conference to inform the media that the state flag was to be restored to its "intended" appearance, that "THERE ARE LIMITS!" was to become "THERE ARE NO LIMITS," because the artist Frugal Jones's original design included the "NO," and because its appeal to limitlessness made it more American anyway, they knew that much more than a state flag was suddenly in danger.

Jensen announced the change with Jones present, to be sure that his flanks were covered. It was not a difficult thing for him to arrange. He slipped Frugal a thousand dollars, all in ten-dollar bills, in the executive offices earlier in the day. It was more than the young black artist had ever seen at one time. It undermined his conviction that there were, in fact, limits. Especially when Jensen suggested, "This may only be the start, Mr. Frugal. A commission for a major work of art is being considered, even now, in the executive offices of your state. One of our great industrialists is involved. It could really mean a great deal to a young artist looking for his first major commission."

But Frugal Jones was luckier than Rico Far. He did not have to travel to Paris to discover what integrity was all about. He simply asked his mother what she thought of the thousand dollars he came home with and how he got it. She told him it was wrong to take bribes and that he should give the money back and inform the press that he had been foolish and greedy. Which he did. But it was too late. Jensen took the money back with delight and told the media that young Frugal was acting... "Well, like artists do all the time. You know..." and he shrugged a shoulder. "I think he feels that he is due a large commission of some kind just because he designed the saying for our flag." The flag continued to read "THERE ARE NO LIMITS."

Rico Far's letter to Pooch, indicating that he was thinking of returning home, was about the only pleasant prospect on the horizon. Pooch's letter about the governor's death had saddened Rico. He wrote Pooch saying that while he had discovered that there was much beauty left in the world he was not as sure as he was in the past that he could do much about it, except to try to chase down the whole question of "integrity" in his own life.

Pooch's return letter, which began with the line, "I have seen cruelty, Rico, close up, face to face, and wearing the name of art," had gotten to him even more. Pooch described the tarring and feathering of Pester and what Allison had reported she had seen at the show in Chicago. The "tragedy with sound of its own making" seemed to Rico suddenly to describe what he had been reading in the French newspapers about Mexico itself. He was now determined to fly to Yucatán as soon as he scraped the money together and to get his mother out of Mexico and into the United States. Events along the Mexican border had, however, also taken on a new life of their own.

LIVES
OF
THEIR OWN

THE AMERICAN SECRETARY of the interior's helicopter banked in low above the refugee camp near Ojinaga, just across the Rio Grande, a half mile inside Mexico, in Sector 5 of the Rio Grande Wall. The camp looked empty. It was anything but. Inside its corrugated tin huts, its makeshift lean-to shacks of cardboard and canvas, its holes dug into the ground and covered with odds and ends of factory debris, used pallets and plastic packing cases, a quarter of a million people lay quietly, or sat quietly, on the sand. It was too hot to move, either for the healthy or the sick. And water was short again. The government tanker-trucks had not been around for two days and people were hoarding the little water they had kept stored in tin cans, wine bottles or crockery. Some of the truckers had the habit of selling the water for a few pesos a gallon instead of distributing it free as they had been ordered to do by their government.

Water that had been taken from the Rio Grande was available too, of course, but it was polluted. Camps upriver from the Ojinaga site, especially the big one near Ruidosa, used the river as a latrine and for washing clothes. Warnings were posted all along the river, telling people that the river water was dangerous, polluted with the typhoid bacillus and with a virulent new intestinal amoeba that attacked the lining of the lower bowel and caused severe ulceration and bleeding. Most people assumed the warning signs were the work of the freshwater mongers. Some were.

There would be no incident with the Mexican authorities. The secretary's tour of inspection had been cleared with Mexican officials before the Americans had left Washington. Mexico was as anxious for the bugs to be removed from the new border control facilities as were the Americans. There had been some very dangerous border incidents as the new laser-beam system was put into operation.

The old brick and concrete wall had been a bad joke, and the high-voltage electric fence that had been added to it, or laid alongside it in eastern border sectors, looked as bad on television as the wall itself. Nor was it effective. An illegal simply had to throw a piece of metal against it, such as part of the roof of his house, to blow a hole in it. A cluster of refugees would burst through and the usual story would follow on television that evening in the United States, pictures of sunken eyes, desperate women with children in their arms too sick to walk, an old man covered with sores, clothed in rags and dragging some pitiable remnant of his household belongings, perhaps a small mattress or a chair, behind him.

The laser system was not a complicated device. In fact, as scientists who built it boasted, it was elegant in its simplicity. And it had not been long in building. The idea of using a system of lethal laser beams instead of barbed wire or an electric fence was the product of the imagination of a young well-groomed scientist working at Oak Ridge, a

251

whistle-blower who found inefficiency in government an intolerable outrage. He had gone on television in Tennessee to say that the situation at the border was absurd, given the advances in laser-beam research over the last several decades. It was possible, he said, to establish a series of laser-beam stations, one every few miles, depending on the roughness of the terrain, the beams from one station overlapping the emission station of the next, like shingles on a roof, so that a military unit was necessary only to guard the anchoring beam station. A beam station would require only a small emission building, slotted on one end so that lasers could be shot out the slot, each six or eight inches above the other, up to a height of fifteen feet. The effect would be an impenetrable wall of laser signals emitted in random, half-second bursts. Power to drive the system could be taken from any electric power plant along the border, coal-fired or nuclear.

There would be attempts to tunnel under the laser wall, of course, but a seismic system would be installed to put a stop to it before it even started. The flaw in the system was that it was brutal. Despite warnings, despite patrolling squad cars along the border roads with large PA systems attached to their roofs, blurting out the severest kinds of warnings about the lethal quality of the wall, people continued to try to penetrate it. Horrifying news stories were the result. Newsmen seemed to relish going into graphic detail describing what the laser did to its victims. The lasers "do not kill in the same manner as a bullet. They bore a hole through the victim, about the size of a dime. The wounds are self-cauterizing, so there is little blood. But there is usually a good deal of steam and some acrid fumes. At times it is possible to look completely through the body of a victim, as if one were looking through a pipe that had been driven through the body."

A broadcaster in Mexico City referred to the wounds that the lasers were drilling through his countrymen as "this contemptible" form of "ventilation" of "vessels of the

Holy Ghost." And there had been pickets around the American embassy in Mexico City for days with placards referring to "gringo delight" in venting the Holy Ghost from Latin American citizenry.

So from a technical standpoint the laser beam wall had been a notable success. No one got past it. From the PR point of view it was disaster. And that accounted for the secretary of the interior himself being asked by the president of the United States to visit the wall to find out what could be done. He was told to take along whomever he wished, scientists, economists, PR people, anyone he needed. "But goddamn it, Bill, I want that problem solved and solved now!" thundered the chief executive in the oval office. "Those immigration and border control people are as useless as tits on a boar. So get down there and get this thing straightened out." Hence the secretary's party in the helicopter above Ojinaga.

"Take her down to about five hundred feet," said the secretary on his intercom to the helicopter pilot. "I want to see things in this sector close-up."

"This is one hell of a situation, Bill," said the undersecretary for border security problems. "This shantytown is forty miles long in this one spot alone. Up the way a bit there's one that's even bigger."

"Remember when all we had to quarrel with Mexico about was the sewage from Tijuana that moved up the coast and forced San Diego to close its beaches? How I wish we had nothing more than polluted beaches to worry about these days."

"It's pretty grim down there, Bill. I was down on the ground yesterday near the Big Bend laser facilities. Met Salvador Morales there for a quick lunch in his headquarters. Morales is all right. Got his feet on the ground. Doesn't spend all his time blasting Uncle Sam like so many others in the Mexican government. He knows there are just too damn many people to handle. And he's objective about those flooding up from below his border, from Honduras and Guatemala. He wants his government to put up the same kind of laser thing we have here."

"It's only a matter of time until every border has one of these systems. It'll coop up a lot of people, but they might as well starve to death in their own backyard as in their neighbor's."

"That's a pretty hard line," said the secretary. "For the love of God, don't talk like that to the newspapers."

"I'm used to catching hell on this one. Mention the fact that every day thousands of people die in these places and someone will call you a damned gloom and doomer."

"Well, you do lean that way you know, Tim. Don't you believe in the right to a short life?"

The secretary was serious. It was the kind of thing that drove the undersecretary up the wall. There was no reasoning with the man. "You know damn well what I mean. This fucking population thing."

"Well if there is such a 'thing,' fucking sure as hell did it," the secretary said, laughing.

"I don't think it's funny, Bill."

"Tim, I'm sure men like your friend Morales would be the first to say that unless they get a handle on birth rates, and fast, their goose is cooked." He added, "I guess I should say the Mexican eagle is cooked."

"Morales and I toured the shantytown for almost twenty miles. God, Bill, the smells would knock you down. And it makes you feel like it's all so damn hopeless. We sent a lot of grain down here, as you know. Gone in a few months. Never saw so many people living on a handful of corn or wheat and dirty water from that river."

"That 'gutter' is more like it, Tim."

"I know, I know. It's *bad*. Like drinking out of a sewer."

"Well, our grain surplus, as they used to call it, is down to a three-month supply. Even if it wasn't, how are you supposed to export it if there's no money on the other end to pay for it."

"Well, I wouldn't worry about that side of it. The ag

people say the shortage is temporary. New wheat strains are coming on line. You've got to be more of an optimist, Tim."

The word *optimist* was another word that was very big in the White House and around the departments the last few years. The President had ordered engraved desk plaques for every executive in the government above GS 14 grade. They said, "OPTIMISM SPOKEN HERE!" He had even taken to sending around little brochures cooked up by his PR people, such as "The Joys of Freefall Optimism," and "An Insomniac's Guide to Optimistic Thinking."

It had gotten under the undersecretary's skin. To the undersecretary, optimism and hope were different. As his minister liked to put it on Sunday, "Hope rests on faith, and therefore entitles the human heart to a permanent claim on a measure of fear and trembling." Optimism, on the other hand, usually meant wearing a lapel button, in bright blue or yellow, on one's pin stripe, and an eagerness to applaud an after-dinner speaker who peddled jovial banalities. So the undersecretary's response to all the desk-plaque optimism was to have a homily prepared in needlepoint and framed for his wall. It read, "A pinch of pessimism three times a day helps drain sap from the head."

The undersecretary turned as if to look across the cabin and out the other window. "Shit," he said to himself, "I have never met a man who called *himself* an optimist who did not have a lazy mind." His boss the secretary had one of the laziest minds in Washington. Over the years it had even made it impossible for his common sense to survive. When the undersecretary went looking for the secretary's common sense he could no longer find it. The lazy mind was there, but nothing else. "Well," he said to the secretary, "one way or the other we will have to face this thing."

"We'll face it, Tim, but as an economic development problem, an EDP, *not* as some dead end the pessimists can gloat over." The secretary had always been impatient with the undersecretary's growing sense of desperation over the "population thing." It was out of step with the president's outlook, and his speech before the Washington Press Club a month earlier was mainstream gloom and doom. He was getting very irritated with Tim.

"Hard to put an upbeat look on this thing, Bill, once you've been through one of those shantytowns, once you've watched them bury their kids in the sand."

"Tim, I'm under orders to find the positive side of this thing, and I damn well intend to. The president told me the day before yesterday that he wants a can-do attitude in the cabinet. He ran for office as a can-do optimist and he got elected as a can-do optimist. So that makes me a can-do optimist, if you get my drift."

The undersecretary stared through the window toward the ground. He had heard it all a thousand times. His lips tightened. He remembered the pamphlet that had come across his desk the week before from the can-do optimist in the oval office. It was titled, "Shrinking Your Doubts With Optimism." He grinned. Reminded him of a cure for piles, just the thing for the asshole he worked for.

"This could be a potential boost to our economy, bigger than anything we've ever seen, Tim. There are a lot of people down there who don't have a damn thing. That's an enormous market potential when you think about it."

"A lot of purchasing power, all right," said the undersecretary dryly. "Every time one of those poor creatures dies, we lose a customer."

"Don't be sarcastic, Tim," said the secretary. Then his lips pursed. He was thinking. "Tim, what if we put in some automated factories down there? Would that help? The president is high as hell on robotics."

"With that wife, I don't have to wonder why."

"You can knock off that kind of remark too. The First Lady is a charming woman. I mean an automated factory that is suited to the market down there. To produce sombreros, perhaps. What do you think?"

"I think it's a thought that deserves more thought," said the undersecretary, then mumbled, "The wretched refuse of your teeming shore... I lift my lamp beside the golden door..."

The secretary shrugged. He hadn't a clue what Tim was saying. "Well, let's get those folks from the aft cabin to tell us what they have in mind. Bring Jerry Angina and his pretty young aide up here." The Secretary was first attracted to Angina by the publicity attendant on his Chicago show. The man might be an artist, but he was a PR genius. He could be of use. "I want to hear their ideas on this whole thing. They've been over every inch of the border, Angina says. Spent months doing their homework I'm told."

"Weeks, not months, Bill. I'll go get them." The undersecretary left the private cabin of the secretary and went to the large aft cabin where Gerald Angina and his aide Anne Jells sat with four of the secretary's people around a conference table. Angina had spread his drawings for the border project out on the table.

Jells was a young woman, perhaps twenty-five years old, attractive, trim looking, with good bone structure. She wore her reddish-blonde hair in a short cut, with bangs that swept down across one side of her forehead. She was dressed in a white cotton jump suit, with a small red kerchief at the throat. A star performer in Angina's stable of interning artists, Jells often traveled with Angina when he worked on major commissions. Gossip had it, naturally, that they were lovers. But that was questionable. She was too smart and too ambitious to allow love to complicate her life. She did not really care if Angina was a genius, the "notorious fraud" that Bombastini said he was, or simply mad. Passion for success overrode any desire to discriminate. But one way or the other she intended to use

Angina, to squeeze what she could out of her association with him. Some day she would top him, even his idea of wrapping tragedy, brilliant as it was. So she stayed as close as possible to him while he was working on major projects. She studied details of the projects and could reel off statistics and cost figures on them with the smooth, monotone effeciency of a taxi dispatcher. On the Mexico project she had made herself indispensable.

"The secretary wants you and you to come up front," said the undersecretary, pointing to Angina and Jells.

The undersecretary considered Angina's ideas for making the laser facilities less of a public relations problem plain damn ludicrous and more cruel than ever. "Bring some of those drawings for this sector," he added. "He wants details." As the two of them got up to go forward, the undersecretary looked back to the secretary's stenographers and photographers and said, "They'll be back. So warm up your equipment."

Angina considered the border project the chance to produce the ultimate piece of art. Mexico was to become a giant "wrapped tragedy." Angina was going to wrap it in principle only, of course. "This is where I make my mark, Anne," he told Jells. "This is going to be one for the ages. If people think the Berlin Wall represents wrapped tragedy, wait until they see this project. Wrapped Mexico, for Christ's sake! Can anyone top that? I'll be damned if they can. This is big, I mean *big*."

"We have been having some very constructive bilateral talks with Mexican government people, Jerry," the secretary said, as he motioned Angina and Jells to seats opposite him around the small conference table in the center of the front cabin of the helicopter. "We think that they will go along with our laser system. Provided we can make the whole thing somewhat less obvious than it it now. The lasers work well enough, but the system hasn't helped our two countries get along better."

Angina and Jells took their seats. Angina could tell that

Jells was impressed. He leaned over to her and whispered. "You think this is flying high, Anne? Stick around." Then he was all business. He outlined quickly what he proposed. The secretary leaned forward to listen.

"I propose," Angina began, "to build a twenty-foot-high wall of beautiful, colored, softly textured vinyl on each side of the laser system, close to it, no more than fourteen inches from it. Vandals will try to cart off some of our art, you can be sure—"

"Until they learn not to screw around with American property backed by a laser," said the secretary, interrupting.

"Periodically the vinyl will be poached, here and there. But it's cheap and can be easily and quickly replaced," said the artist.

"And it will stretch... from sea to shining sea, as we say?" asked the secretary.

"From sea to shining sea," assured Angina. He continued to outline the project, systematically, coolly. "It will use aluminum struts and steel cable designed to accept winds up to one hundred and fifty-five miles an hour. No wind has ever blown in this area at anything more than about a hundred and ten miles an hour, hurricanes and such. Ours is a safety consideration. But it's a must if this is to be done properly."

"We understand," said the secretary. "Proceed."

Angina proceeded. "We propose to use blues, pinks and greens on the south fence, cool tones. These people get pretty hot down on that desert. On the north side, we propose to use sand and buff tones, with some red, so that the wall will blend with the desert, seem to become part of it. It will make the border seem a *natural* thing, thanks to the illusion. Our people don't need to be reminded constantly of the need for this wall." He paused, then said, "They're on a guilt trip as it is." Angina had added the last line to play to the secretary's PR instincts.

"Of course, of course," said the secretary. "I was briefed

in Washington on your special talent in that connection, as well as your success at Chicago."

"Thank you, Mr. Secretary. Our approach goes back to the Great Wall of China, perhaps Hadrian's wall. It is classic."

The secretary was having difficulty keeping up. Simple ideas, with an optimistic spin on the ball, were his thing. "Well, I suppose the function of our work here and the Great Wall's is similar," he said. "A need to keep barbarians out." He paused, grinned, suddenly uneasy. Being quoted suggesting that the Mexicans were barbarians and that Angina's wall would be a kind of high-tech Great Wall of China could set the president's bleeding ulcer off again. "Now don't any of you go leaking a quote from me using words like *barbarian*, for heaven's sake," he added quickly. "It's only a manner of speaking. Though for obvious reasons there may be certain parallels." The secretary rather liked the comparison of the Great Wall of China with the new wall on the Mexican border, now that he had thought of it.

Before the secretary could carry his historical insight further, Angina took over the conversation again. The vinyl wall was a symbol, he said, of the human tragedies contained by it. The starving masses on the south side of the wall were tragic; the grand and powerful nation to the north forced by circumstances to use the laser wall was tragic. It was a case, Angina said, of "bisymmetrical tragedy." He then launched into a description of the details of the project. He intended, he said, to keep a meticulous record of everything related to the erection of the vinyl wall, including the expected occasional incinerations of Mexicans still intent on getting through the wall, as well as complete video documentation of grieving Mexican families after an "incident." It would include sermons at the gravesides of laser-beam victims. It would be the first total synthesis of high technology and aesthetics. A small library would result. A copy of everything in the library could be given as a gift from the United States to the government of Mexico.

The secretary was a bit taken aback by the scope of the artist's plans. "All this filming, all this documentation and such..." He drew in a heavy breath. "Well, our budget doesn't really allow for such in-depth documentation. Oversight committees in congress would not sit still for it. Especially our bleeding hearts, some of whom have... have relatives down there on... the other side."

Angina quickly reassured the secretary that such costs could be met. His effort to document everything about the wall would be paid for by The American Foundation For New Freedom, a patriotic group based in Dallas. It had money to burn, a lot of it from old oil money still churning up profits after being invested in pharmaceuticals. The foundation would build the library to house the documentary materials at the University of Texas–El Paso, and the library would be called "The Mexican–American Peace and Freedom Through Understanding Library."

"Well, thank God you did your homework on this one, Jerry," said the secretary. He sighed, leaned back in his chair, visibly relieved. "Our Latin congressmen would raise holy hell. About the only solution to this border problem they have come up with is the recommendation that our state department print booklets on the rhythm method and drop them from the air on shantytowns along the wall. Well, then," added the secretary, "as we swing up the border toward El Paso, suppose you and your aide brief me on the details of the installation. Where we begin. Time lines. Everything. I'll have some critical-path analysts flown in if you think it will help. And, of course, computerize the whole thing."

Angina and Jells filled in as much detail as they could, occasionally asking the pilot of the helicopter to move in low above a particular spot so they could point out special construction considerations. They knew that once the secretary gave the go-ahead the project would move fast, perhaps fifty miles a day. Once the first few sections of the wall were up the rest might move even faster, up to seventy-five miles a day. There was no labor shortage at the border and illegals could be hired by the thousands, then deported. In its own way it was a made to order labor-intensive situation for the American construction planners providing backup to the Angina artists. And once up and functioning it was doubtful the laser beams would be shut down again.

Disregarding some hitches that developed when materials for the wall could not be delivered by plane and helicopter to the border sites on time, things moved well. Angina had established his headquarters in an old humanities building on the University of Texas–El Paso campus. Jells moved about the place, beautiful, efficient, going over inventories of new materials on order, checking computer printouts of lists of various grades of vinyl, color coding orders to be delivered to various sectors of the wall, going over topographical maps. Even when Angina came down with some kind of virus, one of the new "border bugs" that people working on the wall joked about, work proceeded at an impressive pace. The lasers would be shut down for a few hours in a given sector while the vinyl was being put up, then promptly switched on again. Daily progress reports were transmitted to the secretary of the interior precisely between three-fifteen and three-thirty each day. The secretary was delighted. He told the president that the only thing that could prevent them from finishing the wall between El Paso and the Gulf of Mexico a good week ahead of schedule was if Angina got over his virus. It was clear to him that "this young woman Jells has a future in our administration, even if she is an artist."

Things had turned bad in Yucatán. There was trouble around Uxmal in particular. Some Swiss tourists had been killed. The ancient Nunnery Quadrangle had apparently become the headquarters of a particularly vicious gang of

262

bandits. There were twelve of them. According to newsmen who had interviewed the gang leader, a big, hairy, villainous old scoundrel called Wild Man Serrano, the band operated between Merida in the northern part of the peninsula to Villa Hermosa hundreds of miles to the south. The band swept across the countryside on horses, hiding out in scrub country off the main roads. They would strike at night, at anything and anybody, small back-country grocery stores, isolated communities of squatters left over from the days when the Reforma oil fields were still operating, into the outskirts of the larger cities themselves, killing anyone they chose, often by chopping them into parts with their machetes, evidently trying to conserve ammunition for their rifles. There had been several attempts to destroy the gang with helicopter gunships from the Veracruz air-force station. But the military had its hands full in the rest of Mexico, especially on the Guatemalan and American borders. The gang was not brought to heel.

Wild Man had one trait that made him a particularly nasty customer, an excessive curiosity. He had been a seminarian in his youth and had retained an abiding interest in the notion of life after death. Even when he reached his fifties and was up to his knees in crime of every description—drug running, gun running, brothel operation and acting as a hit man for anyone who would pay him enough—he continued to be troubled by doubts about what went on beyond the grave. So by the time he became sixty-five or seventy and increasingly concerned about dying, he took to a mean habit. He would select some farmer at random from the area where the gang moved and shoot him. But before he shot his victim he would share tortillas with him and wring a promise from him to let Wild Man know what it was like in the land of the dead. When the old bandit did not get back news of a reliable kind and was forced to interpret events of no consequence, such as a horse going lame, as a message from his victim, he would go into an angry sulk, often for weeks, then become depressed. When the depression lifted in a month or two, he would pick another victim and start over. "I seek the truth. How can I know the truth if I am not persistent?" he would ask, as if his feelings had been hurt.

It was a quandary for a man of empirical bent, but lethal for his reluctant research collaborators.

As it turned out, when Rico eventually came back from Paris and reached Villa Rito, Wild Man was off on a raid to the area around Campeche and Rico was able to spirit his mother out of harm's way by traveling slowly southward, well east of the coast road. They then walked and rode what rattletrap buses still operated in the area to Highway 180 and headed north to Veracruz. Sometimes they moved on foot, sometimes on ox-drawn wagons, sometimes they hired the driver of an old jalopy to take them another ten or twenty miles.

Around Tampico conditions were still relatively normal. A large Mexican Red Cross unit was stationed there and was operating effectively with refugees moving up from the south. Rico and his mother spent a week there resting, working with the Red Cross as volunteers. Though Rico and his mother had very little money, compared to many of their desperate countrymen on the move it seemed like a good deal. It was in Tampico that Rico finally got a telephone call through to Milwaukee.

Pooch shouted into the phone, "Try the Eagle Pass border station first. We will be there. They may let you cross. Sara and I will be on the American side. We will try to convince them that we are your sponsors. Sara doesn't look Mexican and her English is from Milwaukee. It may make all the difference."

"No need to shout, Pooch. I hear you fine," Rico replied.

"Well, you must get your mother out as soon as you can. We will drive Sara's car down next week. It's not a Shikel but it still runs. There is a lot in the papers and on television about a new wall. Electronic, with laser beams.

It'll be impenetrable. You must get across before that is completed, unless they let you in because you are really an American citizen. Do you still have your passport?"

"Yes, but you know what good it was when we tried to use it eight months ago."

"I know, but you'll need something."

"We should be able to get to Eagle Pass in two weeks. I must let mother rest for a week at least. We had a very tough time coming up from Villa Rito. Bandits. We had to circle a long distance out of our way. And the buses . . . a lot of breakdowns. Bandits stop them too. But they did not rob us. I don't know why. The army is trying to stop them. But there are too many of the miserable bandits."

"If they do not let you through Eagle Pass go to the canyon. Find Chi Chi Tepic. That little coyote is still making a living, you can be sure of that. We will come down the road through the park, Highway 385, that same as we used before. We will have Sara's car, as I said. We will be staying at the Hotel Merriment in Eagle Pass."

"How is Sara?"

"Fine. Her father is sick. More angry than sick, I think. Because Jensen is trying to break up his club."

"What club?" Rico had never heard anything about Steinberger's club except a little gossip that he had dismissed.

"The gold-hoarding club . . . But Wilhelm got even with Jensen, but good."

"I know this call is costing me money, Pooch, but what the hell are you talking about?"

"When Wilhelm, Sara's father, found out that the governor, the acting governor, this Jensen sonofabitch, was cracking down on old people trying to hoard a little gold, he got mad as hell. He waited for the governor to hold one of his afternoon press conferences. Jensen is trying to come on like he was old Monkopf, a man of the people. Wilhelm showed up walking on his wooden leg. They let him up close to Jensen. Thought there was going to be some good television in it for them. A photo opportunity. Wilhelm hauled off and kicked the governor in the crotch with his wooden leg. That leg is made out of an oak table leg, remember?"

"Pooch, be serious—"

"I *am* serious. The governor went down. Curled up like a corkscrew. Wilhelm got him right in the nuts. Then he said that if the governor rolled over he would ram his wooden leg up his behind."

"*Pooch?*"

"Swear to God, kid. Sara's father was put in jail, but he is a hero around town now because he said he was defending the old people from a tyrant. He never liked the other governor either, but he *really* detests Jensen."

"I'll be damned," was all Rico could say.

"It's really cut into Jensen's chances to become governor. First the thing with Pester and now this with Wilhelm. Jensen was laid up for three days. A lot of jokes going around about the acting governor's 'true blue balls.'"

"Is Sara Okay?"

"She's fine. And her father is out of jail. Jensen was afraid to hold him, I guess. Now Sara's father is talking like a Fritzlander. He and I have something in common now, Rico. It sounds strange, but it's true. That's why we want you up here too. We're going to back this guy Phalen for governor, even if he isn't quick on his feet. But he's honest. That's what counts. You don't want competence unless it's hitched to honesty."

"Tell Sara I learned a lot in Europe and that I will never be able to repay her enough. But I will, Pooch, every cent and more."

"She is not worried about that. Allison still asks about you . . . If she knew we were going to the border she would insist on coming along. Would you like that?"

"No. She's still in my mind a lot, but I don't want to get in over my head again. Until we see you then, give my love to Sara."

"So long, Rico."
"Good-by, Pooch."

Rico and his mother, it turned out, could not get into the United States at the Eagle Pass border station. It was the old problem of forged passports and phony visas. They were being turned out in such volume on both sides of the borders that immigration officials had to change their coding procedures every few days, invalidating old passports and visas and forcing people to stand in line for hours to get new ones. As one might have expected the time spent waiting in line came to equal, give or take an hour, the time between code changes. Which meant that the whole process of passport and visa application became a gigantic, slowmotion bureaucratic ritual that exhausted applicants, drove officials half-mad and made functionaries above them feel as if they had finally invited a perpetual motion machine.

Chi Chi Tepic was a last-ditch hope. At La Cuesta, Rico was told that he was still going strong. But when he got to Boquillas he was told that Tepic was no longer about. He had been killed a month earlier, by machete, by angry clients who demanded their money back when one of the big concrete-mixer trucks had corked the tunnel Tepic and his company, then titled Tepic Transport Ltd., had dug under the old wall in the Big Bend Park area.

The portable seismic system the border patrol used tipped the scales against Tepic. They waited for him to lead a dozen illegals into the tunnel and then corked it. Five of the illegals were entombed. The remaining seven presented the small, printed "warranties" to Tepic while they were still in a state of shock. Tepic tried to joke his way out of the situation. He died with his corny joke about being named after a famous golfer still on his lips.

When Rico and his mother Margarita Far reached the spot where Pooch and Rico had crawled under the border almost a year earlier, the beautiful new vinyl screens of the laser system were already up. They went to the wall precisely at nine o'clock in the morning on the tenth of September, as they had arranged during Rico's call to Pooch at Eagle Pass. They found themselves standing opposite Pooch and Sara, unable to do anything but talk.

"Can you hear me, Rico?" Pooch shouted.

"Yes, but it seems strange talking through this plastic wall."

Pooch shouted, "It's beautiful to look at but lethal. For God's sake, don't try to get through it."

"I know, I won't. Everyone on this side knows it works, the lasers, I mean. This plastic is only fourteen inches from the beams. That's why the vinyl is stretched so tight. It's not just to make it look nice. They're afraid of an accident if the wind blows too hard."

There was a moment of silence. Other people were gathering about them.

"What shall we do?" Rico shouted.

Pooch didn't know. "Is your mother with you?"

"She's right here."

"Is she okay?"

"She's fine." Rico introduced his mother to Pooch and Sara and asked Margarita to greet Pooch and Sara in Spanish, which she did.

"We are worried about you both," said Pooch. "We will have to continue to try to get you into this country, but it will be very difficult."

"We may have to go back to Villa Rito. The government is trying to get everyone to go back to where they live. A lot of people don't know where that is. My mother wants to know if you and Sara are going to be married. She's heard a lot about the two of you from me."

Pooch looked at Sara. She nodded yes. "Yes," he shouted through the wall.

Rico translated the message to his mother. She responded in Spanish to Pooch, "I hope you have a large family, my dear friends."

268

Pooch replied, "We are not kids anymore."

"That should not matter if God wills it," shouted Margarita, as best she could, her voice reedy and weak sounding.

"Rico?" shouted Pooch.

"Yes?"

"Allison has taken a plane to Mexico City. I don't know how she found out you were back. She swore she was going to find you somehow and get you out. I warned her not to try, because of the way things are around Merida and Campeche. She refused to listen. She left the day we left. She said she would demand that the authorities allow you to leave. She said her father would make Shikels in Mexico if necessary."

Rico stared at his mother, then translated the message to his mother. She said, "The young lady will never reach our village. She does not know how to travel in Yucatán, not the way things are now. Not with wild dogs like Serrano loose."

"Couldn't you stop her?" shouted Rico.

"Of course we couldn't. You know that as well as we do. She is in love with you, Rico."

Margarita shouted at Pooch. "Mr. Grenada, things will be all right. God looks after this country, you know. He looks after all of us."

The sun was setting high in the sky and it was becoming very hot. "We are going to have to go, Pooch," said Rico. "Mother can't take this sun. And water is hard to get."

"So soon? Will you write?"

"Yes," said Rico, "and remember, Pooch my friend, you must return to do what you can for your wonderful state. You know what the old governor stood for."

"I will. And you must introduce some of his ideas into Mexico too."

"You may not believe it, Pooch, but someone has already been doing that in a refugee town along the border here. I saw a paperback copy of *Small is Beautiful* in Eagle Pass."

Pooch said, "Someone is exporting revolution."

"Well, we must say good-by, Pooch."

"Don't do something foolish now, back in Yucatán. Giving your life up for something has never struck me as a way to live."

No one laughed.

"Good-by, Sara. Good-by, my friend."

"Yes, good-by," shouted Pooch, his voice trailing off.

"Well, Pooch, maybe things'll get better soon and we can..." Rico just could not bring himself to say good-by and mean it.

Pooch was in pain. Sara was standing next to him, choking back tears. "Well, why don't we discuss this whole thing, I mean the way we can get you out..."

There was a long silence.

"I guess we have to be leaving.... We should be heading..." said Rico.

"*Where* are you heading? You can't just head for nowhere."

"Most people do, Pooch," said Rico, trying to be funny. His throat was tight. "Everything will be fine."

"I know everything will be fine. It's just that I was thinking... well, hell... I don't know what I was thinking. We just have to say goodbye, son, for a few weeks or so."

"Right... well, good-by. My mother says it too."

"Sara too. She's right here, but she doesn't feel like talking..."

"I guess we had better move along then..."

Pooch took Sara's hand and began to lead her away. She protested. "But we may never see Rico again."

Pooch looked at her. "Sara, dear," he said, "we can't see him now."

There was silence for a time on Rico's side of the wall. "Well, good-by then, you two..."

Pooch and Sara had walked too far from the wall to hear Rico.

The plastic wall stood tall, shimmering in the sun, a

forbidding thing, but oddly beautiful as sections of it bent and twisted over the green-gray, scrub-colored hills that rose to the west. It had no end. It simply dissolved into the heated sky above a spot where sunlight ricocheted off a distant bend in the Rio Grande. To the east it seemed to skip and leap across boulder-strewn ridges, then suddenly disappear behind a sandy ridge. In places the wall seemed to sag from the heat, in others grow more taut and unrepentent. Sunlight danced along its aluminum struts and steel cables. There wasn't a sound anywhere, it seemed, for miles.

Six weeks after Rico Far and his mother said goodbye to Pooch Grenada and Sara Steinberger, the plastic wall was complete, from the Gulf of Mexico to the Pacific Ocean. The secretary of the interior received a wire from Gerald Angina.

It was a wrap.